LOSERS CLUB

BY YVONNE VINCENT

By Yvonne Vincent:

The Big Blue Jobbie
The Big Blue Jobbie #2
Frock In Hell

Cover design by Paul Francis

First published in 2021 by Yvonne Vincent.
Copyright © 2021 Yvonne Vincent. All rights reserved.

For Mr V and the Cherubs

I love you this much

∞

A WEE NOTE FROM THE AUTHOR

This story is set in the Northeast of Scotland, where they speak a dialect of Scots called Doric. I've kept the local words to a minimum and tried to give a flavour of how the people are, which is kind, decent and very direct. In the village where I lived as a child, everyone said hello as they passed you in the street, even if they'd never met you before, the grapevine worked faster than fibre broadband and there was always someone on hand to helpfully point out that you'd put on a few pounds.

Things have changed with the march of time, but even in the towns, there is still that sense of local people supporting local people. There is still that strong streak of decency. And a spade is still a spade.

Here's a quick guide to some of the words I've used:

> Quine – a girl or young woman
> Loon – a boy or young man
> Glaikit – foolish, stupid (yon glaikit coo – that stupid cow)
> Fit – what
> Vratch - wretch
> Stramash – an uproar
> Fechtin' – fighting
> Foos yer doos? – how are you?
> Teuchter – yokel
> Feel gype – stupid idiot

PROLOGUE

Under the cover of darkness, two men pulled the small RIB up the shingles. They gave the boat a last heave and staggered back, wet, exhausted and thankful to have made it safely to shore. Peering through the rain, they could just make out the lights of their most recent home, as the larger vessel turned and made its way back out to the open sea.

'Well, thank goodness that's done wi',' said the older of the men, 'C'moan, Mustafa laddie. Let's get you up tae the hoose and get some dry clothes on ye.'

Mustafa stared after the man who had just expertly guided them through the choppy waves into the tiny cove. He'd spent a week with this man since setting sail from Gibraltar, and by the end of the first hour had asked for an interpreter.

'Fit d'ye need an interpreter for Mustafa laddie? Div ye nae ken English?' was the response, so Mustafa had resigned himself to the fact that he was just going to have to figure out what bonnie quines, fine loons and "yon glaikit coo Elsie" were later. After almost a week of living at close quarters together, he'd only realised the day before that the man was called Old Archie. He'd spent six days wondering why everyone on board kept asking him how he liked an allergy until his ears, finally attuned to the Scots dialect, managed to pick out the words Aul' Erchie.

Heaving the small bag containing everything he owned in the world onto his shoulder, Mustafa started up the cliff path after Old Archie. The older man was picking out the route with a torch and Mustafa hurried to catch up. Panting slightly with the effort, he arrived next to Old Archie, and together they made their way to the top of the path.

The two men hauled their weary selves up the last few feet and stood atop the cliffs, surveying the rows of little cottages huddled together against the wind and rain. Old Archie switched off his torch and they made towards the glow of the streetlights. Just as they reached the outskirts of the village, Old Archie stopped, turned to Mustafa and whispered, 'It's the Isle o' Vik, nae doontoon Tripoli, laddie.'

After a moment's hesitation, Mustafa silently slipped the gun into his pocket and followed Old Archie as he rounded the children's playground and walked past the shuttered chip shop, with its faded "O Fryer of Scotland" sign, to a cottage on the end of a row. Not a soul stirred as Old Archie quietly turned a key in the ancient, peeling front door and the two men crept into the dry, welcoming warmth of the house. Neither man noticed the shadowy figure emerge from the alley next to the chip shop and make its way towards the cottage. Neither heard the front door of the cottage open or the figure move down the hallway towards the kitchen, where the men were now peeling off their waterproofs.

A kettle rumbled on the ancient stove, almost ready to whistle its cheery warning, and Mustafa turned to hang his wet gear on the radiator behind the door. By the time he heard the single soft phut of the silenced shot, Old Archie was already on the ground, a small trickle of blood running down his forehead and dripping into the hood of his jacket.

CHAPTER ONE

'Off! Get off ma damn boat,' boomed Captain Rab's voice over the speaker. He tooted the horn twice to underline his point, as the small ferry chugged into Port Vik. There was a flurry of activity and rather a lot of tutting, with the passengers hastening towards their vehicles becoming entangled with those on foot, snaking their way towards the exit. Hector and Edith glared at their mother, who was balancing their empty plastic bottles and sandwich wrappers on top of the overflowing bin.

'I don't see why we had to come here, of all places,' muttered Hector. 'All it does is bloody rain. Why couldn't we stay with dad?'

Penny gave up trying to play bottle Jenga and sighed. They'd gone over this a thousand times and she was rapidly running out of ways to avoid telling Hector that his dad was a cheating arsehole whose idea of fatherhood was extravagant gifts and empty promises. Alex Moon didn't want the twins cramping his bachelor lifestyle and had cheerfully waved them off with their mother, safe in the knowledge that none of them could ever again catch him shagging, oh cliché of clichés, the au pair. There was no point in hurting Hector with the truth. At sixteen, the twins were essentially spotty, resentful bags of hormones, prone to extreme bouts of angst and the shared conviction that everything they did was someone else's fault. Okay, mostly Penny's fault. She loved them very much but, for the past two years, Penny had consoled herself by privately thinking of her little darlings as Detestosterone and Beastrogen. She really ought to stop thinking like that before she accidentally said it out loud, within earshot of the twins. There was a near miss recently when, still seething after an argument with Edith, she'd left a voicemail on the school answering machine, saying that Beastrogen Moon would be late because she was getting her fangs checked. This was followed up a few minutes later with a second message pleading temporary insanity and "please, please don't tell her I called her that." Then a third message – "Sorry, me again, forgot to say, Edith Moon, definitely Edith, dentist appointment tomorrow morning."

Righty-ho, Penny thought, if I'm going to stop calling the twins rude names, then I really should stop thinking of their father as The Wankpuffin - they'll eventually figure out his wankpuffiness for themselves without any help from me. In the meantime, she had to find a way to help the twins build a new life, far from the friends, school and home they'd known since forever, on an island in the middle of the North Sea where, yes, all it did was bloody rain.

'Come on,' said Penny, avoiding the argument, 'Let's get to the car. Granny and Grandad will be so excited to see you.'

Twenty minutes later, they were trundling through the centre of Port Vik, the suspension of Penny's battered old Renault rendered dangerously low under the weight of their worldly goods. A lifetime…three lifetimes…of possessions strapped to the roof and squashed into every conceivable space. It seemed strange, thought Penny, to be coming back to live in the place that she couldn't wait to put behind her twenty-three years ago. Not much had changed, though. Nothing ever really changed on the island.

'Oh, look!' she cried, trying to push some enthusiasm into her voice, 'There's the church hall where we used to go to discos. I had my first kiss there when I was fourteen.'

No response from the back. She glanced in the rear-view mirror and saw that Hector and Edith were wired for sound and oblivious to the world. Penny turned to the cage beside her, where two beady little eyes regarded her, unblinking.

'At least you're paying attention, Freddie. I promise, when we get to Granny and Grandad's house, we'll find you a safe place, away from that horrible cat.'

The little creature twitched his whiskers, as if to say, 'I have no idea what you're talking about because I'm a bloomin' hamster, you big weirdo.'

As they passed her old school, Penny noted that the portable cabins they'd used as additional classrooms had finally been replaced with a shiny, new building. At least the kids these days wouldn't have to freeze all winter and melt all summer. She recalled a particularly hot day when the sex education teacher, Murray Hancock (or, if you were a pupil, Furry Mancock), used an over-ripe banana to demonstrate how to put on a condom. Everything had gone limp in the heat and, as he rolled the condom down, the pressure became too much for the banana, resulting in some definite oozing. Unaware that he'd put an entire class of fourteen-year-old girls off using condoms forever, old Furry mopped up the soggy mess and sent them on their way. It was only when Penny's best friend, Eileen, touched Kenny Bates' willy for a dare, that they realised willies didn't split down the side and ooze black stuff. Poor Kenny. The unforeseen explosion meant he had to put up with 'Come on Eileen' being played at every church hall disco for the next two years.

Penny smiled inwardly. Growing up here hadn't been that bad. The twins would soon get used to the slower pace and the dodgy Wi-fi.

'Come on, you two. We're nearly there,' she shouted at the zombies in the back seat.

Hector and Edith removed their earphones and sat forward, their heads colliding as they leaned towards the gap between the seats so they could peer out the front windscreen for the first glimpse of Granny and Grandad's house.

'Ouch! Muuuum! Edith headbutted me.'

'I did not! You stuck your head in the way.'

'You did. Mum, tell her.'

'Don't be a fucking moron, Hector.'

'You're a fucking moron.'

'Stop swearing. Both of you.'

'Well, it's his fault for putting his stupid head in the way.'

'She nutted me on purpose with her big forehead.'

'My forehead is not big!'

'Yes, it is. It's like this, look.' Hector put his hand across his fringe and pointed to his forefinger. 'Hairline starts here. Big forehead weirdo.'

'At least I'm normal size. Teeny tiny little man.'

'Oi! Ant and Dec in the back. Shut up and get your things together. We're here.'

Penny slowed the car and pulled to a halt in front of Valhalla, her parents' ugly 1970's bungalow. The once white pebble-dashed walls looked grey, and the brick-clad bay window was the only feature in what was otherwise a giant, bland box. Just a couple of miles outside Port Vik, it was one of a row of eight identical houses, separated from the main road by low walls and wide gravel drives. Under the lowering sky, Valhalla looked quite depressing, but looks could be deceiving. Inside was a riot of colour, thanks to her mother's eclectic views on interior design. Mary Hopper held firm to the idea of bold is beautiful, both in life and in her choice of decor. Penny shuddered at the memory of the living room wallpaper circa 1990, which was supposed to be a repeat pattern of petals but actually looked like a neat array of inflamed…well, the least said about that the better. She hadn't been able to take any friends home for a year, until her mother tired of the petalginas and replaced them with flamingos.

As Penny turned the engine off, the front door flew open and her mother charged towards the car. Hector and Edith quickly clicked open their seatbelts and jumped out to greet their grandmother. Enveloping the twins in a huge hug, Mary looked over their heads at Penny, who remained sitting in the car, taking a moment to breathe before she entered the maelstrom that was her mother's world.

Hearing a rap on the window, Penny looked round to see her father opening the passenger door. 'Hello, Penny-farthing. My goodness, who's this little fella?' asked Len, eyeing the furry ball at the bottom of the cage.

'This is Freddie, Dad. Alex got him for Hector for Christmas. I hope it's okay. I know it'll be a pain keeping Mojo away from him, but I couldn't leave him. You know what Alex is like. He can't even keep a houseplant alive.'

No problem,' said Len, lifting the cage from the passenger seat and placing it gently on the gravel. 'We'll put you in Hector's room, Freddie. If he keeps the door shut, you'll be safe from Mojo.'

Penny heaved herself out of the car. She was carrying a few extra pounds these days and felt the difference. She'd nearly sprained a wrist trying to cut her toenails the other day and had made a vow to reduce the accursed belly. Too much separation chocolate and rather a lot of divorce wine. With a possible lack of portion control when it came to ice cream. Which was ironic, given her job.

She made her way round to her father, who by now was attempting to open the boot. She put an arm around his shoulders and gave him a squeeze. He was a small, mild-mannered man, much shorter than the six-foot whirlwind that was her mother. She could feel his bones through his burgundy sweater and mused that she and Hector may have inherited their slight stature from Len, but Mary was definitely the genetic source of her large bottom.

'Leave the cases, Dad. We'll get them later. Why don't you take Freddie in and pop him somewhere the cat can't get him?'

Before she could fully dissuade her father from his attempt to break into the boot, Penny was swept up in a flurry of pink chiffon, cashmere and Chanel No. 5. Her mother had lifted her into a tight embrace and was slowly crushing her ribcage.

How are you darling? Oh, Penny, it's just awful, what you've all been through. My, you've put on a bit of weight. Not that I'm judging, but all the slimming classes and life coaching stuff you do…well, you're not really role modelling it, are you? Have you seen the hydrangea? Your father planted it last year. They're supposed be blue or pink and we've no idea how ours has turned out yellow. What's that, dear?'

'Mum, put me down. I can't breathe.'

'Oh sorry, dearie.' Mary released her hold on Penny and continued to chatter as they made their way towards the front door. 'Do you remember Martin MacDonald? No? You must remember. You broke his tooth when you walloped him with a plastic train in nursery?' Penny was shaking her head no, but her mum ploughed on. 'Well, he married that Rachel Jenkins. You know, the one who got the genital warts from a German tourist and had to go to the clap clinic on the mainland after she gave it to half the boys on the island? Didn't you go to school with her? They call her Radio Rachel. Something about being the best transmitter in town. People *are* mean, aren't they? Anyway, Martin and Rachel bought the Vik Hotel in town, and they're looking for a barmaid. I thought it would be a nice wee job for you in the evenings. We could have the twins, and it would get you out meeting people.'

Mary's monologue had taken them from car to kitchen, and Penny seized the opportunity to cut in while her mother took a breath. 'I told you, Mum, I'm going to run some slimming classes, do the online life coaching. See how things go. I've already arranged to hire the church hall on Wednesday evenings.'

'Well, Sandra Next Door could definitely do with a few slimming classes. Greggs on legs, that one.' Mary smiled and waved out the kitchen window. Penny could see Sandra Next Door, watering her begonias and peering over the wall, hoping to catch a glimpse of the new arrivals. No doubt she'd be telling her friends all about how Penny Moon was back with her tail between her legs. 'Going off and marrying fancy telly actors and thinking she could lord it over the rest of us. Now, here she is. No better than anyone else.' Penny could imagine Sandra Next Door poring over the red tops, repeating all the salacious details to the worthies of the Town Guild, when just last year she'd been pleading with Mum to ask Alex to open the Vik Festival. As she watched Sandra Next Door wave back and scuttle off into her conservatory, Penny said a quiet prayer that the woman wouldn't come to her slimming classes.

'Mum, I know you like telling it as it is, but you can't be rude about people's weight these days. It's called fat-shaming.'

'Oh, for goodness' sake, you young people are so oversensitive. What is it they call you? Snowmen? Snow people? Snow...whatsits. Never mind. Come on, Chunky, let's put the kettle on.'

An hour later, soup and sandwiches lodged firmly down the hatch, Penny rounded up the twins to help her unload the car. As they hauled bags and suitcases into the house, a thought occurred to her. 'Hector, where did Grandad put Freddie?'

'It's okay, Mum. He's in my room.'

'Did you check his water and give him some food? He could probably do with coming out for a run around, he's been cooped up since last night.'

Hector rolled his eyes and sighed. 'I'm not an idiot. Yes, I did the food. Yes, I did the water. Yes, I let him out. And before you ask, yes, I kept the door shut so the cat couldn't get in.'

They turned into the hallway, heading for Hector's room, and Penny stopped dead. Hector's bedroom door was wide open. 'Please tell me you put him back in his cage before we started taking in the bags.'

'Erm...'

'Oh, you really are an idiot. Get in there and look for him. I'll shut the front door and get Mojo out of the way.'

Penny grabbed the cat and put him outside, slammed the front door and hastened back to Hector's room. Hector appeared, shaking his head. 'I can't find him anywhere.'

Penny could see that he was on the verge of tears and took pity on him. 'Don't worry. He's probably still in the house somewhere. We'll organise a search. Muuuuum! Daaaaad!'

Len appeared. 'Penny, how many times have I told you? Come and talk to us. Don't shout.'

Penny rolled her eyes and sighed. 'Freddie's gone missing. And before you ask, yes, all the doors were left open. Yes, it's our fault. Yes, the cat could have eaten him. Yes, he could be outside.' She saw Hector pale and hurriedly added, 'But he's probably in the house somewhere. Can you help us look?'

Alerted by the commotion, Edith stuck her head around her bedroom door and asked what all the fuss was about. Despite taking the opportunity to assure her brother that he was "a total bell end", she agreed to help. Len said he had never heard of a bell end, and there was a moment's silence while everyone tried to figure out the most diplomatic way to explain it to him. They were saved by Mary, who came striding down the hall, declaring, 'The tip of your penis, darling. Looks a bit like a bell.'

'You're right, dear. I never thought of it like that. Although my one looks a bit—'

Penny saw the horrified looks on the twins' faces and cut in. 'Dad, can you check the living room. Mum, you do your bedroom. Edith, your room and the dining room. I'll check my room and, Hector, you make a start on the kitchen. When we've finished, we'll join you there and help. Start by emptying the cupboards, everyone. Edith, don't forget to check up the chimney.' She reached into the hall cupboard and handed Edith a torch. Then she reached back into the cupboard and began hauling out plastic bags containing hundreds of other plastic bags, boxes of single winter gloves and an old handheld vacuum cleaner which was missing its charger.

Over the course of the next hour, the search party scoured the house for any sign of the little hamster. The contents of cupboards were turned out and lay in piles in every room. Mary became quite distracted by the stacks of tins on the kitchen table. 'Len, we have thirty-six tins of beans, three of which expired in 2012. Please stop buying beans every time you go to the village shop.'

'Sorry, dear. It's just that after the summer of 1983...'

Mary turned to the twins. 'The island got cut off by storms for two weeks. Your grandfather has been stocking up on supplies ever since. Don't go anywhere near the garden shed. Apparently, it's full of stuff and he's quite funny about it. Sandra Next Door complained when he bought the bigger shed and I just said, "A man has to have his hobbies, Sandra Next Door. Look at your Geoff, always on the golf course." Well, we all know he's not really on the golf course. More than once he's been seen going into the Vik Hotel with Linda from the shoe shop. And you know why she works in the shoe shop, don't you? Enormous feet. Biggest I've ever seen on a woman! She orders in all these fancy stilettos in a size ten, yet you only ever see her in flats. I bet she wears them for Geoff, though. I wonder if he's one of them foot fleshy-cysts.'

'What's a foot fleshy-cyst?' asked Len.

Before Mary could further indoctrinate Hector and Edith with her own special brand of sex education, Penny interrupted. 'Missing hamster, everyone. Remember Freddie? Small fella, brown fur, likes a nice wheel. I don't think there's much more we can do, Hector. We've looked everywhere, and I can only think he must have scarpered out the front door when we were bringing in the bags. We'll go down to the village shop in the morning and put some posters up.'

Hector looked miserable. So miserable that even Edith gave his shoulders a kindly pat. 'Do you think Mojo could have eaten him?' he asked disconsolately.

Penny thought back to the bundle of black fur she'd tossed out the front door earlier. He did have a rather self-satisfied look about him. 'No, I'm sure Mojo hasn't eaten him,' she lied. 'Come on, how about I make us all some hot chocolate and we'll sort it out in the morning. Mum, do you have any hot chocolate?'

Mary reached across the table and pulled three tubs of cocoa powder towards her. 'Do you want the one that expired in 2015, 2017 or 1998?'

CHAPTER TWO

The next morning dawned dark, wet and windy. Penny swept back the bedroom curtains and immediately snapped them closed again. Ugh. Even the weather was in a bad mood. Here she was, divorced, jobless, back in her old bedroom, two teenagers and a missing effing hamster. Coming home had seemed like such a good idea. Get the kids out of the city and somewhere far away from the tabloids. Having the paparazzi parked outside the house all the time wasn't doing any of them much good. Bloody Alex. She might have coped with the affairs, but then there was the tax avoidance scandal. It transpired that for years he'd been putting money into some scheme that he could write off against tax – except he couldn't, and it finally caught up with him.

'So sorry, darling, we'll have to sell the house. Big tax bill and all that. Do you think the kids would mind going to the local school? I'll make it up to them,' he'd said when the story broke in the press.

She'd noticed that he didn't sell his precious vintage Jag. Or get rid of the au pair they neither needed nor could afford. Monique was due to go home to Belgium soon anyway, and Alex had argued that it would be cruel to cut her experience short. Except, as it turned out, it wasn't life experience that Monique was getting. It was sexual experience. Everything was falling apart and catching them shagging was the last straw. Penny filed for divorce and, taking her share of the proceeds from the house, she had packed up their lives and come home to Mum and Dad to lick her wounds.

Flopping back down on the squishy mattress, which sagged in the middle as the result of an exuberant trampolining session with Eileen aged twelve, Penny eyed the half-empty wine bottle on the bedside cabinet, feeling some regret. Above her on the wall, Chesney Hawkes gazed into the middle distance.

'I used to fancy the pants off you, Chesney,' she told him. 'You really were The One and Only. Who'd have thunk it, eh? One minute I'm standing on red carpets in designer dresses, the next I'm back in my old bedroom talking to a poster. Drowning my sorrows isn't going to make it better, though. What d'you reckon, Chezza? Time to stop feeling sorry for myself and move on, I hear you say? Not sure I'm quite there yet, but I'm doing my best.'

She opened the bedside cabinet drawer and rummaged around. What other remnants of her teenage self were in this room? Aha! She pulled out a mix tape that had been made for her by her first boyfriend, back in the days when a lazy eye and terrible acne were no barrier to romance. Things were so much harder in these days of influencers, where appearance was everything. Nowadays, wee Jimmy Space would be doomed to years of romantic drought and an unhealthy interest in onanism. Penny wondered what he was up to now. Probably trundling around DIY shops on a Sunday, with a wife and three lazy-eyed children in tow. She leaned over the edge of the bed, opened the small cupboard below the drawer, made contact with hard plastic and thanked the dear Lord that Mary and Len never threw anything away. Pulling the tape recorder out, she looked up at the wall above the bed. 'Fancy a bop, Chesney? Bit of old school pop? Well, cross your sexy fingers that this thing still works.'

Ten minutes later, Penny's bedroom door flew open and Edith marched in, with a face like she'd just won the lemon sucking world championship. 'What are you doing, Mum? It's eight o'clock in the morning. You woke me up! Turn it down!'

'I can't hear you,' Penny roared back, as Salt-n-Pepa pushed it real good. Hips gyrating, she was pulling Chesney in on an imaginary rope, even though she suspected this was distinctly pervy on her part, what with him being permanently frozen at nineteen and her being a fat-arsed forty-something in tartan pyjamas.

Edith stomped over to the bedside cabinet, intending to switch the music off. She stared at the machine, with its array of knobs and buttons, and shouted, 'What the…how do you work this thing?'

Penny ignored her. As Push It segued into Let's Talk About Sex (nicely done there, Jimmy my boy), she wondered if she should try twerking. 'I'm going to try twerking,' she shouted at Edith. 'Aaaany minute now, my bottom is going to start bouncing at the Chezster.'

Edith threw a disgusted "Oh My God" look at her and slammed out of the room. Grinning to herself, Penny switched off the tape recorder. No point in antagonising Edith further and, truth be told, the dancing had cheered her up immensely. She pulled on her dressing gown and padded through to the kitchen in search of coffee.

'Morning, love. Was that you playing the music?' Len plucked a mug off the mug-tree and waggled it at her. 'Coffee?'

'Yes please, Dad. I was listening to an old mix tape. Remember Jimmy Space? He made it for me, and it got me thinking about him. Any idea what he's doing now?'

'I think he left the island years ago. His dad's still the vet in town, but I remember hearing that his mum died. Your mother knows more about the goings-on than me, ask her.'

'I'll have to go down to the village later to put some lost Freddie posters up. I'm going to put some posters up for the slimming class too. Do you need anything from the shop?'

Len smiled and winked at her. 'Maybe a tin of beans? Just joking. Your mum threw away all the out-of-date tins last night, but I think she's going to the big supermarket in town later.'

'Great. Maybe she can go round the shops in Port Vik and put some posters up there for me.'

'It's a bit far for Freddie to walk. I doubt he'll be found in town.'

Penny rolled her eyes. 'Slimming class posters, Dad. I brought boxes of stuff with me to get things started. Hector and Edith designed all the leaflets, posters and record books as a project for their Business Studies class, while I did the website. Moon-Lite Life Coaching. It's more than just slimming classes. It's a whole lifestyle approach. I can do a lot of it online, but a big part will be real life slimming clubs and exercise groups. I'll trial it here, tweak it, then roll it out across the country. The marketing stuff only arrived just before we left, so I haven't even seen it yet. Shall we take a look?'

Penny and her father took their coffees through to the living room. Ducking down behind the sofa, she selected a large box and pushed it towards Len, who fished his trusty penknife from his pocket and slit the tape neatly down the centre. Excited, Penny pulled back the cardboard flaps and tore the plastic shrink wrapping from a stack of leaflets. She peeled one from the top of the stack and, pausing for a moment to savour the anticipation of seeing her new business in print, she slowly turned the leaflet over.

'What the bloody hell…Hector! Edith!' Penny stormed out of the living room and down the hall, banging on Edith's bedroom door as she passed. She reached Hector's room, opened the door and roared, 'Get out of bed now. I mean it. NOW!'

Hector and Edith appeared at their bedroom doors, watching their mother's back as she strode off, yelling, 'Living room, both of you.'

Mary stumbled blearily into the hall, wearing a purple satin nightdress, her blonde fringe creating a halo behind the eye-mask pushed back on her head, and yesterday's mascara turning the fine creases below her eyes into a road map of a life well-lived.

By the time the three of them reached the living room, Penny had torn open packs of posters, leaflets and record books. As they entered, Penny shook a handful of leaflets at the twins and hissed, 'What the hell were you thinking?'

Mary took one of the leaflets from her and, with a slight note of motherly condescension, said, 'It's a lovely design, darling, but I don't think Losers Club is the best name for a weight loss group.'

'How the heck did this happen?' Penny hissed at her offspring. 'It's supposed to be Moon-Lite.'

Hector looked mutinous. 'It's not our fault. We texted you to ask about the name, and you said Losers.'

Vehemently denying any such thing, Penny grabbed her phone and frantically scrolled through her texts. Ah, here it was.

Hector: Doing the flyers now. What name did you decide on in the end?

Penny: Am busy. Will talk later. Losers.

'It's obvious I meant later losers. Like a joke, you know, "laters, losers." I didn't actually mean…oh, bugger…why didn't you phone me to check?'

'It's a weight loss thing. We thought you were trying to be edgy, in a mum sort of way,' said Edith.

Penny sighed and sank to the floor. She sat there, cross-legged, head bowed, running a hand through her dark thatch of hair. 'What am I going to do? I can't call a bunch of overweight people losers. It's like fat-shaming. May as well go the whole hog. Put an advert in the Vik Gazette asking if there are any fat losers out there who wish to join this big fat loser right here.'

'Snowflakes!' exclaimed Mary. 'That's what they call them. Snowflakes.'

'Mum, it's not snowflakey to be hurt when other people judge you for your body size.'

'I get things down off supermarket shelves for short-arses all the time, and you don't hear me crying about how awful it is to be tall.'

'Mum…oh, never mind. Well, it's too late to change it all now. Losers Club it is. Let's just hope people think it's quirky or ironic or something. I'll change the website and we'll start getting the leaflets and posters out today. Edith, can you go into town with Granny and cover some of the shops? Hector, you're with me.'

Hector and Edith shot Penny resentful looks and went back to their rooms. For once, they were in total agreement that this was all Mum's fault.

Hector dragged a laptop from the bottom of his yet to be unpacked suitcase, causing an avalanche of balled up socks to tumble onto the floor. He didn't notice. He was intent on downloading a picture of Freddie for his missing hamster posters. Freddie's cage stood empty in the corner of his room, and Hector suppressed a brief flicker of guilt. After all, this was Mum's fault too. If she hadn't made him help with the suitcases, then he wouldn't have left his bedroom door open.

By the time Hector had made a poster, argued with Edith for use of the bathroom, had a full meltdown because she had used all the hot water, and thrown on some clean underpants beneath yesterday's clothes, he was a seething ball of resentment. It took all his willpower to remain polite when he asked Grandad if he could use the printer.

'I know you're upset about Freddie,' said Len, 'but do you think you could go easy on your mother? You've all been through a tough time and she's suddenly faced with having to make a living to support the three of you.'

Shoulders squared, Hector drew himself up to his full five foot four. If Grandad wanted a man-to-man chat, then Grandad needed to hear some home truths. 'To be honest, Edith and I don't want to be here. We want to be in London with Dad. We don't see why Mum had to drag us to the back of beyond just because *she* didn't want to be with Dad anymore. If she's that desperate for money, Dad will give her some. He's probably paying a fortune in maintenance for us anyway. And she worked when we were in London, so she could have stayed in her job there.'

'Oh laddie, you've seen the papers. Your dad doesn't have a bean to his name right now, and your mum could barely support you on a part-time job in London. All I'm saying is, you should appreciate that this isn't easy for her either.'

Hector stiffened. 'I've spent my life seeing rubbish in the papers about my dad. I'm surprised you're buying into it, Grandfather. As far as Edith and I are concerned, Mum has made her bed, and it's unfortunate that Edith and I must share it with her. Now, can I use your printer please?'

Len sighed. Given time, the twins would settle, but there was a long, bumpy road ahead of them and their mother. 'Okay, I'll help you set it up. It probably just needs one of those Wi-fi thingies and Granny's password to make it work.'

By 11am, the family were good to go. Hector was clutching a handful of Freddie posters, Penny had loaded stacks of Losers Club leaflets and posters into both cars, Mary was having a heated debate with Len about which brand of fabric softener brought him out in an embarrassing rash and Edith was still in her room carefully pencilling on a pair of horrendous eyebrows.

'If you end up with a purple bottom again, don't blame me,' said Mary. She turned to her daughter. 'Honestly, it was like living with a human baboon. Eeeeediiiiith! I would come in there and tattoo a couple of slugs on your face if it would make you hurry up! That's the nice thing about boys. They don't make a fuss. Do you remember the time you shoved tissues down your bra to make your boobs look bigger and they all fell out into a puddle, and you insisted on going back to the car in case anyone saw you with a flat chest? Three hours you sat there, while your father and I went shopping. We did stop for a very nice lunch, mind you. It was at that posh French place,

La Maison. Your father had the fish and I had—'

'Eeeeeediiiiith! Come out here before I have to commit matricide! Where was it you wanted your ashes scattered, Mum?'

'I'll wait in the car.' Mary sniffed and headed outside.

'You and Hector go. I'll chivvy Edith along,' said Len.

Her father really was the most lovely, patient, kind man, thought Penny as she got into her car. Hector got in beside her, making a show of shoving in his earphones, presumably to signal that under no circumstances did he want to talk to her. I wonder what heinous sin I've committed to offend him today, Penny thought. She started up the engine and wound down the window to wave cheerio to her mother. As they set off down the drive, she could have sworn she heard a male voice bellowing, 'Eeeeeediiiiith!'

Penny drove slowly. The village was only a mile away, but the wind had grown stronger, and she could feel it buffeting the car. Having once almost come a cropper to a falling branch on this road, she was wary. The rain which had been steadily falling all morning, was now a torrential downpour, and she was quite relieved to find a free parking space directly outside the village shop. Holding their coats over their heads, she and Hector dashed inside, almost taking out a pensioner who was attempting to leave. Mrs Hubbard, the shop owner, greeted her like a long-lost daughter.

'It's just grand to see you, quine. How are you managing after the divorce? We read about it in the papers and I said to my Douglas, "I don't know how she's put up with him all these years." But you never know what really goes on in a marriage, do you? Who's this you have with you? Is this Hector? My, what a…a…medium sized boy you are. I haven't seen you since you were about ten. Come on in and we'll look for a sweetie for you. Do you still like wine gums?'

Mrs Hubbard ushered them to the counter, behind which stood row upon row of old-fashioned sweet jars, brimming with traditional delights such as humbugs, kola cubes and large pan drops. The shop stocked a range of basics and newspapers, but Mrs Hubbard's Cupboard was known across the island as the place to come for sweets and home-made ice cream. Even Hector, whose icy countenance could have frozen the nipples off a polar bear, thawed slightly under her warm welcome. Of course, the free bag of wine gums helped. As he rummaged through the bag, looking for a black one, Penny broached the reason for their visit.

'You haven't changed a bit, Mrs Hubbard. Still as gorgeous as when you sold me my first single cigarette for twenty pence in 1992. Would you mind if I asked for a wee favour? Hector's hamster went missing last night, and we were hoping to put a poster up in your window, in case anyone from the village finds him.'

'Oh, you know how to flatter a woman, young Penny. Of course you can put the poster up.'

'And another wee favour? I'm starting slimming classes. A weight loss group.'

'Aye, I did think to myself you'd put on a few pounds since I last saw you.'

'No, not for me. Well, I'll be doing it too. You're right, I have put on a few pounds. But I'm starting the group for other people, and I'll be leading it, hopefully by example. I wonder...could I put a poster up and maybe leave some of these leaflets on the counter please?'

Mrs Hubbard took one of the leaflets and looked at it thoughtfully. 'Losers Club? Are you sure about the name? Is this one of these new-fangled things where words mean the opposite of what they used to mean?'

'No, it's like lose weight – as in "you are a loser of weight." Not loser like a useless person. That would be ridiculous!' Penny's high-pitched laugh, even to her own ears, had a faintly desperate quality to it. 'Anyway, do you think you could help me promote this?'

Mrs Hubbard gave her a reassuring pat on the arm. 'I will, dearie. And, even better, I'll come along myself. Now, have you heard the latest news?'

'We only arrived on yesterday's afternoon ferry, so I haven't had time for a catch up yet.'

'Well, Old Archie the postman was found dead in his cottage this morning.'

'No! What happened?'

'Do you remember Elsie from the library? She hadn't heard from him for a couple of weeks, so she went round to check he was okay. Looked in the kitchen window and saw him lying on the floor. And, this is the shocking bit, he'd been shot through the head.'

'Shot?!' Penny's exclamation was loud enough to distract Hector from his wine gums.

'Who was shot?' he asked. Maybe this island wasn't so dull, after all.

'The postie,' said Mrs Hubbard. 'And, even stranger, there was evidence that somebody else had been in the house with him. An extra set of waterproofs was on the radiator.'

'Why was he shot? Who shot him?' Hector asked.

'That's what we all want to know, Hector. Poor Elsie. She's in a right state. She thinks nobody knows about her and Old Archie, but we've all seen the library van parked outside his house at odd hours. There's only one thing Old Archie was taking out, and it wasn't a library book.'

The thought of old people doing it was too much for Hector. 'I'll wait for you in the car, Mum. Thanks for the wine gums, Mrs Hubbard.'

'What a polite boy you have there,' said Mrs Hubbard. 'Anyway, as I was saying, Elsie called the doctor. Doc Harris called the police, but Sergeant Wilson went to a meeting in Aberdeen and can't back get to the island because of the storm.'

'Is PC Henry still on the job?' asked Penny. 'He must be knocking on a bit by now.'

'No, dearie, he retired and went to live with his sister in Spain. He was replaced by PC Holmes and Sergeant Wilson, ooh, must have been ten years ago now. It took us years to break them in, then the weekend before last, PC Holmes got drunk during a lock-in at the village pub and decided to round up the sheep at Hillside Farm using the squad car. The car's a write-off and, as Doc Harris puts it, PC Holmes is cluttering up the morgue. That's why Sergeant Wilson had to go to the meeting in Aberdeen.

'The long and short of it is that the morgue's full, so we've put Old Archie in my big ice cream freezer for now and locked up the house. My Douglas isn't too happy about it. We had to squeeze the ice lollies into the other freezer. The doc said it wouldn't be hygienic to keep the Calippos with a corpse.'

'Good Lord,' said Penny. 'What happened to the person who was with Old Archie?'

Mrs Hubbard shrugged. 'No idea. He must have scarpered after he shot him.'

'Wow. A murderer on the island, with a gun!'

'Looks like it. Doc Harris says Old Archie was probably killed the night before last. No ferries went out yesterday because of the weather forecast. Today's storm was due to hit yesterday morning and they say it will be with us for a week. Your ferry only came in because Captain Rab's a mad devil who refused to be stuck in Aberdeen. This means that...' Mrs Hubbard left a dramatic pause, '...whoever killed Old Archie must still be on the island.'

'Has everyone been warned that there's a murderer on the loose? Does everyone know?'

'The police said to keep it a secret until they can get here, so of course the whole island knows.'

Penny was well aware of the island grapevine. It was faster than fibre broadband and a more effective deterrent than any police force. There was never any chance of skipping school or snogging a bad boy in secret when she was young. Someone would always spot you, and by the time you got home, your mother would be by the door, wooden spoon in hand, ready to help you see the error of your ways. If there was a murderer running around the place, he wouldn't last long.

'At least he went out on a high,' said Mrs Hubbard. In response to Penny's quizzical look, she continued, 'He just won Postman of the Year. His picture was in all the newspapers. He was even interviewed on BBC Scotland by that Eddie Miller. Oh, now there's a man with a nice speaking voice and a strapping pair of thighs. Did you see him when he did the celebrity swimathon for Children in Need? He was definitely smuggling more than one budgie in those…goodness, listen to me, gossiping away. I'll let you get on and I'll see you on Wednesday, dearie.'

Penny thanked Mrs Hubbard for her help with Losers Club and made her way to the car. As she got in, the wind whipped the door from her grasp. Risking another blast of rain, she leaned out, grabbed the handle with both hands and slammed the door to. She had been planning to deliver leaflets door to door, but she'd need to go back home and find some more waterproof clothing first.

Hector reluctantly removed his earphones and handed Penny her phone, which she'd left in the car while she was in the shop. 'Grandad rang. He says can you bring him back an ice lolly?'

CHAPTER THREE

Penny pulled another chair into the centre of the church hall and surveyed her afternoon's work.

'Thanks for helping, Eileen. Do you think twenty chairs is enough?'

Eileen set her sweeping brush aside and stood, hands on hips, considering the scene before her.

'To quote the road signs outside the old people's home, I think twenty's plenty. You've got the tables, with all the books and leaflets. Cash box. Scales. It just needs one final touch to cheer it up.' She grinned, clearly pleased with herself, and went to fetch a bag from the side of the room. 'Here, I got the kids to make you this.'

Penny's eyes widened as Eileen pulled a roll of white material from her bag and began to unfurl it. The grand unfurling went on until there, in shaky foot high letters across the banner, the words "LOSERS CLUB" were revealed. Oh, my flipping word, thought Penny, this is quite the opposite of cheering anything up. I'm about to become the leader of the saddest sounding group ever. Note to self – the island football club have the hall booked for 9pm. Do not forget to take down the banner.

'What can I say? I'm speechless,' said Penny, brightly.

'Good. I knew you'd be pleased. Shall we put it up outside, above the door?'

'Ooh, tempting. The whole town will see it there, but it'll get wet and we're a bit short on time. How about we string it across the stage for now?'

Eileen looked momentarily disappointed, but her habitual smile soon returned when she dug further into the bag and produced some blue balloons. 'Here, I got you these as well. Thought we could tie them next to the banner.'

Penny took one and blew it up. She eyed it sceptically. 'Hooray it's a boy?'

'They were left over from Karen Green's gender reveal party. I don't really hold with those gender reveal parties.'

'Too American?'

'No. I just think what if the baby came out and it wasn't a boy? What if it was an alien or something?'

Penny sometimes wondered how on earth her best friend had survived into adulthood.

'You do have two children? You do know how these things work, don't you? No. Don't answer that. Thank you for the balloons and banner. It was very kind of you and we have...' Penny looked at her watch, '...ten minutes to put them all up. Do you want to do the banner or the balloons?'

'I'll do the balloons. My Kenny always says I'm very good at blowing.'

Lord have mercy, thought Penny. When Eileen married Kenny Bates, he of the prematurely exploding todger, her own mother had described it as the melding of two morons. Ever loyal, Penny had told Mrs Campbell that she was being very harsh, and that Eileen was the sweetest person on the island. The sweet part was true. However, when Eileen and Kenny got back from their honeymoon, Penny had to concede that Mrs Campbell had a point. Eileen complained that the holiday hadn't been at all like they thought it would be.

'How so?' Penny had asked.

'Well, it's supposed to be the city of romance, isn't it? It took ever so long to get there, it was full of Americans and we never found the Eiffel tower.'

'These Americans...lots of cowboy hats and Texan accents?'

'Aye, it was very strange and not what I expected.

Still, we had a great time. If you're ever in Paris, go to Le Big Bronco Steakhouse and say hello to Monsieur Dwayne for me. Lovely man. Taught us some actual French.'

'The main thing is that you enjoyed yourselves.'

'We did. Two weeks of sunshine and good food. It made me realise how uncultured we are on Vik. Not even the staff in La Maison speak proper French. Kenny took me there for a meal when we got back. I asked for the Connard à l'Orange, and the waiter looked at me like I had two heads. I did that thing British people do when they're talking to foreigners. Where you just repeat yourself more loudly. In the end, I was shouting "Connard à l'Orange" at the poor man, and the manager asked us to leave. I had to give them a one-star review. Very poor customer service.'

'Oh dear. I think this Monsieur Dwayne may have been a bit of a tinker. Perhaps avoid speaking French in front of your granny until she recovers from the stroke.'

Now, tying the banner to two chairs on the stage, Penny smiled down at her friend, who was quite red in the face from her efforts with the balloons. She felt a rush of affection for the woman. Grabbing the ball of string, she clambered down from the stage and began to pull the balloons into bunches. This may not have been the slick, professional start she'd hoped for, but it came from a kind heart, and she'd take that over professionalism any day. She put an arm around Eileen's shoulders and gave her a hug. 'I'm so lucky to have you. It's almost seven and our audience awaits. Shall we pop these onto the stage and open the main doors?'

Seven o'clock came and went. Ten past. Quarter past. The two friends sat alone in the circle of chairs, watching the big clock above the door as the seconds ticked away. From behind her, Penny could hear a faint hiss as one of the balloons slowly deflated. She cleared her throat and abruptly stood up.

'Right, that's it. Nobody's coming. It's a complete failure.'

'Give it until half past,' suggested Eileen. 'Maybe something's happened. Maybe people don't want to go out in the storm.'

'This is Vik. We're practically twinned with Tornado Alley. If people here didn't go out in storms, they'd spend three hundred and sixty-four days a year indoors!'

Penny was about to continue her rant, when a tall figure stumbled through the door. The newcomer was swearing and wrestling with an umbrella, sending a spray of water and curse words in the direction of Penny and Eileen.

'Sorry I'm late lads. How the fuck do you put these fucking things down? Ah, press the wee button, got it. What a fucking nightmare I had getting here. The big tree came down on the main road and—'

The man stopped talking as he looked up and spotted the two women. They watched, dumbstruck, while he fumbled with the cords at the neck of his anorak and pulled back the hood to reveal a tanned, craggy face and a mop of brown hair. Ooh, he's a bit Liam Neeson, thought Penny. I wouldn't mind being rescued from some baddies by him.

Her mind had just happily segued into a very rude place, when the man said, 'Bugger. This isn't the football meeting, is it? Not unless the players have got much less hairy since last week.' He caught sight of the banner on the stage. 'Although the way we've been playing recently, I might be in the right meeting after all. Losers Club?'

'It's a weight loss group,' said Penny. 'Football doesn't start until nine.'

'You must be doing a good job,' said the man, looking around the hall. 'The buggers are so thin I can't see them.'

Penny bristled. 'It's our first meeting, and nobody is here yet,' she said, sharply.

'Well, let me be your first customer. I could do with losing this belly.' The man patted his small paunch with one hand and offered the other to Penny. 'Jim Space, local vet and part-time goalie.'

'Goodness, I didn't recognise you.' Penny shook his hand. 'Penny Moon. Or Hopper, as was. This is Eileen Bates. Used to be Eileen Campbell. You might remember us from school?'

'Nope. Sorry, can't place either of you.'

'Oh, come on. Let's talk about sex baby? Push it real good?'

Jim winked at her. 'We've only just met, but if you're up for it, then who am I to say no.'

'For God's sake, I'm talking about the mix tape you gave me when we were fifteen. You must remember. You snogged the face off me at the fourth year school dance.'

'Bugger me. Penny Hopper! I remember you. You were a skinny, wee, flat chested thing with braces. My, you've grown a bit.'

Penny glared at him. 'You were hardly Patrick Swayze. I see you got the eye fixed.'

'Fair comment. Neither of us was a catch. I only asked you to the dance because you were in my league.'

Eileen could see Penny's hackles rising and hastened to defuse the tension. 'Okay, you two old lovemuffins. That's enough banter. Are you staying or going, Jim?'

'Considering it'll take me an hour to get back round that bloody fallen tree, I may as well stay,' said Jim.

'How nice,' snapped Penny, before remembering that he was her first and only customer. She forced her mouth into a smile. 'I mean, how nice to welcome you to Losers Club. There's a £20 joining fee, which covers your record book, your induction and access to the Losers Club website, where you'll find a range of nutritious recipes and top tips for a healthy lifestyle. Thereafter, it will be £5 a week. If you follow Eileen, she'll weigh you and issue your record book.'

Penny turned away from him in time to see Mrs

Hubbard come in, her dripping wet coat adding to the small puddles created by Jim's brolly. She removed a headscarf, which had clearly given little protection against the torrent outside. Her usual soft silver waves had retreated into tight, steely curls, and water was running down her collar.

'I'm sorry, dearie. It's blowing a hoolie out there, and a tree has almost blocked the main road.' She stripped off her coat and cardigan to reveal three jumpers and a pair of heavy-duty trousers. 'Always get weighed at your heaviest first time. It makes you feel great about yourself next time. I haven't even been for a number two today. Don't worry, next week I'll be here in my swimming costume, raring to go. Is that Eileen over there, doing the weighing? What a bonny lass she is. No, no dear. There's no need for a welcome speech. You'll be very busy in a minute because I've just seen Gordon and Fiona in the car park, and I know Elsie from the library is definitely coming. She popped in past the shop to visit Old Archie this morning, and I gave her one of your leaflets. She could do with the company, if nothing else.'

Mrs Hubbard gave Penny a friendly pat on the arm and tottered off in what appeared to be steel toe-capped boots.

Penny reckoned Eileen was right. It looked like people were running late due to the storm. That was a relief – imagine starting Losers Club and being the only member.

Sure enough, a few minutes later, a couple arrived, followed by an older woman who Penny recognised as Elsie the librarian. Elsie stood to one side, hanging her damp things on the pegs by the door, as the couple introduced themselves to Penny and handed over a plastic tub. Once she'd directed them towards Eileen, Penny approached Elsie and said how sorry she was to hear about Old Archie.

'It's just such a shock,' the older woman said, softly. 'I knew he was going away for a week or so, but when I hadn't heard from him, I thought I'd better check. Finding him like that...and he was so happy when he won Postie of the Year. Forty-five years of his life dedicated to delivering the mail in all weathers. This,' Elsie gestured towards the storm outside, 'wouldn't have made a jot of difference to him. He was a good man. We both loved people over the years, yet we always drifted back together. Whatever happened, we always had each other. Always. I don't know what I'm going to do without him.'

Tears welled in Elsie's eyes and Penny could feel her own misting over. Her heart went out to the quiet, dignified woman in front of her.

'It's a huge blow, especially to you. You're among friends here, Elsie, and I hope you can at least take some comfort from that.'

Elsie grasped Penny's hand. 'That's very kind of you. When you were younger, I always thought how like your mother you were, but I can see I was wrong. There's a big dose of your father in there too. Such a lovely man, your dad.'

'I didn't know you were friendly with my parents.'

'Mainly your dad, really. He's been helping me with a community project.'

'Well, Dad's always been one for giving to the community.'

'And he's doing a grand job. Now, if you'll excuse me, I'll go over and see Eileen. Her Kenny has promised to fix the library van, and I need it up and running so I can get out to the pensioners. Sometimes I'm the only visitor they'll see for days.'

Penny watched Elsie shuffle over to the weighing station and reckoned that no matter what the scales said, the woman was carrying the heaviest burden in the room. She looked at her watch. Half past seven. Better get started. However, just as she was about to leave her post by the door, another newcomer arrived. Penny's heart sank, and she could feel her sense of optimism being swept away by the broom of doom. She knew this woman. This woman ironed her tea towels and ruthlessly judged others by the cleanliness of their houses and the whiteness of their laundry. She was like an emotional vampire with a vacuum cleaner.

Penny plastered on a smile and said, 'Sandra Next Door, how lovely that you could come.'

Eventually, weighing done and record books received, the group sat in a circle of chairs in the centre of the church hall. Penny took a deep breath, ready to make the first speech of what she hoped would be her brilliant new career.

'Hello everyone and welcome to Losers Club. Eileen will have told you about the website, and there's more information in your record books, but I want to tell you a little bit about how this will work and my own qualifications.

'I have a joint honours degree in psychology and nutrition, and I previously worked as a nutritionist in the sports industry. The journey we are all about to embark upon together isn't so much a diet, as a change of lifestyle. I won't be telling you what you can and can't eat or how much you should exercise. However, I will ask you to hit certain nutritional targets, and by doing so, you yourselves will adjust your diet. You each filled in a questionnaire when you were weighed, and I will email an individual plan to you tomorrow. In your record books there is a food diary, which I'd like you to keep. Each week, we'll discuss as a group how you are getting on, and I'll be available for one-to-one coaching. As we get to know each other, we'll agree exercise goals. This can be as a group or as one or two individuals.

'Now, I don't know if or how well everyone here knows each other, so we'll have a quick round robin where you introduce yourself to the group, and if you have any questions or concerns, please feel free to speak up. Who would like to go first?'

A hand shot up and Penny had to concentrate very hard on keeping her expression neutral.

'Hello. I'm Sandra Next Door. If you're not telling me what I can and can't eat, then what am I paying you for? Also, you're not exactly Twiggy yourself.'

Cow, thought Penny. 'Thank you, Sandra Next Door. A very interesting point of view. Who's next?'

Gordon and Fiona, a pair of shiny-faced thirty-somethings, introduced themselves as relative newcomers to the island. They'd moved to Vik seeking a simpler, self-sufficient lifestyle and lived on a smallholding near the village. Fiona gestured to the plastic box she'd given Penny earlier and said, 'We've brought along some snacks made using our own vegetables, and we'd like to share them with you, our new friends.'

Penny fetched the box and some paper plates and placed them on the low table in the centre of the circle. Inside the box was a colourful salad, the vegetables chopped and carved into intricate shapes. The group duly oohed and aahed, before enthusiastically tucking in.

Looking rather pleased with herself, Eileen dug into her bag and pulled out a round, pink tin. 'Gordon and Fiona, it's like you're actually psychic. Here, I've brought some healthy fruit and veg based pudding. Carrot cake or lemon drizzle?'

Penny's objections went unheard in the rush for cake.

'The thing is,' said Gordon through a hipster beard full of cake crumbs, 'we'd like to go vegan, but we can't give up this sort of thing. Cake and cheese. Mmmm.'

'Or, the best of both worlds, cheesecake! said Jim.

There was a chorus of mmms, and Mrs Hubbard commented that she did a delicious strawberry cheesecake ice cream cake. She would bring one in next week and they could try some.

'Helloooo,' said Penny. 'Weight loss group, not MasterChef final.'

'You said you weren't going to tell us what to eat,' complained Sandra Next Door.

'I'll bring some more veg and dips next time. We've had such a massive crop of tomatoes this year, I don't know what to do with them all,' said Fiona.

'It's all down to the right fertiliser. What are you using?' asked Jim.

'We make our own. We have one of those composting toilets.'

Jim's forkful of salad froze midway to his mouth. 'You mean…'

'Oh, yes,' said Fiona serenely, unperturbed by the look of horror on Jim's face. 'We use our own poop.'

Several people in the circle paled, and there were mutterings of "not very hungry, after all" as paper plates were piled back onto the table. Seemingly undaunted, Elsie continued to munch her salad. 'Bless you, sweet girl. I'll have some soup. Is it tomato?'

Mrs Hubbard nudged her. 'Turn up your hearing aid, Elsie. Poop! Anyway, you don't need to worry about diets. You've always been slim. I don't know how you do it.'

'I take my false teeth out at 6pm every evening. Unless I'm going out, of course.' She bared her teeth at the group, as if to reassure them. 'Now Archie's gone, I'm not going to get out very much. I only came here for the company because I don't want to be sitting in the house on my own, thinking about him. It was this or the crochet group, and with my arthritis, well…'

The short silence that followed was broken by Jim asking, 'Do the police have any idea what happened?'

'I don't know,' Elsie replied. 'They just said they'd be here as soon as the storm settles and to keep the house locked until then. It was very strange, though. He was wearing waterproofs, and there was another set hanging on the radiator behind the kitchen door. The kettle was on the stove, and there were two mugs, like he'd arrived from outside with someone and was making them a cup of tea. One of the kids next door said he saw a RIB down on the beach, but I expect it's washed away in the storm by now. It made me wonder if he'd been out on a boat with someone. But why? It's all very mysterious. I looked through the books and newspapers in the library in case there was a pattern, and there was nothing about Postmen of the Year being shot.'

'And if they were going to kill him, they could have pushed him over the side of the boat, not waited until he was making them a cup of tea,' said Jim.

'Which implies that the person he was with, wasn't the person who shot him,' said Penny. 'Ooh, we're quite good at this, aren't we?'

Anxious not to be outdone by Penny, Sandra Next Door said, 'Which means there was a third person there, and he or she is the killer.'

'What with the ferries being off, they couldn't have left the island,' said Mrs Hubbard.

'They could have taken the RIB, but the wind was already getting up. Unless they were an expert sailor, they'd probably have drowned. Also, the second person left his waterproofs at Old Archie's, making it more likely that he or she is a witness who ran off,' said Jim.

'So, somewhere on the island are a killer and a witness,' said Penny.

Eileen clapped her hands. 'Oh, we *are* good at this. We're like the Famous Five and the Secret Seven mixed together. Hang on, that's eleven and we're,' she counted the people in the room, 'eight. We're like the..the..Hateful Eight.'

'I think the lovely Quentin Tarantino might have something to say about that. Let's just stick to Losers Club,' said Penny.

'Losers Club, then. But can we at least have a dog called Timmy like in the Famous Five?'

'No.'

Eileen looked crestfallen. 'Pity. When are we going to start?'

'Start what?' asked Penny.

'Detecting. Solving the mystery.'

'We're not,' said Penny. 'We're a weight loss group, not a bunch of kids who put themselves in harm's way and get rewarded with lashings of ginger beer and a slap-up picnic.'

'I quite like a picnic,' said Fiona dreamily. 'Or a cream tea.'

'With a nice fruit scone,' added Elsie. 'Although the sultanas play havoc with my teeth.'

'And jam and cream,' said Gordon. 'Fiona makes her own strawberry jam. We take the runoff from the composting toilet—'

'Moving swiftly on,' interjected Penny.

Before she could continue, Jim stuck his hand in the air, like a giant child interrupting a teacher, and said, 'I think Eileen's got a point. We can't leave a murderer running around the island. What if they're after the witness? What if the witness was shot as well and is lying injured somewhere? We should at least try to find the witness. Make sure they're okay.'

'I'm not going around the place in a storm, trying to find someone who may or may not be injured,' sniffed Sandra Next Door, patting her stiffly lacquered hair. 'It was probably one of Old Archie's drinking pals, in which case they're more likely to die of liver failure before they die of a gunshot wound, and they were probably too pickled to remember a thing anyway. It's why I don't let my Geoff go to the village pub. A rough crowd.'

Elsie, whose hearing aid was now fully functional and had received every word loud and clear, reddened. She may be a frail, quiet little thing, thought Penny, but sometimes those are the ones you have to watch out for.

'You take that back,' said Elsie, glaring at Sandra Next Door. 'Archie was a good man, and I won't have a word said against him. He liked a pint now and then, but he was *not*, as you say, a rough crowd. He delivered the post to your house for years and never told a soul about those parcels. Except me.'

Sandra Next Door paled and mumbled a quick "sorry". Penny would have given her left buttock to know what was in those parcels. Although, if she ever did find out, she wouldn't tell her mother. Mary still hadn't forgiven Sandra Next Door for reporting Len to the local council when he got the new shed. If there was anything embarrassing in those parcels, Mary would lord it over the woman, like an avenging angel in an M&S Per Una cardigan. Penny looked at Elsie, who appeared to be once more on the verge of tears, and her heart softened. Sod it. This wasn't quite how she'd envisioned her first group meeting, but Jim was right. In the absence of any actual law and order, they could at least look into it for Elsie's sake.

'Okay, here's what we're going to do. Elsie, you have the keys to Old Archie's house, right?' Elsie nodded. 'You and Sandra Next Door go to the house and look for clues.'

Sandra Next Door opened her mouth to object, but Penny forestalled her. 'We're playing to your strengths here. If something's out of place in a house, you're the person most likely to notice.'

'What exactly are we supposed to be looking for?' asked Sandra Next Door.

Penny turned to Eileen, hoping for some help with an answer. Then, realising that any sensible help was unlikely to come from that direction, she turned to Jim.

'First things first,' said Jim. 'See if there are any clues as to the identity of the witness. Any personal belongings, things in pockets, that sort of thing. We're assuming it's a man, but could the waterproofs have belonged to a woman? Wear gloves, touch as little as possible and, when you check the pockets, try to leave everything as you found it. I've watched CSI. The police will go mad if they think we've messed up their crime scene.

'Secondly, try to work out where the shot came

from. Elsie, did anyone take any photographs before Old Archie was moved?'

'Doc Harris took some, but I don't think he'll let us see them. You know what an old stickler he is.'

'You'll just have to go from memory, then. Try to recreate the scene. Look at where he was standing, what he was probably doing at the time. Was he shot front to back or back to front? We can analyse the blood spatter and use laser pens to track the trajectory of the bullet.'

Elsie looked slightly sick, and Penny worried for a moment that Gordon's shitty tomatoes were going to make an unscheduled appearance on the church hall floor. She hoped not. The floorboards hadn't been revarnished in at least a decade, so they'd never get them clean in time for the football club.

'For goodness' sake, Jim. You've been watching too much telly!' Penny turned to Elsie and Sandra Next Door. 'Just take a good look around and try to get a sense of where the bullet came from, if you can. If it's too much for you Elsie, just leave it to Sandra. She has an eye for detail.

'Mrs Hubbard, would you mind checking Old Archie to see if there are any clues as to where he'd been or who he was with?'

Mrs Hubbard looked worried but took a deep breath and nodded stoically. 'It feels a wee bit disrespectful, but the poor man's dead in an ice cream freezer after all. I don't suppose he'd mind a wee frisk.' She patted her friend's hand. 'Oh, I'm so sorry, Elsie. That came out all wrong.'

Before Elsie had time to think about Mrs Hubbard getting frisky with Archie's corpse, Penny continued.

'Gordon and Fiona, could you speak to Old Archie's friends and find out if any of them knew what he'd been doing or where he'd been?

'Eileen and Jim, you're with me. We're going to check with the Coastguard to see if there was any unusual activity at sea the night Old Archie was killed and do some internet research into his background.'

Pleased that they were making progress, Penny punched the air and shouted, 'Yay! Go Losers!'

Seven faces stared blankly back at her for a moment, then everyone rose and started gathering their things together. She lowered her arm. 'I didn't mean go away losers. I meant…oh, never mind. Shall we meet at 7pm on Friday to discuss what we've found out? Village pub or Port Vik pub?'

The general consensus was that the village pub would be quieter on a Friday. After a flurry of finding pens and frantic scribbling, a few of the group exchanged phone numbers and made their way towards the coat pegs by door. Penny watched Elsie as she and Mrs Hubbard untangled their respective coats, cardigans and umbrellas. Neither seemed sure which belonged to whom, and the two elderly women appeared to be having a mild disagreement. Penny was just about to turn back to the hall to begin clearing up, when she caught sight of something out of the corner of her eye. She could have sworn she'd just seen Elsie slip her false teeth into Mrs Hubbard's coat pocket. Definitely one to watch out for, that one.

CHAPTER FOUR

Penny jerked awake to "I am the one and only, You can't take that away from me". For one confused moment, she stared up at Chesney, wondering how he was singing to her, then she remembered many wines with Eileen and much reminiscing with Eileen, followed by both of them loudly proclaiming their undying love for the Chezster and changing their ringtones to prove it. She rolled over and reached for her phone. 7am! Who the actual eff rings someone at 7am?! She didn't recognise the number and considered letting it go to voicemail, but curiosity got the better of her. Although if this was some twat telling her she'd been in a car crash and was due some compensation, she'd hunt them down and... 'Hello?'

'Penny? It's Jim Space. You little fucker.'

'I'm putting the phone down.'

'Sorry, not you. I'm out at Hillside farm. Bloody cow just tried to kick me. Are you at your mum and dad's? I thought I'd stop over on the way back, and we could work out what we're going to do today.'

'It's seven o'clock in the morning!'

'Don't worry, it'll be at least half an hour before I get there. Plenty of time to get the kettle on.'

Jim hung up, leaving Penny dumbstruck for the second time in their short reacquaintance. She growled and buried herself deeper under the duvet. That man was so annoying. What sort of psychopath drops by at half seven in the morning? She couldn't ignore him and hope he'd go away because something told her that he'd just stand there ringing the doorbell until someone gave in. Mum would go ballistic. Hector and Edith would roar and moan on about it for days, until she called them entitled brats and threatened to send them to work in a t-shirt factory in China so they could see how the other half lived. To be fair, that wasn't a bad idea. Not children working in factories, because she was very against that, but the twins getting a weekend job or a paper round. It might make them a bit less entitled. Especially Hector, who could be a pompous little git sometimes. She loved him and would fight to the very death for him, yet when he puffed himself up and said "Mother" in that disapproving tone of his, she sometimes wondered if it was too late to give him up for adoption. Nevertheless, whatever she did today, she had to make time to tramp around the village with him, delivering lost hamster leaflets through letterboxes. She'd make Edith come too. Maybe the twins would bump into some of the local kids and do normal things like smoking behind the bus shelter or kicking a football about, instead of hanging around the house, complaining of boredom, and standing in front of the fridge, yelling "there's nothing to eat."

Penny reluctantly emerged from her nest and got out of bed. If Jim Space thought she was going to make an effort for him, he had another thing coming. He could take her hairy legged in her "Grumpy but Gorgeous" nightie, and if he didn't like it, he could bugger off back to the farm. Actually, maybe not hairy legged. You have to have some self-respect, she decided, slipping on a pair of old pyjama bottoms under her nightdress. She checked herself out in the mirror and, with some satisfaction, noted that her hair was sticking up in fifty different directions, and she hadn't been entirely successful in removing last night's mascara.

'Yep, that should do it,' she told Chesney. 'And I won't even brush my teeth. Scare the beggar off and teach him never again to darken my door before nine.'

A few minutes later, having given in and brushed her teeth because even she could tell that her breath smelled like roadkill, Penny sat at the kitchen table, surfing the news while she waited for the kettle to boil. Every morning she'd read the BBC news, tut over the state of the world and pick out one or two articles for further research. Then she'd surf what she thought of as "the real news" websites for all the juicy details the Beeb had missed out in their efforts to not offend anyone or be sued. Sometimes it was not enough to be discreetly informed that a cabinet minister had been caught in flagrante. One needed to find out that he'd shacked up with a prostitute and spent a hundred grand of taxpayers' money on fine champagne and a set of furry handcuffs. Otherwise, what was the internet for?!

Penny was just about to check Twitter to find out which footballer had taken out an injunction preventing him being named as the man who, according to the BBC, sent "lewd" pictures to "an aspiring actress", when the doorbell rang. She rushed to the door, desperate to get there before Jim could ding dong some more and wake the whole house up. She got there and fumbled the door open, just as he was about to press the bell again.

'Do not touch that bell,' she hissed. 'Come in. I don't know what you were thinking, visiting someone at this time of morning.'

Jim grinned down at her, his eyes moving to her chest. 'Good morning to you too, Grumpy but Gorgeous.' He stooped down to pick up Len's newspaper from the doormat, then straightened up again, this time standing slightly closer.

Penny suddenly became very conscious that she wasn't wearing a bra. Crossing her arms over her chest, she turned away and snapped, 'Close the door behind you. Kitchen's through there. I'll just be a minute.'

As Jim ambled into the kitchen, she dashed into her bedroom and threw on her tatty old blue dressing gown. By the time she returned to the kitchen, Jim had settled himself into a chair and was reading Len's newspaper.

'Who d'you reckon this footballer is?' he asked.

'I don't know, and I don't care,' Penny lied, as she clattered around making cups of tea.

'Then why's your phone open on a Twitter search

for "footballer lewd pictures aspiring actress"?'

Penny snatched her phone off the table and shoved it in her dressing gown pocket. 'Mind your own business.'

Jim sighed. 'Look, I'm sorry to come round so early. I've been up at the farm half the night, and I didn't want to go home, fall asleep in a chair and forget to phone you. I was being selfish, and you've every right to be annoyed.'

As apologies go, that wasn't a bad one, thought Penny. She decided to relent and gave him a brief smile. 'Apology accepted. Toast?'

'Please. I'm starving.'

Penny bustled around, making tea and toast, before pulling her mother's magnetic shopping list pad off the fridge and sitting down opposite Jim, ready to make a to-do list.

Jim offered to come with her to help deliver the hamster leaflets, on the basis that he'd rather power through than take a nap and meet her later. They agreed to call the Coastguard late morning, then go to Eileen's to do some research. Penny hadn't been able to think of a task for Eileen that wouldn't end in disaster, but as long as Eileen was included, she'd be happy. It was going to be weird spending a whole day with Jim, though. He could be intensely irritating, and she was slightly worried that she might accidentally perform an involuntary castration by teatime.

'Do you not have to go to work at some point?' she asked.

'Nope. No more cows' bums for me. Dad's on duty today. He's mostly retired now, but he likes to keep his hand in.'

Penny quickly erased that particular mental picture. 'Have you always worked with your dad?'

Jim took a sip of his tea before replying, 'After uni, I was a vet in Banff for a while, then I moved closer to Aberdeen. I came back to the island a few months ago because Dad's getting on a bit and had some health problems. He's fine now. What about yourself? What led you back here?'

It turned out that Jim was practically the only person on the island who didn't read the gossip columns. Used to everyone she met knowing more about her private life than she knew herself, it was quite a novelty for Penny to fill someone in on what she'd been doing for the last…good Lord, it was almost thirty years. He seemed more interested in her time working with football teams than the fact that she'd married and divorced a famous actor. She'd just got to the part about how if there was a leader board for wankpuffins, the name Alex Moon would be at the top, when her parents arrived in search of breakfast.

'Ooh, wankpuffin. I'll add that one to my swear word collection,' said Mary.

'What's a wankpuffin?' asked Len.

'Who's a wankpuffin?' said a bleary voice behind them.

Penny mentally kicked herself and said, 'Goodness, Edith, it's not like you to be up this early. Come and have your breakfast, then get your eyebrows on because we're going down to the village to deliver hamster leaflets.'

Ignoring Jim, Edith sat at the table, waiting for Coco Pops to magically appear. Mary and Len introduced themselves and began a long tale about all the cats they'd ever owned and all the illnesses the cats had ever had. This gave Penny the opportunity to slip off and get dressed, banging on Hector's bedroom door on the way.

Eventually, Penny managed to herd both teenagers into the car, and they set off in a convoy behind Jim. Parking outside the village shop, she could see Mr Hubbard behind the counter. Presumably Mrs Hubbard was in the back, frisking a frozen corpsicle. She really didn't envy Mrs Hubbard that task, but it made sense that she was the one to do it. Clearly, it couldn't fall to Elsie. Penny wouldn't have even asked her to go to the house if she could have avoided it. Gordon and Fiona didn't know Archie, so the idea of them going through his pockets seemed disrespectful. Sandra would have refused point blank, and Eileen would have switched the freezer off by accident. She wondered if she should pop in and see how Mrs Hubbard was getting on. Maybe after they'd delivered the leaflets.

Penny was very impressed with how Hector had prepared for the leaflet dropping. He'd printed up a map of the village and divided it into three sections. Hector and Edith took the two smaller sections and went their separate ways. That left Penny and Jim to cover the larger section. Handing Jim a pile of leaflets, she directed him left and peeled off to the right, the idea being that they'd meet in the middle.

It didn't take long to cover the ground. In fact, most of the time was spent politely declining the offers of cups of tea when people spotted her coming up the path and came to their doors to find out what was going on. When she met up with Jim again, he was carrying a bag of fresh scones and a fruit loaf.

'I bet these aren't in the healthy eating plan,' he said.

'I haven't even written the plans yet. I went to the pub with Eileen last night, then some twat woke me up at 7am insisting we make a schedule for the day.'

'I wonder who that twat was. If you find out, let me know and I'll punch his lights out,' said Jim.

Penny laughed and said, 'Sure, but don't get arrested because the twat also suggested we investigate a murder and I need him. Listen, I was thinking we could look in on Mrs Hubbard while we're here. See if she's had a chance to search Old Archie yet. What do you reckon?'

'Good thinking, Hamsterwoman.'

As they slowly walked down the road, towards the shop, Penny couldn't help worrying about the little hamster.

'Aw, I hope someone finds Freddie. He's a lovely

wee thing, and I'd hate for him to suffer. Hector's genuinely heartbroken. I know this because even Edith's being kind to him about it. Yet I can't help worrying that Freddie isn't anywhere, and Mojo might have got to him.'

'Yes, it's a possibility,' said Jim. 'I didn't see Mojo when we were at your parents'. What sort of cat is he?'

'The kind that took one look at you, decided that his humans were utter bastards for inviting a vet into the house and went and hid under my bed. He's not any breed, just a black cat. Dad called him Mojo because he said if the cat ever went missing, at least he could put posters up saying he wanted his Mojo back,' said Penny.

They reached the shop door. Jim held it open for her and they stepped inside, turning to shake the rain off their umbrellas. When Penny turned back, she saw that Mr Hubbard was glaring at her from behind the counter.

'Is everything okay, Mr Hubbard?'

'No, lassie, it isn't. My Araminta is through there having a cup of sweet tea to get over the trauma and, by all accounts, it's your fault. What did ye think ye were doing asking a five-foot two seventy-year-old woman to get inside a freezer?'

On the outside, Penny was saying, 'I'm sorry, Mr Hubbard. I didn't ask her to actually get in the freezer. Just check Old Archie's clothing for clues. Is she alright?' On the inside, Penny was thinking, Araminta! Oh, that's a brilliant name, Araminta Hubbard. If I ever get a cat, I'm calling it Araminta.

Mr Hubbard softened slightly. 'Aye, well, Minty's in the back. You can go through and see her for yourselves.'

Penny and Jim trooped through the storeroom at the back of the shop and opened the door that led into Mr and Mrs Hubbard's house. They found Mrs Hubbard in a cluttered little living room, sitting in a burgundy velvet armchair by a fireplace. The flock wallpaper was almost obscured by shelves full of china figurines and miniature classic cars.

'Are you okay, Mrs Hubbard? Mr Hubbard said you got inside the freezer?' asked Penny.

'I'm absolutely fine, dearie. My Douglas is always making a fuss, pay no heed. There's nothing to worry about.'

'Are you sure? Did something happen? Mr Hubbard seemed quite upset.'

Mrs Hubbard looked uncomfortable. In a low voice, she said, 'It was just a wee accident. I'll tell you, but you mustn't tell anyone else.'

Penny and Jim assured her that they were the souls of discretion and would take her secret to the grave.

'It's a wee bit embarrassing,' began Mrs Hubbard. 'When we moved Old Archie up to the shop, we popped him inside some bubble wrap first to preserve the scene. My Douglas has been ebaying his model car collection, so we have loads of bubble wrap in the garage. You know, he got £100 for one of his cars and when he's done, we're going to book a cruise. The Parkins went on a Mediterranean cruise a few years ago, and they said they were so well looked after. Apparently, the ship was beautiful, and the food was wonderful. They said they'd go again in a heartbeat, but Mr Parkin can't get the travel insurance since he had that thing with his bowels.'

'Old Archie, Mrs H?'

'Sorry, dearie, I'm rambling. Well, I've seen the folk on telly in plastic suits so they don't get fibres on everything, and I thought to myself that I may not have a plastic suit, but I do have a birthday suit. So, I stripped down, covered my hands and my hair and got some scissors ready to cut the bubble wrap. I didn't think it would be difficult, because my Douglas had already cut the top bit, so Elsie could see Old Archie when she visited. I just didn't realise how many layers of bubble wrap there were. I was trying to hack my way through it, when I fell in the freezer, the lid came down and I couldn't get it back up again.

'It's just as well my Douglas noticed I'd been very

quiet for a while and came through to see what I was up to. He lifted the lid and there I was, naked as the day as I was born, except for a shower cap and a pair of Marigolds, lying on top of a frozen corpse. At least I wasn't in there too long, and I popped some bubbles to keep me busy. Well, those bubbles are hard to resist, aren't they?'

In the silence that followed, the ticking of the clock on the mantlepiece seemed suddenly very loud. Mrs Hubbard took a sip of her sweet tea and waited patiently. Penny's first instinct was to laugh, and she deliberately avoided catching Jim's eye in case he, too, was fighting off a fit of the giggles. Eventually, she cleared her throat and said in a shaky voice, 'I'm glad you're okay.'

Jim turned away and wheezed, 'I'm just going outside to check on Hector and Edith. They should be back by now and will be wondering where we are.'

Penny watched his back retreating through the living room door and thought, TRAITOR. She turned to Mrs Hubbard and saw to her relief that there was a twinkle in the woman's eyes. Mrs Hubbard's shoulders began to shake and soon she was roaring with laughter.

Through tears, Mrs Hubbard said, 'It was so embarrassing thinking about it in my head, but when I told you…oh…it's really funny. I don't think I've ever done something so daft. And your faces…my word, you should have seen your faces.'

When they'd both calmed down, other than the occasional snort, Penny asked, 'Did you find anything of use?'

'I found a Cornetto under his left thigh, and I gave it to Douglas to put in the other freezer. Oh yes, and there was a receipt for a restaurant in Gibraltar. What would Old Archie be doing in Gibraltar?'

'I've no idea, but it's a good start. Well done. I suppose I better go and see if Jim's managed to round up Hector and Edith. Thanks, though. I'm sorry about the freezer thing, but if it's any consolation, you've really cheered up my day.'

Still giggling, Penny made her way back through the storeroom and out of the shop.

When they returned to Valhalla, Hector and Edith leapt out of the car and made towards Sandra Next Door's house.

'Where are you two off to?' Penny called after them.

'We're going to search all the gardens for Freddie,' Edith shouted back.

'Make sure you ask people for permission before you go trampling through their gardens, otherwise we'll have the police round, and you know how much Granny likes a man in uniform. She'll end up in court for sexual harassment,' Penny warned.

'I really would,' said a voice behind her. 'You know they're not going to ask permission from anyone, don't you?'

'Yes, Mum, I know. But at least when you're in jail I can say "I told you so".'

Mary, wrapped head to toe in an enormous pink plastic mac, was loading a sword into the boot of her car. 'I'm running late for the WI meeting. We're practising in the church hall today,' she said. 'There are some fresh scones in the kitchen. Help yourselves before Len scoffs the lot. I made some yesterday and they've all gone. He's denying everything of course.'

As Mary trundled off down the drive, Jim asked, 'What is this obsession with scones? The entire bloody island runs on sultanas and carbohydrates. Anyway, I didn't know there was a branch of the WI on Vik. I don't recall my mum ever going, and it would have been right up her street.'

'There isn't. It's the Warrior Islanders. Quite the opposite of the Women's Institute.'

As they went indoors in search of a radiator and a hot cup of tea, Penny explained that once a week in the summertime, her sixty-eight-year-old mother donned a leather bikini, painted her face blue and re-enacted a battle from over a thousand years ago, when the islanders tried unsuccessfully to defend their wee patch of Scotland from the Norsemen. With a belly full of stretch marks and a bikini line that would shame a gorilla, Mary would entertain unsuspecting tourists with her fierce battle cries and prowess with a shield. Even when she broke her leg, Mary was still there, bikini line poking over the top of her cast like an unstoppable furry tide, waving her crutches in support of her fellow warriors.

'It's just as well it's raining. You don't want to see what's under that mac.' Penny concluded.

While Penny made tea, Jim called the Coastguard. Penny only heard his side of the conversation which, other than his enquiry as to whether they'd had reports of any unusual activity at sea on the night of Old Archie's murder, consisted entirely of "aye…aye…aye…aye…aye…aye…aye…aye."

'What did they say?' she asked as soon as he hung up.

'No.'

'So, what was all the aye aye aye about?'

'It was one of the boys from the football club. We were male bonding. He was telling me about his wife divorcing him and I was sympathising with him.'

'What was his end of the conversation? Gone, gone, gone?'

'Aye, well, not everyone's as bitter as you?'

'Bitter? Bitter? Bitter?!'

'Aye, aye, aye.'

'I'm not bitter about the divorce, you moron. Or the giant tax bill, mostly. Or even the affairs. I knew a long time ago he couldn't keep it in his pants, but I turned a blind eye because we had a nice life, two kids and, weirdly, we did love each other. What I *am* bitter about is that he shagged the au pair tart in our bed, and Edith was the one who caught them. He tried bribing her with a new iPhone to keep it to herself. She took the phone then agonised for days about whether she should tell me. No kid should be put in that position. Now, she may have forgiven him, but I will never forgive him bringing his shit into our house and for hurting our kids.'

'Ah, I didn't realise.'

'It's the one thing that didn't make the papers, and I'd be grateful if we could keep it that way. Edith never told Hector, and I never will either. He idolises his dad.'

Penny took a deep breath to calm down, then she realised something. Where was her own dad? The house was strangely silent. Normally Len would have heard her ranting and come through to keep the peace. She stood up and, ignoring Jim's protestations that he was sorry and he didn't know, stalked off in search of Len.

Failing to find Len in the house, Penny checked the garden. The wind was driving the rain into an almost horizontal sheet, and within seconds her jeans were several shades darker, and her thin t-shirt was plastered to her torso. Shielding her face to prevent her wet hair from whipping into her eyes, she looked across the lawn. Len was on the other side of the garden, the handle of his golfing umbrella tucked precariously beneath his chin while he locked up the big shed. Having managed to successfully turn the key in the lock without the heavy gusts sweeping him away like a latter-day Mary Poppins, he splashed his way back across the grass. He looked startled when he saw Penny.

'What were you doing?' she asked as they dashed into the house.

'I didn't expect you back so soon. I was just checking on some things in the shed. This storm seems never ending and, you never know, we could get cut off for weeks.'

As she entered the kitchen, Jim spied her sodden state and gave a wolf whistle. "Wahey. Wet t-shirt competition?'

Then he saw Len behind her and immediately apologised.

'Have you got foot in mouth disease?' snapped Penny. 'What with you spending half your life with your hand up cows' backsides, I can't say I'm surprised.'

'Hey, that's not funny. Or epidemiologically accurate,' Jim called after her as she stormed off in search of dry clothes. Muttering, 'Bloody women,' he turned to Len, who had lifted a tea towel from the worktop and was cleaning his glasses.

Oblivious to the storm raging indoors, Len was peering myopically at the plate which had been beneath the tea towel. He popped his glasses back on, smiled at Jim and held out the plate. 'Scone?'

CHAPTER FIVE

In Port Vik that afternoon, the streets were empty as the residents battened down the hatches against the raging storm. The wind howled down the narrow passageways and the streetlights, awakened early under a slate sky, cast a dancing orange glow on the wet pavements as the lampposts swayed and shuddered with each gust. The storm drains had long since given up, and water poured in small rivers down towards the harbour, where it flooded the road and returned to the foaming sea. Jim and Penny drove slowly along the harbour road, towards one of the pastel-painted cottages that were normally so picturesque but today looked drab and patchy, like pretty girls who'd woken up hungover and still wearing last night's glad rags.

Jim deftly steered the Land Rover through the deluge as, next to him, Penny pointed to a pink house near the end of the row.

'That's Eileen and Kenny's. If you pull up the lane to the side, you should be able to park at the back where it's bit more sheltered. I'm glad we took your car. Mine would never have made it through this.'

Jim patted the dashboard. 'Trusty old Phil. He's never let me down yet.'

Penny looked at him like he'd just won the weirdo world cup. 'You named your car?'

'Yep, Phil Tank. Because whenever I'm low on fuel, a wee fill tank light comes on. Don't tell me you've never named your car?'

'I'm not sure what I'd call it, other than a temperamental old rustbucket. Alex tried to get me to replace it with something fancy, but I didn't see the point when we were living in London. I mostly used public transport and only needed the car occasionally to get me from A to B. I'll give some thought to a suitable name for it.'

They knocked on Eileen's back door and, without waiting for an answer, let themselves in. Eileen was sitting at the kitchen table, helping her sons with their homework. As Jim and Penny entered, she told the boys, 'Ricky, clear a space so your Auntie Penny can sit down. Gervais, go and get the chair from the other room for Jim.' She beamed at Penny, who was busy unloading a bag full of chocolate treats and biscuits. 'I'll put the kettle on, shall I?'

'That would lovely. I've brought some of Dad's old jigsaw puzzles for Kenny. The bag's enormous, so I've left it in the back porch,' said Penny.

As Eileen scuttled off to look in the jigsaw bag, Jim whispered to Penny, 'And you thought me naming my car Phil was strange. Ricky and Gervais?'

'Kenny's a big fan. Just be glad they didn't go with her first choice. She loved Rainbow as a kid. If her mum and I hadn't intervened, it would have been so much worse. As it was, we had to compromise.'

Eileen came back into the kitchen and caught sight of her eldest. 'Ricky Zippy Bates, you put down those biscuits right now!'

'Let me guess,' murmured Jim. 'Gervais Bungle?'

'No, we bargained her down to George.'

They settled themselves at the table and listened as Ricky and Gervais embarked on a long tale about a fort they'd built in the woods and how they were worried that the plastic sheeting they'd used to cover it wouldn't withstand the storm. This was, apparently, their finest fort yet and when it stopped raining, they planned to dig out a dungeon so they could catch the island murderer and lock him up.

Eileen hastened to put an end to this talk of murderers. With bribes of chocolate biscuits and a movie, she managed to temporarily banish the boys to the living room, so that the grown-ups could talk. About murderers.

'Pour l'amour de la merde, if I hear about this fort once more, I'll dig the…pardon my French…flipping dungeon myself and put them both in it. Sorry, the school sent all the kids home early because it flooded, and my two are driving me daft.' She parked her bottom between Penny and Jim and pulled the laptop towards them. 'Maths homework. I could never do maths. I'm more of a languages person myself. Right, what are we Googling?'

'Try Archie Henderson,' said Jim.

'Here we go. Archie Henderson is a retired Canadian ice hockey player. Well, I never knew that! Postman of the Year and an ice hockey player. Mind you, he did a good job of losing the accent. You'd never have been able to tell.'

'Moving on,' said Penny, giving Eileen a playful whack over the head with a maths jotter. 'It looks like there are over five million results. We need to narrow it down a bit. Let's try…Archibald Henderson…hmm…over three million. Maybe some of the newspaper articles about him winning Postman of the Year will have some information. Try Henderson postman of the year.'

They scrolled through the articles, finding little of interest, until Eileen suddenly exclaimed, 'Stop! Scroll up. Click on the photo.'

Penny and Jim stared at the photo, confused.

'Look! Zoom in. It's there on the certificate.' Eileen stabbed the screen with her finger, and Penny turned to her in amazement.

'Mon Dieu, Eileen. You wee genius.'

There was Archie, proudly holding up a Postman of the Year certificate bearing the name Archibald Eugene Henderson. Penny quickly typed the name into the search engine.

'No results found. That's unusual.'

She tried Archie Eugene Henderson. No results. She tried Archie Henderson Vik. No results beyond

Postman of the Year.

'He was what? Seventy? He possibly didn't use the internet much, so it's not surprising there's no trace. Let's try birth records. If we get a date of birth, we can maybe search some of the genealogy sites and see if there are any relatives,' suggested Jim.

After an hour of drawing a blank, Jim said, 'Maybe we're doing something wrong. My dad has an unusual name. Google Ivor Space.'

'Three hundred results, none of them relevant,' said Penny. 'Let's have a look for his birth records. What's his date of birth?'

'2nd of February 1950.'

Penny quickly went through all the open tabs, inputting Ivor Space. 'No trace. This is very weird. Let's try my parents.'

There was no trace of Len and Mary Hopper. There was no trace of Eileen's mum either.

'I'll try Araminta Hubbard,' said Penny.

'Wow! Mrs Hubbard was born in 1847,' said Eileen a moment later.

'Oh, maths really isn't your strong suit, is it?' Penny laughed, giving her friend a nudge with her elbow. 'Seriously, though. Don't you think this is strange? Our parents don't exist. Mrs Hubbard doesn't exist.'

Eileen suggested that maybe their parents were aliens. Surely this could be the only reasonable explanation. 'I'm going to ask my mum what planet she's from.'

'Well, the alien theory might explain a lot,' said Penny, who had often wondered the same about Eileen, 'but there's probably some logical earthly reason. Although I can't imagine what it would be. Do you think we should ask our parents, or should we share our findings with the group first? I'm inclined to keep everything within Losers Club for now, simply because we don't want it getting out that we're asking questions, or we'll have half the island coming to us with wild theories. Always assuming Mrs Hubbard hasn't told the entire village yet.'

'What if one of the group is the murderer?' asked Eileen, looking horrified.

'It's hardly going to be Elsie or Mrs Hubbard. Sandra Next Door would have tidied up the mess and hidden the body under her begonias. I suppose it could be Gordon and Fiona, but they didn't know Old Archie, and this is going to sound terrible, they're a couple of big softies. I wasn't on the island at the time, and you can't even work the telly remote, never mind a gun. That leaves...' Penny and Eileen stared at Jim.

'I had my hand up a cow's arse at the time,' he said, holding up the offending hand. 'I have a farmer, nine other cows and a randy mare as witnesses.'

'Is that a randy mare as in horny horse, or do you mean Randy Mair from Hillside Farm?' asked Eileen.

'Both, I suppose. So, are we going to ask our parents?'

They agreed to ask the others about it at the pub the next evening.

Penny and Jim stayed at Eileen's house until Kenny got home from work. A big man in oil-stained mechanic's overalls, he came in swearing, asking who had left a bloody big bag at the back door. He'd nearly tripped over it and was most unfuckin'happy. Penny owned up, and the peace offering of jigsaw puzzles was accepted. Ricky and Gervais appeared, throwing themselves on their dad and gabbling about the movie they'd been watching, while Eileen raised her voice above the hubbub, telling her three boys, two small and one large, to go and wash their hands because the broth was ready. Penny smiled at the happy domestic scene playing out before her. She felt a pang for similar moments shared with Alex and the twins, but she was glad that her friends had so much love and warmth in their lives.

Later, in the car on the way back along the harbour road, Jim remarked, 'What a perfect little family they are. I envy them that. I always wanted a family, but I never met the right person.'

Penny wasn't paying attention. She was sitting forward, eyes scrunched, peering through the rain towards two figures who were standing below a streetlight. Despite the rain, neither was wearing a hood and they appeared to be arguing.

'Slow down,' she said. 'Isn't that Captain Rab? Who's he with? Look at the pair of them, they're soaked to the skin. I wonder what on earth they're doing out in this weather without the proper gear. Stop the car and check they're okay.'

Jim stopped the car and lowered his window. 'Is that you, Captain Rab? Are you okay?'

'Mind your own damn business!' came the reply.

The stranger with Captain Rab had turned at the sound of Jim's voice. He was a young man, perhaps in his early twenties. The rain bounced off his thick-rimmed glasses and plastered his dark hair to his forehead. As he raised his hand to push his hair back, Penny caught a flash of white and was left with the distinct impression that his arm was in a cast.

Jim tried again. 'It's no weather to be outside. Can I give either of you a lift home?'

'Did you not bloody hear me? Stop sticking your nose in and get on your way,' said Captain Rab.

The stranger, however, looked relieved and approached the car window, bending down to ask Jim if he'd give him a ride to the Vik Hotel. Behind him, Captain Rab was roaring, 'Get back here, laddie. I'm not done with you yet.'

'I don't know you, and I don't want anything to do with you, so leave me alone,' the young man shouted back. He got into the car and shut the door, cutting off the responding rant from the other side of the street. 'Sorry about that and thanks for rescuing me. I walked down to see if the Harbour Chip Shop was open, and that lunatic came out of nowhere and started shouting at me.'

'You came out in this weather for fish and chips?' asked Penny in amazement. 'There's a chip shop right next to the hotel!'

'I know. Call me an idiot tourist, but I just fancied a change. I'm Pete, by the way.'

Penny extended a hand. 'Pleased to meet you, Pete. Penny and Jim. Is that a touch of an American accent I hear?'

'Canadian. My mom and dad are Scottish, and they emigrated years ago. So, I'm back in the home country, finding my roots as it were.'

'Were they from Vik?'

'No, they were from the west coast. I'm making the most of my time and touring all over Scotland. Although my schedule has been a little disrupted by the storm. I only booked to stay one night, but the ferries stopped, and I was stuck here. It hasn't helped having this, of course.' He waved the arm in the cast at her. 'I'm almost out of painkillers. However, the island hospitality is legendary, and Martin and Rachel at the hotel have been angels. They've given us rooms at half the normal rate.'

'Us? Are there more of you trapped on Vik?' asked Jim.

'Yeah, a couple of American tourists, an English guy and a Russian woman. We're an odd group, and we've been thrown together in odd circumstances, but we're making the best of it. I just needed to get away from them for a while and thought I'd grab a bite on my own.'

Jim steered Phil along the high street and pulled up outside a large, white building that dominated the town Square. 'Here we are. I hope this storm dies down soon so you can carry on with your trip.'

Pete thanked them, ducked out of the car and, head down against the rain, ran to the hotel entrance.

'Nice guy,' commented Jim, as they drove off. 'Pity about his holiday being mucked about.'

'You do realise what this means, don't you?'

'What?'

'Honestly, I partnered with you because you were the only vaguely sensible one, even if you are a bit annoying.'

'Yet astonishingly handsome.'

'And quite arrogant.'

'But still out of your league. Be honest with yourself, Penny. The only reason you're not throwing yourself at me is because you know you'd be punching above your weight.'

'I could never tire of punching you.'

They bickered their way back to Valhalla where, just as Penny was about to slam the car door in an almighty strop, Jim remembered her original question.

'Pete's holiday being messed up. What does it mean?'

'Suspects, you big idiot. Think about it, a group of people who don't belong on Vik and who were here at the time of the murder.' Determined to have the last word, she gave the door an almighty shove and sprinted towards the house, leaving Jim to ponder their next steps.

The house was in darkness and eerily quiet. Jim's headlights briefly illuminated the hall as he turned the car around, and Penny took advantage of the light to pull off her wellies. She shuffled across the wood floor in her socks and flicked the light switch. Nothing happened. Where was everyone? This felt very spooky. A flickering in the crack beneath the living room door alerted her to another presence in the house, and she crept forwards, reaching out to turn the handle. The door swung inwards, and her heart leapt into her throat as a pale face loomed out of the darkness.

'Hello, Chunky,' said a voice. 'Toasted marshmallow?'

As Penny's eyes adjusted, she saw her mother sitting cross legged in the centre of the living room, toasting marshmallows on a stick over the old camping stove. Len and the twins were supervising from the sofa, sleeping bags wrapped around their knees. Mojo, who was curled up on Edith's lap, deigned to open a sleepy eye to check out the new arrival, decided it was nobody important, and went back to sleep.

'The storm has knocked the power out,' Len explained. 'It's 1983 all over again.'

'So, we've set up camp in the living room, and we're telling ghost stories. We couldn't find the new camping stove anywhere. It's just as well I remembered we had this one in the attic,' said Mary, proud of her ingenuity.

Len shone a torch on himself. His expression was miserable, he was covered in a fine layer of dust and a spider's web hung from his right ear. 'Yes, and she made me go up there and dig it out.'

Penny settled herself into the armchair and asked the twins how their search for Freddie had gone. They shifted uncomfortably in their seats and exchanged glances.

'We searched all the gardens in the row and didn't find any sign of him,' said Hector gloomily.

'That Sandra Next Door's a right cow. She wouldn't let us in her garden until I told her I knew what she'd been up to and if she didn't let us search her garden, I'd tell Granny,' said Edith.

'What has she been up to?' asked Mary.

Edith shrugged. 'I dunno. But anyone that uptight has to be up to something. She was like well-spooked.'

'Ooh, I'd love to know. I bet she has a secret lover. Or maybe she's a "real housewife", you know, not like a housewife who does housework, but one of those…'

Mary continued to speculate, but Penny wasn't listening. She was watching the twins, who were casting meaningful glances at each other and looking rather shifty. Never mind Sandra Next Door, those two were definitely up to something. There was little point in pressing them on it, Penny decided. They'd only deny everything. Anyway, Vik was a place with limited opportunity for shenanigans, and the island grapevine would soon alert her to any wrongdoing. She smiled at the irony of grown-up Penny relying on the very thing that her teenage self had so resented.

As Mary rounded off a monologue on how Sandra Next Door was definitely a lap dancer in Aberdeen because she was always there allegedly shopping, yet she never came home with lots of bags, a thought struck Penny.

'All the lights were on in the village when we drove through it earlier. Has anyone checked the fuse box? Where's the fuse box?'

Len's shoulders slumped and he looked the perfect picture of misery. 'In the attic.'

CHAPTER SIX

Penny awoke the next morning to a rhythmic tapping sound. At first, she couldn't work out where it was coming from. Confused, she stumbled out of bed and opened her bedroom door. Nobody was there yet the tapping continued. It seemed to be coming from the window. Wide awake by now, Penny strode over to the window, flung back the curtains and almost had a minor coronary. Jim was standing outside, clutching a small bunch of what she was certain were begonias from Sandra Next Door's garden. She opened the window and hissed, 'What do you think you're doing?'

'Peace offering,' said Jim, squeezing the flowers through the gap.

'What time is it?'

'Ah, that's why I'm giving you the peace offering. Don't look at the clock. Just focus on the flowers. Is that a poster of Chesney Hawkes?'

'That is indeed the one and only Lord Chezza of the Hawkes, and I'll thank you to keep your opinions to yourself.' She looked at the flowers Jim was waggling at her. 'I'm not taking those. Sandra Next Door's begonias are Mojo's favourite peeing spot.'

Jim cursed, quickly withdrew the flowers and dropped them on the ground. 'Can I come in and wash my hands?'

Penny sighed, closed the window and padded through the house to open the front door.

Jim stood there, grinning down at her. His gaze flickered to her chest. 'Bra off, PJs on. Yep.'

She crossed her arms over her chest, glared at him and stalked off in search of her dressing gown. Slipping her phone into the pocket, she went through to the kitchen, where Jim had found some carbolic soap and was giving his hands a thorough scrub.

'Don't you ever go to work?' Penny asked him.

'Dad's in charge again. Mrs Taylor's dog won't stop chasing its tail. Dad likes taking on the weird ones. He says it helps make ends meet.'

Penny groaned. 'What is it that couldn't wait until…,' she checked her phone, '…at least 8am?'

'I was thinking about what you said last night.'

'What? The bit about you having your head so far up your own backside, you should clean your teeth with a toilet brush?'

'No, the bit about there being visitors on the island. We should interview them. Give them a good grilling. Check the hotel CCTV. Break into their rooms and search them for clues. Take their toothbrushes and get them tested for DNA.'

'Or we could go to the hotel for breakfast, bump into them, have a friendly chat and steer the conversation towards where they were on the night of the murder?'

'Yes, that might work too.'

'Sorry about the toilet brush comment, by the way.'

'And I apologise for saying your breath smells like a cow with parasitic gastro-enteritis?'

'You didn't say that last night.'

'No, but I'm saying it this morning, and damn sorry I am for it too.'

Flossed and brushed, washed and dressed, Penny scribbled a note for her parents and the twins, then left with Jim for Port Vik. He'd phoned ahead to check whether the hotel could accommodate an extra two for breakfast, and when they arrived, Rachel was waiting for them at the front desk. The lobby was beautiful, with its high ceilings, oil paintings of familiar Scottish landmarks and warm oak woodwork. Rachel and Martin had clearly invested in the public areas when they bought the place.

'I hope you don't mind,' Rachel said, 'I've put you by the window. We have some other guests, and I thought you'd like to sit away from them. Be a bit more private.'

This was the exact opposite of what they wanted, but Penny wasn't sure how to tell her that they'd quite like to eavesdrop on the other guests. Rachel had been in the year above Penny and Jim at school, so neither felt they knew her well enough to confess that they were a couple of nosey parkers. There was an awkward silence, broken by the arrival of Martin, who came ambling through from the lounge, wiping his hands on a bar towel. Smiling at Jim, he nodded his head towards Penny and said jovially, 'You better watch out for this one. She whacked me on the nose with a toy train when we were three. I've got PTSD. Post Train Smacking Disorder!'

Everyone dutifully laughed and Martin showed them to their table. 'I must say, it's great that you two got back together,' he said.

'Oh, no. We're not—' Penny began, but Martin had already bustled off to get them some coffee.

Penny gazed around the plush dining room, with its green tartan carpet and ornate fireplace, before her eyes finally came to rest on Jim, who appeared highly amused by something.

'You do realise they think we've just spent the night together and are here for a post-coital fry-up, don't you?' he told her.

Penny rolled her eyes. 'Oh dear. We'll have to break up. How about I throw a glass of water in your face and storm out?'

'Could you wait until I've finished my sausages, please?'

'No problem. You can signal when you're ready. Just say the words "stuck on you" and I'll do it.'

The friendly banter continued through breakfast. Penny idly wondered what it would be like if they were actually a couple. On the one hand, he could be incredibly irritating and slow on the uptake, although she suspected he did this on purpose to wind her up. On the other hand, he was funny, decent and quite good looking. But was she ready for a relationship? She didn't think so. Also, there was the twins to consider. If she brought anyone into their lives, it had to be a relationship that would last. Penny's mind whirred, as she mulled over whether her new friendship with Jim could develop into something else or whether it would be better for everyone, in the long run, to simply stay friends.

In the meantime, Jim was also giving some thought to Penny. She was a sparky little thing and he really, really liked her. Was she wearing a push-up bra? How many sausages could you make from one pig? He'd have to Google it later.

Their inner dialogues were interrupted by the arrival of the other diners, who took their seats at a large, circular table in the centre of the room. Peter sat next to a pale, thin woman, with red curly hair, who was bemoaning the lack of coffee in a high-pitched, whiny voice. The middle-aged man beside her, who hadn't removed his baseball cap, leaned back in his chair to signal to Martin. As he raised his arm, his green T-shirt parted company with his waistband, and the dark-haired woman to his left was treated to the sight of an exceptionally hairy belly spilling over his belt. She quickly turned away, her thin lips curling in disgust. The man to whom she had turned didn't appear to have noticed. He was hunched over a mobile phone, rapidly typing with both thumbs. Only the top of his head, a crew cut disguising a balding pate, was visible.

It wasn't long before Pete spotted Penny and Jim. He came over to their table and declared it awesome to see them again. Penny felt that awesome might be stretching it a bit. Here in the North East of Scotland, the word fine covered the full range of adjectives to describe any state of being, from death's door (not so fine) to absobloodylutely fantastic (awful fine). Penny consulted her inner fine-o-meter and told Pete it was quite fine to see him too.

At the urging of Pete, they joined the other guests, who shuffled around to make room for them. Penny found herself between Pete and the red-haired lady, Jim between the dark-haired woman and the thin man with the phone. The red-haired lady introduced herself and her husband as Ruth and Larry Cohen from Illinois. Penny wondered why Americans always gave their home state as an introductory suffix. She couldn't imagine introducing herself as Penny Moon from Vik. Ruth's nasal whine cut through her inner musings, and she focused her attention on the conversation.

'…And the two of us were rattling around in this big old apartment. So, I said to Larry, didn't I Larry? I said, "Larry, for the first time in our married lives we can go anywhere we want." He always wanted a vacation in Scotland, so here we are.'

Ruth pulled her handbag from the back of the chair and rummaged around inside, disturbing an alarming amount of what appeared to be bottles of pills, before extracting her purse. She saw Penny notice the pill bottles and looked embarrassed.

'Larry hasn't been well,' she murmured. 'He had Guillain-Barré Syndrome, and it left him with some long-term health problems. I'm a walking pharmacy. Anyway, you don't want to hear about that. I was going to show you some pictures of my babies. Of course, they're grown-up babies now. Here's Abigail at her graduation and here's…'

Jim was having less luck with his table partners. The dark-haired woman turned out to be Yulia Klimova, a Russian businesswoman. Jim initially thought she was with Anthony Woodbead to his left, but it turned out that they'd only met since their unexpected stay on the island. However, a certain familiarity between them, something in the way they kept seeking each other out with their eyes, suggested that they'd been indulging in some extracurricular entertainment of an evening.

In response to Jim asking what had brought her to this little corner of Scotland, Yulia told him, 'It is my holibobs. I go places where the office can't find me, for absolute peace and quiet. Where is better for that? I am not like the others. I book here for two weeks, and I find myself in the group. I like these strange little people. I came to be alone, yet I am surrounded.'

She shrugged and, having no more to say, passed the baton on with a glance towards Anthony, who neatly evaded Jim's question by asking questions of his own.

'Do you live on the island?'

'Yes, I'm the local vet,' said Jim. 'I grew up here, went away for a while and now I'm back working with my dad, who's been the vet here for years.'

'And Penny? Is she your...?'

'Friend. We knew each other at school, and we've only recently met up again through a weight loss group.'

Anthony looked pointedly at Jim's plate, which had six sausages on it. 'And how's that working out for you?'

'Well, she can be a bit prickly, but she looks great in pyjamas.'

'I meant the diet,' Anthony laughed.

'What about you? What do you do?' asked Jim.

'Oh, I'm quite boring, I assure you. I'm an accountant. Anyway, how do you know Pete?'

Jim looked over at Pete, who was deep in conversation with Penny. 'We met him yesterday evening. We were coming home from visiting a friend and he was having an argument with someone in the street. We stopped to find out what was going on and gave him a lift back to the hotel.'

'What on earth was he doing out in the storm?'

'He said he was getting fish and chips. It seemed odd that he didn't go to the chip shop in the Square, though. Said he wanted to get away on his own for a bit, then Captain Rab appeared and just started shouting at him.'

'The ferry guy? I remember him from our trip here.

He was quite rude, but he didn't come across as the type to accost people in the street.'

'I don't know,' said Jim. 'We were terrified of him as kids. He lives in one of the cottages down by the harbour, and it was a massive dare to knock on his door and run away. Chap and Run, the game was called. Mind, you had to be fast not to be caught by Captain Rab.'

'We used to play that. It was called Knocky Knocky Nine Doors where I was from.'

'Is that the Newcastle area? I trained as a vet there for a while and that's what the kids on the estate called it.'

Anthony shifted uncomfortably. 'Northumberland. If you and Penny live here, why didn't you have breakfast at home instead of coming out in this weather?'

'This weather's nothing to an islander. We're used to it, although this storm is quite rough, I'll give you that.'

They chatted about the weather for a while, with Yulia joining in to tell them about the snow in Moscow, until they were interrupted by Pete, who was trying to scoot his chair along next to Anthony but was somewhat impeded by the cast on his arm. Anthony stood up and lifted the chair over, then sat back down, looking thoughtfully at Pete.

Pete was thanking Anthony for his help, when the table vibrated and Yulia's phone screen lit up. She checked the screen then stood abruptly, gave the company a terse smile and walked quickly away in the direction of the lobby, clutching the phone to her ear. A few seconds later, Penny excused herself, asking if anyone knew where the ladies' loos were.

With one eye on Penny's hasty exit, Jim tuned into Anthony's conversation with Pete. Anthony was quizzing him about yesterday evening's foray into the storm, and Pete looked as though he regretted having moved over. His fingers twisted nervously around a napkin as he explained to Anthony that he'd simply become tired of being cooped up in this damned hotel. His discomfort was entirely at odds with his earlier bonhomie when he'd introduced them to the group, and Jim couldn't help wondering what Pete was hiding. He decided to wait until Penny returned then make their excuses and leave so they could compare notes.

Jim didn't have long to wait. Penny came back, looking flushed. Whatever she'd been up to, she had definitely visited the ladies because a ribbon of toilet roll was trailing from her shoe. She gave him an expectant look, and he pushed his chair back from the table, saying, 'It was great to meet you all, but Penny and I have to get going. I hope we have the chance to meet again before you leave.'

He stood up and turned towards Penny. 'Erm, you've got some toilet roll stuck on you.'

She gave him a grin of the purest evil, and he realised he'd fallen into a trap. The little witch, he thought, she'd managed to spy on Yulia and still make time to set him up.

'No! Don't you dare, you wee vratch.'

Penny looked towards the jug of water at the table then back at Jim, raising her eyebrows and smiling meaningfully.

Jim glared at Penny, grabbed his coat off the back of his chair and sprinted for the exit.

Penny beamed at the group, who were looking somewhat confused by Jim's sudden departure, and said her goodbyes. She followed him out to the car, stopping only at reception to ask Rachel one final question.

Jim was sitting in the car, looking grumpy. Penny hauled herself up into the front passenger seat and smirked at him.

'Oh, come on,' she said. 'After all the times you've wound me up since we met, a bit of payback was overdue. I wasn't actually going to chuck water on you.'

Jim relented. 'Fair enough, I suppose. Do you want to compare notes?'

'Not here,' said Penny. 'Let's go back to Mum and Dad's. I haven't seen much of the twins in the last couple of days, and I feel a bit guilty. Not that they've probably noticed. They've either been busy searching for Freddie or shut in their rooms playing crap music. Mum keeps complaining about glasses, crockery and food disappearing. I'll have to put my hazmat suit on and conduct a search under their beds at some point.'

When they arrived at Valhalla, everyone had gone out. Mary had left a scribbled note on the kitchen table to say they'd taken the twins into town to get them out of the house and wasn't it about time that Penny enrolled them in school? Penny had thought about this, but she'd wanted to give the twins a couple of weeks to settle in before packing them off to a new school. Yet, for once, her mother was probably right. The routine and social aspect of school would do them some good. Penny parked the problem as something to follow up on later and turned her attention to Jim.

'Do you want to start or shall I?' she asked.

'I'll go first. Yulia Klimova says she's a businesswoman who's just getting away from it all. She booked ahead for two weeks, something we can easily check with Martin and Rachel. You don't check into a hotel for two weeks if you're planning on murdering someone. Fact! On that basis, she's not a likely suspect. The things against her are a) it's weird that a Russian woman would come to Vik for a fortnight's holiday, b) she didn't say what sort of business she's in and c) she talks like she learned English from the Urban Dictionary. Holibobs, for God's sake. But, unless you've found something a bit more concrete, I think we can more or less rule her out.

'Next, Anthony Woodbead. He was *very* cagey. He avoided any questions about himself, and all I got out of him was that he's an accountant who grew up in Northumberland. No idea why he's here, but if it was just a tourist day trip while he happened to be in Aberdeen, why not say so? Also, he seemed very interested in Pete's little jaunt to the harbour yesterday. I'd say Anthony is definitely a suspect. And definitely shagging Yulia.

'Which brings me to Pete. His trip to the harbour didn't quite ring true, and I think there's more to the Captain Rab thing than he's letting on. However, Rab's an angry man and a bit of a bully, so I have some sympathy for Pete. It could have happened like he said, but he seemed damn uncomfortable when Anthony was asking him about it. The thing that makes me inclined to rule out Pete is the cast on his arm. Yes, you can hold a gun in either hand. But he struggled to lift a chair one-handed. It wasn't that heavy, so it leaves me wondering if he could hold a gun steady one-handed. Okay, your turn.'

Penny gave Jim a self-satisfied smile and said, 'I have something which might change your opinion of Yulia. I followed her out to the lobby, where she was talking to someone on the phone. I went into the loos and kept the door open a crack so I could listen. I didn't catch it all, but I heard her telling the person on the other end "if Max won't do it then tell Alexander to shoot him." She was clearly ordering a hit or something. She must be mafia or some sort of assassin.'

'Shit, that's serious stuff,' said Jim, impressed by Penny's stealthy sleuthing. 'Let's keep Yulia in play. What about the others?'

'The American couple, Ruth and Larry Cohen, aren't a good bet. Larry's recovering from some serious illness which has badly affected his arms and legs. Ruth told me about it. He's on a whole load of medication and can only walk short distances. Ruth has a handbag full of pills, so I think she's telling the truth. They're empty nesters, enjoying their first holiday since the kids left home. Larry definitely couldn't have done it and Ruth seems very genuine. I would rule them out as suspects.

'I didn't get much out of Pete. He seemed a little over-anxious to please, but he didn't say anything to make me rule him in or out. I agree with you. Yesterday's trip to the harbour and the argument with Captain Rab doesn't quite sit right with me. I say we keep him as a suspect.'

Jim pulled Mary's magnetic shopping list notebook off the fridge and slid Len's crossword pen out from under the newspaper. 'Let's make a to-do list. Our suspect pool is Yulia the Assassin, Anthony the Shifty and Pete the Quarreller. We'll need to do some internet research on them. What else?'

'We don't know that they're the only outsiders who are staying on the island. The murderer could have arrived days before and be staying with relatives, although as I said, it's unlikely a murderer would have planned on hanging around. We need to know who arrived on the day of the murder and who didn't leave on the evening ferry. Who do we need to call to check the ferry manifest?'

Jim looked perturbed. 'That would be Captain Rab. Which one of us Losers is going to ask him? I don't want to, but I think it makes sense that you and I do it because it'll give us a chance to ask him about the argument with Pete. Mind you, I'd like to be a fly on the wall if Sandra Next Door was questioning him. She's almost as bad-tempered as he is.'

Penny rolled her eyes in agreement and continued her stock take of the evidence. 'The only other two leads at the moment are Old Archie's receipt from Gibraltar, courtesy of Mrs Hubbard, and the fact that Old Archie and our parents don't appear to exist. I've no idea how or if those things are connected to the murder.'

'Aye, I'm not sure what to do about those things yet. We haven't found out anything about the witness either. Let's wait and see what the others have when we meet them at the pub later,' said Jim.

They agreed that it was probably about time that Jim went to work, and Penny knew she really ought to get on with writing the nutrition plans before Sandra Next Door started voicing her dissatisfaction to the village gossips. However, first she'd phone the school and ask about enrolling the twins.

After Jim had left, she dialled the number for Port Vik Academy. Used to automated voicemail services, with their multiple options for every conceivable teenage problem (press 1 to report an absence, press 2 to leave a message for head of year, press 3 if overnight your child has sprouted an indecent amount of body hair/enormous zit and is refusing to leave the house ever again), Penny was surprised when an actual human being answered.

'Hello, Port Vik Academy, how can I help you?'

'Hi. I was wondering how I can enrol my children.'

'No problem. I'll take some details then make an appointment for you to come in and see the Head Teacher this afternoon.'

'Who is the Head Teacher these days?'

'It's Mr Hancock. Murray Hancock.'

Oh bugger, thought Penny, better start the inner mantra straight away. I must not say Furry. I must not say Furry. I must not say Furry. Oh bugger, bugger, bugger, I'm definitely going to say Furry.

CHAPTER SEVEN

The twins made an enormous fuss about meeting the Head Teacher that afternoon. They'd arrived home just before lunch and Penny, sure that at the very least they would be curious to see their new school, greeted them with the wonderful news that she'd done a good parent thing. Instead of cherubic cries of "I can't wait to walk the hallowed halls of learning and let my wee brain soak up the wisdom of Furry," there was slamming of doors and angry declarations that they didn't have time to go to school. They were very busy.

'Busy doing what?' Penny shouted back. 'Because practising make-up, watching YouTube and masturbating twelve times a day does not count as busy.'

Hector puffed out his chest, crossed his arms and glowered at her. 'Mother, you've been an absent parent for most of this week, so are in no position to judge. If you choose not to pay attention to us, please don't expect us to dance to your tune. We'd have been better off if we'd stayed with Dad.'

Ooh, two can play at that game, you pompous little sausage. Penny smiled sweetly at him. 'You're right. I haven't spent enough time with you. Let's spend the whole weekend together. What shall we do? How about a lovely hill walk?'

Hector realised he'd been neatly hoisted by his own petard. He could never play the absent parent card on Mum again. If he refused to spend time with her, she'd lord it over him forevermore with "Well, I did offer, but…". If he agreed, she'd lord it over him with "I spent two days yomping up hills with you!" In fact, she'd probably make him yomp up hills with her every bloody weekend just to make sure he could never call her an absent parent again.

'Alright, I'll come to the meeting,' he said sullenly. 'And I don't masturbate twelve times a day.'

'Who says I was talking about you?'

'Oi!' exclaimed Edith.

The school meeting went rather well, all things considered, although Penny got Murray Hancock and Furry Mancock completely confused and told the receptionist they had an appointment to see Hurry Fancock. She emerged triumphant, with the offer of places for the twins beginning the following week. The twins were less thrilled. They pleaded with her to let them start the week after, as they had many, many things to do that they absolutely refused to tell her about. They claimed trauma over the missing Freddie and declared that any decent parent would have arranged counselling by now. Penny's answer to this was to remind them that Granny was a trained counsellor before she retired. Would they like to talk to Granny about their feelings? The twins agreed that, whilst they were very sad and worried about Freddie, trauma was perhaps taking things a bit far.

Penny felt a pang of parental guilt and decided that she ought to have put more effort into helping them search for Freddie. Did they want to do another search of the gardens with her? The twins assured her that they'd already searched very thoroughly, and they were positive that nothing more could be done. In fact, they were suspiciously keen that she *didn't* search the gardens. Mulling this over on the drive home, Penny made a mental note to check there was nothing missing from Len's binocular collection, in case they'd taken to spying on Sandra Next Door on behalf of her mother.

They arrived back at Valhalla to find Mary and Len having one of their very rare arguments. They were standing in the living room, and between them on the floor was a long metal object.

'I don't care what you say,' shouted Len. 'You are not putting that thing up in my shed.'

'Why do you always have to be so difficult? It's only until Penny gets her own place, then we can put it up in her room again.'

'My shed is not a dumping ground for your hobbies.'

'Well, that's rich coming from you. I know you've got your old golf clubs in there.'

'Okay. I give in. I'll put the pole up somewhere else for you, but it's NOT going in my shed.'

'Fine! You can put it up in here.'

'Fine!'

Len stomped off to find his toolbox, and Mary smiled weakly at Penny and the twins.

'What a stramash,' she said, shaking her head sadly. 'I keep telling him, it's very good for the core, but he's never been supportive of my pole dancing.'

Penny sighed. 'Really, Mum? I wonder why. Listen, I'm off to get ready. We're having a Losers Club meeting at the pub in the village this evening.' She eyed the pole and added hopefully, 'Pilates is very good for the core too.'

Making her way towards her room, Penny gave a shudder as, behind her, she heard Edith say, 'This is so cool, Granny. We can do a TikTok, and you'll be famous.'

She shuddered again, as Mary's delighted cry rang through the house. 'Len! Pass me my leather bikini. We're doing a Tok Tik.'

The pub wasn't very crowded for a Friday night, and Penny suspected that the weather had kept a lot of the regulars at home. The islanders were a hardy lot, but after nearly a week of high winds and torrential rain, everyone was tired of doing battle with the roads. With only a handful of locals propping up the bar, the Losers Club were able to pull a few tables together and make themselves comfortable.

Jim had given Penny and Sandra Next Door a lift to the pub and had left Phil in a sheltered spot behind Elsie's library van in the car park. Penny was fairly sure the van was council property and that the council would take a dim view of Elsie taking it to the pub. She worried that Elsie would be in trouble if someone reported her. Tongues wagged all over the island, but they were particularly waggy in the village. She should have a word with Elsie about it.

Jim offered to buy the first round. Dry white wine for Penny and Sandra Next Door, half a cider for Eileen and a vodka and cranberry juice for Fiona, who confided that she had raging cystitis, and every time she peed it was like someone was stabbing her in the hoo-ha. Penny suspected that Fiona may have had a few vodkas before the rest of the group arrived. Craft beer for Gordon, a lemonade for Elsie because she was driving and a Jägerbomb for Mrs Hubbard.

They each took it in turns to report what they'd found. Mrs Hubbard went first, telling the group about the receipt from Gibraltar.

'That's strange,' said Elsie, 'he told me he was going to visit Bob McLardy. He's a postmaster in Dundee. They met at some work thing years ago and kept in touch. What on earth was he doing in Gibraltar?'

Penny thought for a moment. 'If Old Archie came in on that RIB, he must have come from Gibraltar. Assuming the witness arrived with him, then they both came from Gibraltar. Jim, did you ask your friend at the Coastguard about any ships from Gibraltar when you were doing your male bonding?'

Jim shook his head and smiled ruefully, 'No, I was consumed with thoughts about how he was much less bitter than you.'

'Ha, ha. Very funny. Phone him in the morning and ask him to check. What about you, Gordon and Fiona? What did you find out?'

Fiona gave a small burp and giggled. Gordon put his hand on her arm. 'I've got this, my love. Fiona did extensive research in the pub all week, and you were right, Sandra Next Door. Old Archie's friends do like a drink. In fact, Fiona's research was so thorough, she was sick on the floor of the van three times and googled how to make tomato vodka. Old Archie's friends thought he was away visiting a friend in Dundee. They said he liked to socialise in the pub, but otherwise kept himself to himself. He'd go fishing with Captain Rab at the weekends sometimes, which you probably already know, Elsie.'

Elsie said she knew Old Archie was friendly with Captain Rab, as far as Rab was friendly with anyone. They both loved boats, and the captain kept one at the loch on the other side of the island.

'If Captain Rab wasn't stuck in Aberdeen, he'd be a good suspect,' mused Penny.

'It's not very likely,' said Jim. 'If he captained the evening ferry to Aberdeen, it would have been a stretch for him to sail back to the island, shoot Old Archie then sail back to Aberdeen again in time for the morning sailing. Remember, he would have been expecting to take a boat load of tourists to Vik in the morning, until he was told not to sail because they expected the storm to hit. He then lost the heid and sailed in the afternoon, which was the ferry you arrived on, Penny. Anyway, he wouldn't have sailed on his own. Plus, there'll be records of shipping movements from Aberdeen, so it should be easy to check. I'll ask my friend at the Coastguard tomorrow.'

Sandra Next Door was looking agitated. 'Do you want to hear what me and Elsie found out or do you want to sit around debating ferry times all day?' she asked. Without waiting for an answer, she ploughed on. 'Mrs Hubbard looked at Old Archie's body for us, and we think he was shot from front to back through the head.'

Elsie gave a quiet moan, and in an uncharacteristically kind gesture, Sandra Next Door said, 'Would you like to sit this one out, Elsie? Here, take this.' She handed Elsie some money. 'Why don't you and Mrs

Hubbard go and get the next round in?' She glanced meaningfully at Mrs Hubbard, who took the hint and hustled Elsie off in the direction of the bar.

'As I was saying, he was shot from front to back, which means he was facing whoever killed him. The spray of blood was over the stove. That kettle is completely ruined, and it was a very nice kettle. A proper old fashioned one. That's a crime on its own! Alright, alright, I'm getting to it,' she said in response to Penny's impatient sigh.

'All of this means he was probably facing the kitchen door when he was killed. Elsie says he never remembered to lock his front door, so it's…oh, what's the word they use on the telly…*credible* that his killer came into the house. There's certainly nothing to indicate that someone broke in or that he was shot through the window. Elsie is sure the window was closed when she found him because she looked through it and saw him lying on the floor.

'There didn't seem to be anything missing or moved, although neither of us can be certain about that. Now, here's the good bit. We checked the waterproofs on the radiator. They were probably a man's, going by the size of them. But you'll never guess what we found in the pocket. Go on, guess.'

Sandra Next Door's face bore a look of self-satisfaction as Penny, Eileen, Fiona, Gordon and Jim guessed in turn. To their suggestions of a receipt, a book, a tumble dryer (Fiona really needed to dial back on the vodkas), a fish and cigarettes, Sandra Next Door gleefully replied, 'No, no, for goodness' sake Fiona, no and no.' She dug into her handbag and produced a freezer bag containing a black, metal object.

'Is that a gun?' gasped Gordon.

'Yes,' said Sandra Next Door triumphantly. 'The witness was carrying a gun. Sort of blows your Captain Rab theory out of the water, doesn't it, Penny? Maybe the witness and the shooter are one and the same.'

Penny ignored the sly dig. 'If the witness is the shooter, then he's the biggest dimwit since the invention of poorly lit cleverness. What sort of killer shoots someone, reaches behind the door, pops the gun in his pocket then runs away, leaving his coat behind? Anyway, didn't we say before that if he arrived with Old Archie on a boat then he'd have offed him long before they arrived at the house?'

'Maybe the shooter left the gun,' said Sandra Next door, determined not to be outdone.

'Then the shooter is also the biggest numbskull since the invention of anaesthetised craniums. He shoots someone, leans behind the door, spots a handy pocket and thinks "ooh, that looks like a good place to hide a gun"?'

'Penny's right,' said Jim. 'The cliffs are practically outside Old Archie's door. You'd just chuck the gun off a cliff if you wanted to get rid of it. By the way, Sandra Next Door, you need to put that gun back. The police will go mad if they think we've tampered with evidence.'

'I'm confused,' announced Eileen. 'Who did what to which gun?'

'It looks like there were two guns. One belonging to the witness and one belonging to the murderer,' Penny told her.

'So, who shot Old Archie?'

'The murderer!' they all chorused.

'And who's the murderer?' asked Eileen.

As everyone tried very hard not to imagine battering some sense into Eileen with one of Elsie's largest library books, Gordon patiently explained, 'It looks like Old Archie has gone to Gibraltar and returned by sea, accompanied by someone else. This person had a gun in his pocket. When he and Old Archie returned, they were taking off their waterproofs in the kitchen when someone came into the house and shot Old Archie. The murderer ran off, and so did the other person who was there.'

Eileen nodded thoughtfully. 'Right. Does that mean Old Archie wasn't the intended victim? I mean, the killer could have mistaken him for the other person.'

Penny looked at her friend in astonishment. 'Well deduced, Eileen!'

'Or it could have been aliens on a random killing spree.'

And there we go, she's back, thought Penny.

Their discussion was interrupted by the return of Mrs Hubbard and Elsie with the drinks. It was the same round as last time, except Mrs Hubbard appeared to have opted for a cocktail. Elsie looked even more upset than she had before they went to the bar.

'Elsie's not talking to me because I asked Bertie behind the bar for a Sex on the Beach,' Mrs Hubbard murmured to Fiona, who hiccupped and said Elsie should count herself lucky that Mrs H hadn't fancied a Screaming Orgasm.

Penny took a sip of wine and summed up for the benefit of Mrs Hubbard and Elsie. 'Bottom line,' she concluded. 'We know what happened, but we don't know who the intended target was, we don't know who the killer is and we're no nearer to finding the witness. However, Jim, Eileen and I do have some leads.'

She nodded at Eileen, encouraging her to share the results of their internet research. Eileen looked blank, then nodded gravely back. Suppressing a smile, Jim picked up the baton.

'We got nothing from the Coastguard, but then we did the internet searches, and that's where it gets interesting. We got nothing from the internet. Literally nothing. Before winning Postie of the Year, Old Archie didn't exist. We checked birth records and ancestry sites then, thinking that maybe we were doing something wrong, we searched for people whose details we knew. Again, nothing. They didn't exist either. Not our parents and not you, Mrs Hubbard. We were hoping you could explain it.'

Mrs Hubbard took a long sip of her cocktail, her face obscured by the pink paper umbrella. The silence stretched. And stretched. Eventually, she lowered her drink and fixed her eyes on the table.

'I'm sorry, dearies. I can't answer for your parents, and I won't answer for myself. Let's just say that things happened in my past that I don't want to remember and leave it at that. What I *can* tell you is that it has nothing to do with Old Archie's murder.'

Penny, Gordon and Eileen tried to press Mrs Hubbard for more information, but she refused to be drawn. Beside her, Elsie had a rather pinched look and was staring into the middle distance, as if she hoped that by avoiding eye contact, their attention wouldn't turn to her. Fat chance. Sandra Next Door, with all the subtlety of a rottweiler shaking a rabbit, asked, 'And what about you, Elsie? Do you exist or are you so ungrateful to us for looking into Old Archie's death that you'll sit there and lie your face off too?'

Elsie fiddled with her hearing aid and said, 'Pardon? Sorry, this blasted thing. I can't hear you.'

'I said,' shouted Sandra Next Door, 'are you...oh never mind! You heard me fine.'

Elsie ignored her and, trying to defuse the tension, Jim said, 'Let's park that one for now. Anyway, that's not all we found. Listen to this.'

He recounted their run in with Pete and Captain Rab and their subsequent breakfast with the trapped tourists. Everyone agreed that Yulia Klimova, Anthony Woodbead and Pete were definitely hiding something.

'Our next steps, then, are to call my pal at the Coastguard and ask about ships from Gibraltar and the ferry movements from Aberdeen, do some internet research on Yulia, Anthony and Pete and ask Captain Rab for the ferry manifests. Penny and I thought we could speak to Captain Rab in case we can also get some information about his argument with Pete, but if anyone else wants to do it...?'

Unsurprisingly, there were no takers. Nobody else was daft enough to take on the irascible captain. However,

Eileen did offer to do the internet research. Unwilling to sift through fifty printouts about aliens to find one nugget of actual relevant information, Penny offered to help her the next day. Jim offered Penny a lift, and they hatched a plan to once more commandeer Ricky and Gervais' homework laptop.

'And don't forget to put the gun back, Sandra Next Door. You can't go about with it in your handbag,' said Penny. She clapped her hands together and smiled at the group. 'That was a good evening's work. Well done everyone. Give yourselves a pat on the back. Yay! Go Losers!'

Mrs Hubbard immediately stood up and put on her coat.

'No, I didn't mean go. I was cheering us on!' Penny explained.

Mrs Hubbard shook her head and gave Penny a wan smile. 'I'm sorry,' she said. 'I just can't…I'll see you all on Wednesday.'

She bustled out the door, a far sadder figure than she had been just half an hour previously, bowed down by troubles and memories she'd rather forget.

Elsie watched her leave and, pulling on her own coat, said, 'Come on Eileen. I'll give you a lift home.'

Penny hugged Eileen and promised to see her tomorrow. To Elsie she said, 'I meant to check, is it okay for you to drive the library van for personal journeys? Sorry, I'm not trying to interfere. I was worried that some of the old gossips around here would report you.'

'Believe you me,' said Elsie, 'most of the old gossips around here look forward to seeing the library van. They won't say a word.' She tapped the side of her nose and, slipping her arm through Eileen's, shuffled off towards the exit.

After Elsie and Eileen had gone, Gordon hefted Fiona off her chair and steered her towards the ladies, declaring that he was not going to clean up sick for a fourth time this week. This left Jim, Penny and Sandra Next Door to finish their drinks. Penny was just about to take a sip of her wine when Sandra Next Door gave a squeal.

'What's the matter?' asked Penny.

Sandra Next Door didn't reply. Instead, she held out her glass and shook it slightly. There, at the bottom, was a neat set of false teeth.

CHAPTER EIGHT

Penny awoke early the next morning with a thumping headache, a sore throat and a mouth that tasted like she'd been sucking off a sperm whale. She hadn't slept well. When she got home last night, she'd finished half a bottle of wine that had probably been in the fridge since 1986 and heated up some leftovers from dinner. She went to bed, expecting the wine to send her straight to sleep, but her brain had other ideas. It wanted to churn over the night's events. She told her brain, 'Calm down. Think about nice things like fluffy clouds and flowers.' Her brain replied, 'I wonder what happens to you when you die.' In the end, having decided to get up and watch some telly, she went to switch the living room lamp on, bounced off Mary's pole and cracked her head on the coffee table.

Now, the noise of the wind hurling the rain at her window in great blasts was making it impossible to go back to sleep. Penny rolled over in bed and reached out for her phone. 7am and no wake-up call from Jim. Perhaps she should go to his house and give him a rude awakening. She looked up at Chesney and opened her mouth to ask what he thought, but no sound came out. She tried again. Nothing. Her phone rang and she stared dumbly at it. She'd spoken…thought…too soon, she decided, wondering how she was going to answer and tell Jim to eff off. She cut the call and texted him:

"Am ill. Lost voice. Eff off."

Jim texted back:

"Will not eff off. Am at front door. Will ring doorbell."

Penny dragged herself out of bed and shuffled miserably to the front door. She caught a glimpse of herself as she passed the hall mirror and did a double take, before realising that it was not, in fact, the zombie apocalypse. Just a middle-aged woman in "I'm Sexy and You Know It" pyjamas, with dark circles under her eyes and hair that looked like she'd brushed it with the arse end of a hedgehog. She opened the door and gazed up at Jim, every atom of her being conveying deepest, darkest misery. He looked at today's pyjama offering, gave her a lascivious wink and saw himself to the kitchen. She shut the front door and followed, no longer caring if the girls perked up under the PJs and pointed straight at him. Although these days they were more likely to point in the direction of his feet. She could probably tuck them into the waistband of her pyjamas if they misbehaved. Penny grabbed Mary's magnetic shopping list pad off the fridge and scribbled "bad throat. are you going to work today?"

'I've been up at the farm since 3am, so Dad's covering again. Karen Green's cat has diarrhoea. I don't do cat poo, but dad says it's not to be sniffed at.'

Penny rolled her eyes and wrote "groan. put kettle on + get me paracetamol. am dying."

A cup of tea, two paracetamol and half an hour of surfing news websites, while Jim read Len's newspaper, improved Penny's throat and restored her voice to a hoarse whisper. She wasn't yet ready to try toast but croaked that she might manage some ice cream. What, she thought, was the point of having a sore throat and not taking advantage? Jim considered muttering the words "nutrition plan" at her, but she was sitting far too close to the bread knife for comfort.

By the time she'd had a shower and got dressed, Penny felt much better. Her voice had settled on husky, and she was quite enjoying the fact that everything she said sounded incredibly sexy.

She stared at herself in the bathroom mirror and said, 'Hey babe, I'm going to brush my teeth now.'

Mirror Penny stared back and replied, 'Ooh, go on

then, you saucy minx.'

'I totally will. And I'll get those bristles right to the back,' said real Penny.

'I love it when you push them in deep,' said mirror Penny.

'I'm going to rub them all over my tongue - jeez! Dad, you frightened the life out of me!'

Len was standing behind her in the open doorway, clutching one of Mary's Louboutins, ready to stiletto someone to death. He took a couple of steps forward and swept back the shower curtain.

'Sorry, Penny-farthing. I thought I heard someone in here.'

'It was me. I was just...just...brushing my teeth and my voice is a bit funny. Sore throat. Put that down, Dad. That's about three hundred quid's worth of shoe you're holding.'

'Really?' said Len, gazing in wonder at his weapon of choice. 'Your mother said she got them in a sale in Marks and Spencer when she visited you in London last year.'

'Ah, yes. I'd forgotten about that,' Penny lied, no stranger to sneaking in the odd extravagance under the radar herself. 'Still, twenty-five quid's worth of shoe isn't something you'd want to waste on a burglar, is it?'

Len looked rather disappointed by the lack of burglars and handed Penny the shoe. 'Don't tell your mum.'

'I won't,' said Penny, discreetly checking the size in case she needed to borrow them someday. 'As long as you don't tell anyone about the...erm...tooth brushing.'

They went through to the kitchen, where they found Mary making Jim a bacon sandwich.

'Morning,' she chirruped, flitting around the kitchen in a pink satin robe. 'Jim says you have a sore throat. Could you manage a bacon sandwich? Len, pass me the bread. I'd offer you all a sausage, but I can't find them anywhere. Honestly, the twins are eating us out of house and home. I bought a salami the other day and it's gone as well. Len, did you hide the salami?'

'No, dear,' said Len, rummaging in the bread bin. 'There's no bread in here, but I've found these.' He shook an orange packet at her. 'Do you want me to butter your crumpet?'

As Jim choked on his tea, Penny growled, 'Are you two doing this on purpose?'

Two round pairs of eyes turned innocently in her direction.

'What?' asked Mary. 'And why do you have my shoe? That's one of the very special shoes I bought in the sale.'

'I found it in the hall. Edith must have been trying it on. Listen, while I have you two on your own, I have something I wanted to ask you about. Jim and I were doing some internet research the other day and—'

'Morning. Bacon crumpet?' said Mary, as Hector dragged himself into the kitchen, wearing nothing but a faded pair of "Santa's Little Helper" boxers. Penny had bought them as a stocking filler last Christmas, back when they were a happy family. Back when they had no idea that this was the last Christmas the four of them would spend together under one roof. Back when Alex was merely a bit of a cockwomble at times and was yet to achieve full wankpuffin.

'Why are you staring at my boxers, Mum?' asked Hector.

'Sorry. I was remembering last Christmas.'

'You mean before you ruined our lives and dumped us in this shithole? Ouch! What the fu—. Ouch!'

Hector clutched his ear, the lobe stinging where Mary had smacked it twice with the greasy spatula.

'You don't talk to your mother like that,' she warned him. 'Stop thinking about yourself for once and realise that your mum has lost as much as you. Now, go and put some clothes on, and come back when you're prepared to show some respect.'

'Go Granny,' muttered Penny once Hector was out of earshot.

'He's angry, but he'll come around eventually,' said Mary. 'Just make sure he knows you love him, even when you don't like his behaviour. Edith seems to be settling in a bit better and starting school will do them both good. Get them out meeting people their own age, instead of hanging around with old fogies like us. I've been encouraging them to go to the village, but they seem to want to stay here. Which reminds me, could you look under their beds for my crockery? We're down to our last four plates. Now, bacon crumpet?'

'I better not. Trying to eat healthy,' said Penny, conveniently forgetting the two scoops of luxury vanilla she'd had an hour before. Jim stared at her in disbelief and she looked away, willing him to say nothing. She wondered how her mother could be so bonkers, yet so wise. And how her father, a retired bank manager, could miss the fact that her mother was blowing the family fortune on shoes. Ah, well. Every cloud and all that. At least they had the same foot size.

Before she left, she went to see Hector in his room. He was sitting on his bed, sullen and uncooperative, refusing to look away from the video game he was playing on his laptop. Penny knew that whatever she said, it was unlikely to penetrate the shell of teenage angst. However, she could at least try.

'I understand why you're angry, I really do. I can't change what's happened, even though I wish I could make everything right again. We need to find a way forward together, because I love you and I love Edith, and we all deserve to be happy. There's no money - genuinely no money. Even if we had stayed in London, you'd have had to move schools and move to a much smaller house. Your dad and I would still not have been together, and you would be living with me because he's taking every bit of work he can get to pay off this tax bill. I would have struggled to support us in London. The money from the house sale wouldn't have gone far. Up here, we have a safety net. We have Granny and Grandad, I can afford to buy us somewhere to live, and if Losers Club doesn't work out, I can get a job in a shop or something to keep us going.

'Your dad agreed to all of this, and he knows he can visit any time he likes. You can call him, e-mail him, whatever, as much as you want. Just know that we both love you, and we are both trying to do our best for you.'

A tear slid down Hector's nose and he angrily wiped it away. 'I don't want things to change. It feels like you took what money he had and made us go as far away from him as possible.'

'I really didn't. The press was horrible, so we were always going to come to the island for a bit of peace and quiet anyway. Your dad and I looked at the money situation and decided it made sense for us to move here. Honestly, he really is okay with this. It lets him get on with work.' And shagging anything that moves, thought Penny.

'I'm just so angry all the time. Angry with you, Dad, Edith, everyone. It's like this frustration that keeps building up inside of me, and I want to throw things or hit someone or...' Another tear slid down Hector's nose. This time, he let it fall onto the blankets.

Penny put her arm around him, giving him a reassuring hug. 'It's really scary feeling out of control like that, but also really normal for people your age, especially with the life changes you're going through. I think there's a punchbag somewhere from when Granny went through her kickboxing phase. How about I ask Grandad to hang it up in the shed for you, so you can go out there and get rid of that negative energy whenever you feel like it?'

Hector smiled weakly. 'Grandad's definitely not going to agree to that, but thanks anyway. You don't even want to know what he's got in that shed. Can you tell Gran I'm sorry for being horrible?'

Penny was just about to ask exactly what did

Grandad have in his shed, when a voice said, 'You can tell her yourself,' and Mary appeared, bearing a plate laden with bacon crumpets.

'Here you go, Hector. All is forgiven, and I'm sorry for whacking you over the earhole. You can probably get done for assault for it these days but, eech, the number of times I chased your mother round the garden with the wooden spoon. There was a reason we were so slim and fit in those days. Couldn't catch the little devil and we'd both end up laughing. Of course, that was before Sandra Next Door moved in. There used to be a lovely couple next door, Rosie and Robert. He worked up at Hillside Farm, until he got caught fiddling with the cows and they had to move away to the mainland. Shame really. Rosie and Bovine Bobby were such good neighbours, always happy to lend you a pint of milk.'

Hector gave a snort of laughter and took the plate of crumpets. Giving him a kiss on the head, Penny said, 'I'll leave you to play your game. I'm going out with Jim for a while, and I'll be back around lunchtime.'

'You've been spending a lot of time with Jim. You and he…you're not…?'

'No!' exclaimed Penny, horrified that her son would think she and Jim were…whatever she and Jim weren't. Yet she couldn't deny there was some chemistry there. If chemistry was the name for feeling slightly randy whenever Jim was around. Better not tell Hector that, though. 'We're just friends. Jim, myself and the rest of Losers Club have been looking into what happened to Old Archie.'

'Have you really?' said Mary, mildly envious that her daughter had such an exciting new hobby. 'Is there anything I can do to help?'

'Me too,' said Hector, momentarily forgetting his troubles in the face of this exciting news. 'What can I do?'

Penny thought for a moment. She didn't particularly want to drag the kids into this or have her mother meddling, but it was good to see Hector so enthusiastic about something for a change.

She told them what the group had discovered so far. 'The one thing we don't have is any information about the witness, other than that he came from Gibraltar by sea. We think they probably came in at the beach at the bottom of the cliff path near the chip shop in the village. Someone spotted a RIB down there. You probably won't want to do this, what with the filthy weather, but could you have a look on the beach and maybe trace their route to see if there are any clues? Also, the killer must have been watching Old Archie's house and seen them arrive. Check if there are any good vantage points and have a poke about for clues. Highly unlikely you'll find anything, thanks to the storm, but no harm in trying.'

Mary promised she'd drag Edith out to help and Len too, if they could prize him away from his precious shed. 'Honestly,' said Mary, exasperated, 'the longer this storm goes on, the more convinced he is that we're all doomed. I caught him sneaking out of the kitchen with a six pack of baked beans the other day. Lord knows where he bought them because I've told Mrs Hubbard and the supermarket in town that they're not to sell him beans. The man is a bean hoarder!'

Penny left her mother to expostulate further to Hector about his grandfather's annoying habits and went back to the kitchen, where she apologised to Jim for being away for so long.

'It's okay,' said Jim. 'Your dad and I were doing the crossword. Three down. Some can't, but I varied it ably. Two words. Five letters and seven letters.'

'Mixed ability,' rasped Penny.

'Well done, dear,' said Len, looking over Jim's shoulder at the newspaper. 'That gives us a letter for ten across. Story. In part a legend. Four letters. Second letter a.'

'Tale. Dad, can I ask you something? Losers Club

has been looking into Old Archie's murder, and while we were doing some research into his background, we came across something strange. We couldn't find any birth records for him, you, Mum and some other people on the island. Why is that?'

'I've no idea. Were you doing the search properly? These Wi-fis can sometimes get things mixed up. It's all to do with pop-ins and log-ups and load-downs. Things have to go in so many directions that they get confused. That's what routers are for. They tell the pops, logs and loads where they're supposed to go. Anyway, I won't bore you with the technical details. Looking into Old Archie's murder, eh? I hope you're as good at murder clues as you are at crossword clues. Now, I think the bathroom's free, so if you'll excuse me.'

Len tucked the newspaper under his arm and wandered off to spend some quality time ingesting the day's news while he expelled last night's fish curry. In fact, Penny realised, the fish curry was probably to blame for the foul taste in her mouth when she woke up this morning.

'Are you starting to get the feeling that there's something they don't want to tell us?' she asked Jim.

'Definitely. Mrs Hubbard, Elsie and now your dad. I haven't had a chance to ask my dad yet. I wonder if Eileen has asked her mum. It's weird, isn't it?'

'Very. I hope it's something exciting, like they were all in a famous rock band in the seventies, blew their money on coke, changed their names and moved to Vik to detox. It would certainly explain why Mum blew her top when she found weed in my pocket when I came home for the summer during university.'

'You did drugs at uni?' Jim was shocked. He'd never had Penny pegged as the type to do drugs.

'Lord, no. I tried weed once, fell asleep on the floor and threw up in my flatmate's shoes. I brought the rest home for Kenny. Him and his pals were in the middle of their wonder years, as in "I wonder what the heck's going on." They spent ages seventeen to twenty-one either in the pub or stoned out of their heads, sometimes both. There was a big group of us who used to hang out together and have house parties. For goodness' sake, don't tell the twins. My late teens are no role model for them.'

'I missed out on all that,' said Jim. 'I was too busy getting enough Highers to study to be a vet. I went off to Glasgow at eighteen and spent my summers on work experience.'

'You probably did yourself a favour in the long run. Look at me, divorced and homeless, with two kids,' said Penny.

'Yes, but you've had a full life. I never settled down with anyone. Not many women out there for a country man who takes off at a moment's notice to shove his hand up a cow's arse.'

'I'm a firm believer that there's someone out there for everyone.'

'Maybe so. Maybe I've already met her?' Jim gazed meaningfully at Penny, and she felt her stomach swoop. Not yet, she thought. I'm not ready for that yet.

Penny was saved from answering by Edith, who padded into the kitchen, yawning, 'Met whooooo?' She flumped down at the table, ignoring Jim, and pointed mutely at the cereal cupboard.

'Never you mind,' said Penny, leaning over to kiss the top of her head. 'Sort out your own breakfast. You've got important business to do this morning. Granny will explain. Jim and I are off out, but I'll be back by lunchtime.'

Edith looked appalled at being expected to go to the effort of pouring out her own cereal.

'There are no clean bowls,' she shouted to a retreating Penny.

'Get one from under your bed,' Penny shouted back.

There was an awkward silence in the car on the way to Port

Vik. Eventually, Penny could bear the tension no longer.

'Sorry, I hope you didn't think—' she rasped, at the same time as Jim said, 'Look, I didn't mean to—'

Jim glanced at her, and they both laughed nervously.

'Let's just hope Captain Rab's in the mood to help us,' said Jim. 'Shall we swing past the library afterwards and make that special delivery?'

Penny checked her handbag. It was fortunate that Sandra Next Door was still carrying a roll of "evidence" freezer bags last night. There, bobbing gently in the village pub's finest cheap sauvignon blanc, were Elsie's false teeth.

CHAPTER NINE

Captain Rab lived in one of the cottages opposite the harbour. These days, most of the ferry tickets were sold online or on board, but he still kept an office of sorts in his front room, where tickets could be purchased in person whenever he happened to be at home. Consequently, his house was easy to find, and even if there hadn't been a large "Ferry Ticket Office" sign above the door, the shabby exterior, with its peeling paint and dirty windows, spoke of a man who lived alone and was uninterested in keeping up appearances.

The captain himself was a short, pigeon chested man, with receding brown hair, a year-round tan and a thick, yet neatly trimmed beard. His house may have been shabby, but Captain Rab hadn't let himself go. Standing on his doorstep, glowering at the unexpected visitors, he didn't look a day over fifty, Penny thought. He was almost exactly as she remembered him from thirty years ago, when he'd roared at the fourth-year school trip that there was to be "nae fechtin', nae drinkin', nae runnin' and nae snoggin' on board," although she realised that he must be in his seventies by now.

'Aye? What do you want? The ferry's nae goin' today,' snapped Captain Rab.

'We're sorry to bother you. We wondered if we could ask you about the people who arrived on the ferry on Saturday. Maybe see the manifest?' asked Penny.

Captain Rab's eyes widened in surprise, before returning to their habitual scowl.

'Why do you want to see the manifest?'

'Could we come in and explain?' asked Jim. 'We're getting soaked out here.'

'No,' snapped the captain. 'Either tell me why you want to see it or bugger off.'

Jim sighed. 'We met some of the people who came in on the last ferry, and we wondered if there were any others trapped on the island.'

'And why would you be wanting to know that?'

'We…uh…thought we might see if they needed anything. Good works for the island community, that sort of thing,' said Penny brightly.

Captain Rab glared at her. 'A right pair of nosey buggers, aren't you? If they're not up at the hotel then they're staying with someone. In which case they don't need anything from the likes of you.'

He made to close the door, but Jim put a hand on the edge to stop him. 'Can we ask you about Pete, then? The person you were arguing with the other night?'

'No, you can not. I don't know what you're talking about, and if you know what's good for you, you'll mind your own business,' said Captain Rab, before slamming the door closed, leaving Penny and Jim, astounded and soggy, to agree that they'd probably get more out of the peeling slab of wood before them than they would its ill-humoured owner.

They made their way across the road to the car, quickly got in and sat in silence for a moment, the windows steaming up from their breath. Jim switched the engine on and ran the heater yet didn't immediately drive off.

'That could have gone better,' he said.

'I don't know why we're surprised. Maybe we should have set Sandra Next Door on him. She'd have got the truth out of him *and* made him clean his house. Hang on. What's this?'

Through the hazy window, Penny caught sight of movement in one of Captain Rab's downstairs windows.

'He's watching us, the old curtain twitcher!' she exclaimed. 'Quick, move Phil down the road a bit where he can't see us.'

Jim obligingly pulled away, did a U-turn and parked further down on the same side of the street as Captain Rab's house.

'Do you think he's up to something?' asked Jim.

'I don't know if he's up to something or if he's just being a bad-tempered old coot, but it looked like he was checking to see if we were gone. Let's hang around for a few minutes and see what happens,' said Penny, slumping down in her seat so that she was less visible. She prodded Jim in the side. 'Get down, will you. And keep the heating on so the windows stay clear.'

'That means leaving the car running, you idiot. Folk will notice a car running.'

'Don't you call me an idiot. Folk will notice there's somebody inside the car if the windows steam up, you big twat.'

'For fucks' sake, I'll back the car up a bit so it's less obvious that the engine's on.'

'Do you have to swear? You're always swearing.'

'Since when did you become a prude, Miss Weedhead?'

'It was once. Once. I thought we'd established that I'd lived a life and you hadn't.' Penny went in for the kill. 'And what were you going to say to me this morning just before Edith came in?' she asked in her bestest most innocentest voice, knowing full well that he wasn't going to admit to liking her right now.

Jim's cheeks reddened, and he squirmed in his seat. Pain in the arse bloody woman, she knew how to make things awkward.

'I'll back the fucking car up,' he snapped, snatching a minor sweary triumph from the jaws of defeat.

With the car parked further down the street, they were able to keep the windows clear, although the rain obscured the view, turning the few passers-by into amorphous dark figures. The waves battered the harbour wall, and Penny felt the car rock as gusts of wind tore at everything in their path. She hadn't minded the storm at first. It felt like a cleansing after a few weeks of muggy days and nights spent battling the twins, packing their lives away into storage boxes and mourning a past that was tantalisingly recent yet forever gone. She'd kept telling herself "just six months ago I was planning our next family holiday, never realising what was ahead" or "just five months ago I was signing for a new dishwasher, and here I am signing divorce papers." Eventually, she had realised that she'd have to stop thinking of her life in terms of before and after the divorce. She couldn't keep grieving for what was. She had to think of it all as the next step towards something different, otherwise she'd drown. And she couldn't drown. The twins needed her. It was the thought of the twins that kept Penny going because, no matter how awful they were being right now and no matter how deeply she was hurting, she and Alex had to make life okay for the twins, so she came up for air and swam on.

Sitting here beside the world's most curmudgeonly vet, Penny decided that she'd had quite enough of wind and rain now, thank you very much, and surely it was time for some sunshine. There would be other storms, other rainy days, but as they neared the end of what for her had been the most miserable summer of her life, did she and her babies not deserve a few warm rays in which to start making a few happy memories of the next part of their journey?

She poked Jim in the side. 'Scootch down, there's somebody coming.'

She and Jim sank lower in their seats, peering over the dashboard to get a glimpse of the tall, slim, hooded figure crossing the street outside Captain Rab's house. They watched as the person stopped at Captain Rab's door, knocked and waited. Ten seconds or so later, he stepped inside the house.

'Who was that?' croaked Penny

'How the fuck should I know?' said Jim, still simmering after their row and determined to get some good swears in.

'For goodness' sake,' Penny hissed.

She drew up her hood, opened the car door and jumped out, ignoring Jim as he shouted after her, 'Sorry. I didn't mean it. Get back in the car!'

She put her head back round the car door and said, 'Stop shouting and come on. We're going to take a look through Captain Rab's windows and see who's visiting him.'

'In this weather? I'm already soaked. I'm not going all the way up there to look in some old man's windows. He could be getting his end away or anything. Maybe he has a sex dungeon in his living room or maybe there's a coven, and he's the grand wizard.'

'Have you been taking conspiracy theory lessons from Eileen? Anyway, wizards probably don't even have covens.'

'I could stay here and google it, while you go and look in old men's windows?' Jim offered, a hopeful look in his eyes.

'No chance. Get your butt out here now.'

With a sigh, Jim switched the ignition off, pulled his hood up and joined Penny on the pavement. Together, they walked quickly up to Captain Rab's house and ducked low outside his living room window. Penny slowly raised her head above the window ledge and peered into the living room before quickly ducking back down.

'I can see them, but they're at the back of the house looking at something on a table,' she whispered. 'Follow me. There's a lane up the side of the row and a path that runs along behind all the houses. We can sneak through the back gate and get a better look.'

'Have you totally lost it? We can't go breaking into someone's garden!'

'Do you want to see who the visitor is or not?'

'Well, yes, but…'

'Then grow a pair and follow me.'

Without waiting for a reply, Penny squat-walked

past the window. She looked behind her. Jim was squat-walking in her wake. She couldn't help but smile, thinking to herself that they must look ridiculous.

When they reached the edge of Captain Rab's cottage, Penny and Jim stood up and quickly walked to the end of the row where, sure enough, there was a lane. They turned into the lane and walked up a short incline until the came to a narrow path on their left that ran in a straight line between the back gardens of the harbour cottages and the houses further up the hill. Jim could see fence upon fence running into the distance, broken only by one high wall halfway along the row. He had a sinking feeling that this wasn't going to be as simple as pushing open a back gate.

Sure enough, as they drew level with Captain Rab's cottage, it became clear that the man had added an extra level of security. Embedded between two walls was a solid, smooth metal gate. Jim gave it an experimental shove and it did not budge.

'That's that, then,' he told Penny. 'Shall we go back to the car?'

'Give us a leg up,' she said.

Jim shook his head. 'No way. We'll get caught.'

'And what's going to happen? We get arrested? There's no police! The worst that could happen is the wrath of Captain Rab. Eileen and I used to play along the back of these houses all the time. Half our friends lived in them. Trust me, we won't get caught.'

There followed a hushed argument, with Jim steadfastly refusing to boost Penny onto the wall and Penny making dire threats against his dangly bits unless he did as she asked.

'It's strange, but when you say "bend over and let me stand on you, or I'll cut your cock off with a bacon slicer" in that voice, it sounds more like an invitation to some weird sex game than a threat,' said Jim.

Penny glared at him then jumped up at the wall, the toes of her wellington boots scrabbling for purchase as she clung to the top, backside sticking out, looking for all the world like a defective Spiderman after a few too many of Aunt May's pies. Jim sighed and, musing to himself that with great power comes great responsibility, put a hand on her bottom and pushed hard upwards.

Penny felt herself lifted onto the top of the wall, where she wobbled and narrowly missed tumbling down the other side. With a leg either side of the wall, she scooted along towards the gate, where she could see two wheelie bins parked and ready to take out for Monday's collection. She swung her other leg over and carefully lowered herself onto the bins, praying that they were full enough to stay upright under her weight. Crouching on top of a green bin and looking behind her, she could see Jim pulling himself onto the top of the wall. Her own ascent may not have been elegant, but his wasn't much better. As she slithered off the bin, her coat riding up to expose a belly that she'd have preferred to keep firmly under wraps, Jim slid onto the blue bin then jumped down to stand next to her.

The garden had been levelled into the hillside, with steps down to the back door. Where Jim and Penny stood, they could just see the tops of the windows, meaning it was unlikely that anyone inside the house could see them. However, anyone looking out an upper story window nearby would have a bird's eye view of the intruders.

Penny once more crouched and waved at Jim to do the same. 'Stay low and follow me.'

She moved forwards, using the grass along the edge of the garden path to muffle the sound of her boots, then stepped carefully onto the gravel and tiptoed down the steps, holding onto the metal handrails to keep her balance. The kitchen window opposite was covered by a closed blind. Stooping low, Penny made her way towards the window at the back of the living room. She could hear Jim quietly swearing behind her and turned to see that his pocket was caught on one of the handrails.

Ignoring Jim's struggles to free himself, Penny

leaned forward and peeked in the window. Two men were standing at a dining table, looking down at what appeared to be a map. The shorter of the two was clearly Captain Rab, but the other had his back to her. He had removed his hood and she could make out a short crew cut.

There was a muffled thump and a muttered, 'Fuck,' behind her, and just as she drew back from the window, she caught a glimpse of the taller man's face as he turned in the direction of the noise.

Jim was lying on his back on the path, and Penny, made lithe by fear, ran up the steps and vaulted over him, hissing, 'Run,' as she streaked across the lawn towards the bins at the back of the garden. She could hear Jim scrabbling to his feet in her wake and keys jangling in the back door lock. Hurling herself behind the green bin, she curled into a ball and silently willed Jim to hurry up. She heard the blue bin beside her rattle as he tucked himself, panting, behind it.

They were just in the nick of time. Penny was concentrating hard on keeping her breath shallow and ignoring the urgent hammering of her heart, when she heard the back door burst open and Captain Rab's voice shout, 'Who's there. If that's you blasted kids again, I'll have your parents told and your guts for fish bait, you wee shites.'

Penny could hear him growling to the other man that it was probably the local kids. She heard him climb the steps and mutter triumphantly that, whoever it was, at least they hadn't got away scot-free. Peering around the edge of the bin, she saw Captain Rab bend down and pick up something shiny, before making his way back down the steps and into the house.

They waited for a full minute after the back door closed, both of them shaking from the adrenaline rush, before slowly emerging from behind the bins. Cautiously standing, Penny could see that the living room curtains were now closed. She put a finger to her lips and signalled to Jim that it was it was safe to come out, then pointed to the back gate, where a key sat in the lock. With one ear open for any sound at the back door, they crept towards the gate and turned the key. It opened with a gentle creak, and Penny peeked around the edge to check the back path. All was clear and they slipped through the opening, Jim locking the gate behind them and sliding the key back under the gate.

'I near shit myself there,' he said, leaning against the wall to catch his breath.

'I haven't been that scared since Eileen and I skived school and got spotted by one of the teachers while we were trying to buy a litre of cider in the middle of the afternoon. We legged it out of the shop, taking the cider with us, and hid under the bridge near the woods. I walked all the way back to the village, half drunk and desperate for a pee, thinking I was so clever because I'd timed my arrival to coincide with the school bus. Mum was waiting for me and chased me a mile up the road to the house, roaring that the school had been on the phone, and I was grounded for a month. I don't know why she bothered chasing me. She'd have caught me anyway. All she needed to do was follow the line of pee up the street. Yes, that was the day I pissed myself in front of everyone on the school bus and that's why they called me Spend a Penny Hopper, or Spenny for short.'

'I'd forgotten we used to call you Spenny,' laughed Jim. 'Come on then, Spenny. I reckon if we go up this way, we'll come to the lane at the other end of the row, near the car.'

Wet and windblown, they made their way, giggling, up the path. In her relief at having escaped capture, Penny had quite forgotten about the man she'd seen in Captain Rab's cottage. It was only as they reached Jim's car that she remembered.

'By the way, I got a look at the man—'

She was interrupted by a torrent of muttered curses and turned to find Jim frantically searching his pockets.

'What's the matter?' she asked.

'Car keys. I've lost the fucking car keys,' Jim said,

his voice rising in panic.

'Bugger,' said Penny. 'Captain Rab has them. I saw him pick something up off the path. They must have fallen out of your pocket when it got caught on the handrail. Does it have your name or anything to do with your car on them?'

'No. That's the one saving grace. The keyring is one of those ones with names on them. It just says "Phil."'

'Thank goodness for that. Captain Rab will be hunting high and low for a burglar called Phil.'

'Aye, that's as maybe,' said Jim. 'But it doesn't do us any good right now. How are we going to get you home?'

'Bugger. Do you have a spare key at home?'

Jim nodded. 'I'll phone my dad and get him to nip down with it.'

'Let's see if Eileen's in. No point in standing here in the rain if we can scrounge a cup of tea in a nice, dry kitchen,' said Penny, tucking her arm into his and steering him in the direction of Eileen's house. 'By the way, I've decided what to call my temperamental old devil of a car.'

'What?'

'Captain Rab. Now, you'll never believe who the captain's visitor was.'

CHAPTER TEN

'Let me guess,' said Jim, as they approached Eileen's back door. 'Pete?'

'Warmish.'

'Captain Rab's brother?'

'Captain Rab has a brother?'

'No idea. Are you being clever? We assumed it was a man, but maybe it was a woman. Elsie?'

'Freezing.'

'Mrs Hubbard. She's having it off with Captain Rab. Ooh Minty, you sexy silver mermaid, hoist your main sail over my mast and be damn quick about it.'

'That's disgusting,' said Penny. 'And you're as cold as Mrs Hubbard's lemon meringue ice cream.'

'If it was Sandra Next Door, she'd have cleaned his windows the minute she saw the state of them. Who am I missing? Yulia?'

'I'll give you a clue. It wasn't a woman.'

'Was it one of Eileen's aliens?'

Penny rolled her eyes at him. 'It was Anthony Woodbead.'

'Well, bugger me! What was he doing there?'

'I don't know! Maybe we should take a walk back to Captain Rab's and ask him. Oh, and ask for your car key back while we're at it.'

'Well, bugger me,' said Jim again.

Penny turned the handle on Eileen's back door and pushed. Nothing happened. The door was locked. She knocked then pushed her face against the glass, trying to see if there was any sign of life inside the house.

'It looks like there's nobody home,' she told Jim. 'Call your dad and ask him to meet us here. We can at least stand under the edge of the porch out of the rain.'

'Yes, boss.'

Jim pulled his phone from his pocket and clicked on "Dad." Penny could hear the ringing tone, followed by a muffled voice. 'Hello?'

'Dad, it's Jim. I've lost my car keys. Could you come down to the harbour with the spare?'

'Hello? Hello?' said the muffled voice.

'Turn the phone the other way up,' bellowed Jim.

'It's this infernal thing. I don't know what he was doing buying me an iPhone for Christmas. There was nothing wrong with my old phone.'

Jim held the phone close to his mouth and yelled, 'DAD the phone's upside down.'

He waited a moment, hearing only some rustling sounds, then the call was disconnected. He sighed and scrolled through his contacts, clicking on "Work."

Penny heard a female voice answer and Jim said, 'Is that you, Jill? I'm trying to get hold of Dad. Is he there?'

After a few "ayes" and "uh-huhs", Jim put his phone back in his pocket and told Penny that his dad was at Mrs Richardson's checking on Napoleon, her French bulldog, but that he'd be back in an hour.

'Do you normally do house calls? Apart from farms, of course. Can't see anyone taking their cow to the vet.'

'You'd be surprised. The Robertsons up at Braemuir once took three sheep into the surgery. There was a Border Collie in the waiting room, and all hell broke loose. It took an hour to calm them all down and sort everything out. But you know what they say – all's wool that ends wool.' Jim gave her a lopsided grin. 'Seriously, we do house calls to the people who can't get to us.'

'You're good people, you and your dad. So, what are we going to do now? We can't stand under Eileen's porch for an hour,' said Penny.

'My house is only about twenty minutes' walk away

if we cut through the woods,' suggested Jim, frantically trying to remember if he'd tidied his boxers off the bathroom floor and done the dishes.

They set off up the steep lane, the wind at their backs pushing them along. At the top of the bank, they stopped to catch their breath and looked down at the inner harbour where the fishing boats, like toys from this distance, heaved and tossed in their haven, while the sea flung itself in raging bursts against the wall outside. The ferry held firm against the onslaught, but Penny could see that a couple of small yachts had not fared so well. The sight brought home to her the precariousness of island life. In some of the cottages down there were people whose livelihoods depended on the sea, and in the houses around her were people who depended on the ferry for their supplies, their medicine, their mail. Used to living in London, where food from every corner of the globe could be delivered by a man on a bike at the touch of a button, Penny was uncomfortable with the thought that already the supermarket in Port Vik was running low on stock. They weren't going to starve, the island had farms and Fiona's shitty tomatoes after all, but perhaps it was time to start saving Len's Gazettes for loo roll.

Turning onto the main road, Penny and Jim found themselves temporarily shielded from the wind by houses on their left and a long, high dry-stone wall on their right. The barrier was intersected by lanes which ran up to the High Street and formed wind tunnels, which would catch them off guard, the blasts throwing them sideways as they passed by. The normally busy streets were empty, and Penny couldn't help but envy the people snug inside their living rooms, gorging on a diet of home renovation programmes and funeral plan commercials.

At the end of the road was a small car park, with a path running into the woods. On fine days, the woods were full of joggers, dog walkers and day-trippers who'd taken a wrong turn. Today, the car park was empty, and any sound from the road was drowned out by the roar of the trees as the wind whipped and slipped between their branches. Under the slate skies, the woods took on a dusk-like gloom, and Penny couldn't help feeling quite skittish as she spied the path leading into the dark tunnel of trees ahead.

Within the woodland itself, the roar of the trees above them was muffled, and their progress was punctuated with the unnerving thud of falling branches either side of the path. Penny squealed as a wild rabbit, fleeing the incursion, leapt from under a bush and streaked off in search of a safer place to forage. Chuckling, Jim offered her his hand.

'My, you're a jumpy one,' he said, as she ignored his hand and attached herself to his entire arm.

'Can't help it,' Penny replied. 'A bunch of us used to come up here in the dark and scare the pants off each other with ghost stories. Mind you, that wasn't the only pants removal that went on in here. When Eileen and I were eight, we found a stash of used condoms. Only, we thought they were balloons.'

'Please tell me you didn't,' said Jim, looking slightly sick.

'Oh yes. Blew them up and took them home as a surprise for our parents.'

'I think I might throw up. What did your parents say?'

'Nothing. Eileen and I always called them the salty balloons. We even went back and looked for more! Then, when I was about fifteen, I was having a huge row with Mum and told her she never appreciated anything I did. She asked what I meant, and the first example that sprang to mind was her binning the salty balloons. She told me to go away and have a think about why the balloons were salty. My face was probably like yours is now.'

'Jeez. And you went on to study nutrition. Talk about early influences,' laughed Jim.

'I think it was somewhere around here that we

found them,' said Penny. 'Yes, see over there. The big rhododendrons behind the green bench. It was somewhere in there.'

She let go of Jim's arm and veered onto a narrow mud track, beaten into the grass over years by the feet of randy islanders and adventurous children. Jim hurried to catch up with her.

'Careful there,' he said, putting an arm out to steady her as she skidded. 'Are you after more balloons? Because these days the shop in town has them in a variety of flavours, without the extra sauce.'

'No, I just spotted something in the trees over here,' Penny said, pointing to what appeared to be a ramshackle construction of branches and plastic covered in hanks of dead grass. 'This must be Gervais and Ricky's fort. They've done a good job. I'm surprised it's still standing after all this weather. Mind you, Kenny's going to go ballistic when he finds out they've pinched his tarpaulin.'

Penny and Jim pulled a makeshift door aside, bent down and looked inside the fort. Dark and cavelike, it smelled of damp and pine needles. There was a small stash of tinned food at the back, along with a sleeping bag, a couple of torches and a pile of rocks. Two water pistols, fully loaded, had been stashed by the entrance, ready to repel intruders.

'Looks like if they couldn't drown the enemy, they were planning to stone them,' commented Jim, looking around the small space. 'What's this?'

He knelt down, crawled inside the fort and retrieved a small, metal object from the floor. Scooting backwards, he passed the object to Penny, then squeezed out of the doorway and stood up. Penny stood with him, holding the object up so that they could both examine it in what little light penetrated the trees.

'I think it's a money clip,' she said. 'It looks expensive. Proper silver. Why would the twins have that?'

'I doubt they would. Makes me wonder if someone

else has been here,' Jim said, taking the money clip from Penny and putting it in his pocket. 'We better let Eileen know, in case the boys run into a stranger and…well…better safe than sorry. Come on, let's get back to the main path.'

By the time they arrived at Jim's house, Penny was a miserable, squelchy mess. She'd taken a welly off to shake out a stone and accidentally stepped in a patch of mud. She'd tucked the muddy sock into her pocket then spent the next ten minutes complaining that her welly was giving her bare foot a blister. By the time they arrived at Jim's house, he was a red-faced, sweaty lump. He'd gallantly offered Penny a piggyback so that she'd shut up about her sore foot. She did shut up about the foot, but instead spent the rest of the journey complaining that he was jiggling, and it was making her wellies fall off, until Jim curtly told her that the best cure for a sore throat was to keep your mouth closed. By the time they arrived at Jim's house, Penny and Jim were arguing so loudly that curtains twitched in the windows of the houses on either side. His well of gallantry exhausted, Jim unceremoniously dumped Penny at the bottom of the garden path, telling her, 'There you go, you heavy lump. You can walk the last wee bit.'

Ignoring the impulse to give Jim a swift kick up the backside with her good foot, Penny limped behind him into the house. It was a solid, stone farmhouse on the outskirts of Port Vik. A hundred years ago, it would have stood a good distance from the town and been surrounded by fields. However, with the passage of time and a population swelled by incomers seeking a rural idyll, the fields had been swallowed by kit houses, a new primary school and a leisure centre. Jim's house was now a charming anomaly in a crop of white, pebble-dashed insipidity.

Penny was curious to see how Jim lived. He didn't seem to spend much time at home, had never married and, outside of football, didn't have any hobbies that she knew of. She was, therefore, pleasantly surprised when he led her into a comfortable living room, dominated by a nubuck leather sofa and a large television. The colour scheme was soft and neutral, in complete contrast to the riot of purples, reds and golds that Penny had become used to at Valhalla. In fact, he didn't even own a pole-dancing pole. Having removed her wellies at the front door, Penny hopped towards the sofa, trying to keep her wet, muddy trouser leg off the cream carpet, and sank down, grateful to at last be somewhere dry.

'Off! Off the sofa! Sit on the pouf,' yelled Jim. 'Your arse has been hanging out the back of your coat for the last ten minutes and you look like you've pissed yourself. You're not ruining my good leather with your wet backside.'

'For goodness' sake, do you have a towel?' asked Penny, struggling back to her foot and hopping into the hall.

Jim reached into a cupboard and flung her a towel.

'I'm going to take my trousers and knickers off. I'll need something a bit more substantial than this, you big pervert,' she said, holding up the small hand towel.

'Aye, there's a fair bit of acreage to cover there. I might need to nip back and get the tarpaulin off the fort,' Jim snapped, lobbing a bath sheet at her and stomping off in the direction of the kitchen, leaving Penny to strip in the privacy of the hall, with its big glass door and road outside.

'It's just as well you don't keep your house keys with your car keys,' she told him as she wandered into the kitchen a few minutes later, wearing her makeshift skirt, her knickers rolled into a discreet ball inside the trousers in her hand. The kitchen, she noted, was large and modern, yet the traditional stove gave the room a homely feel, an ambience that was reinforced by the large, scarred pine table in the centre of the room.

'When you're a vet, you only make that mistake once,' said Jim. 'Years ago, I dropped my keys and had to wait two days for them to come out the other end of a pig. Come over here, woman. You can wash your trouser leg in the sink and chuck the lot in the drier.'

As Penny rinsed the mud off her trouser leg and gave it a quick wash with some dish soap, she realised that she had a knicker quandary on her hands. If she chucked her damp undercrackers in the drier, it might blow the smell of gusset around the place. If she washed them and Jim noticed, he might think she had a smelly hoo-ha. Either way, she was potentially going to be exposed. And it wasn't even smelly. Not really. Okay, probably a bit after being locked in damp knickers. Mind you, it was itchy. Did damp knickers give you thrush? Jings, crivvens and help ma Boab, she probably had a fandango like a fermented herring, but because it was her own, she couldn't smell it. She wasn't going to risk it, she'd have to wash her knickers.

Penny dunked her knickers in the water and quickly added a drop of washing up liquid. All the while her brain screamed that here she was, half-naked in the house of a man she'd known less than a week, if you didn't count school, with a fur-china that could scare off a skunk. Where was Chesney when you needed him? He wouldn't judge a bush by its odour. He'd sung "you are the one and only you."

'Can you smell that?' asked Jim.

'It's *not* my fanny!' blurted Penny.

There was a moment's stunned silence, then Jim cleared his throat and said, 'Erm, I think it's my trousers. I put them in the drier while you were getting changed. I should have just put them in the wash because they smell like a wet dog farted in them. That said, I'm relieved it's not your fanny.'

As they dried off, Jim called his friend in the Coastguard.

'Hiya, Andy, foos yer doos? I'm hoping you can do me a wee favour and check a couple of things. Did we have any ships from Gibraltar go past the island last weekend? Aye... aye…aye…aye…aye… aye…aye…aye…aye. And what about the Aberdeen ferry? Did it stay in the harbour

Saturday night? Aye... aye...aye...aye...aye... aye...aye...aye...aye. Aye, cheerio.'

Jim hung up and yawned. 'I could do with a cup of tea,' he said, stretching his arms and yawning again.

Penny gave him a poke in the stomach, cutting him off mid-stretch.

'Oof. What did you do that for?' he asked, hunching forward.

'Aye... aye...aye...aye...aye... aye...aye...aye...aye?'

'Oh, aye. His wife died. A tree came down on her car on the loch road and killed her instantly. He's quite pleased. He told me he'd have said she was taking him to the cleaners if she'd had any intention of leaving him the shirt on his back. Anyway, he says the funeral's next week, every expense spared.'

'Not the wife, although that's quite harsh. The ship and the ferry?'

'Aye, there was a ship from Gibraltar which sailed close to the island. He'll text me the details. The ferry was in Aberdeen until the Sunday afternoon, though. But,' Jim held up a warning finger to stop Penny interrupting, 'he said that a smaller boat with no GPS could have come and gone without a trace.'

'So, Captain Rab could have come back to the island,' mused Penny.

'Theoretically, yes. He has the experience to navigate without GPS and didn't Elsie say he keeps a boat at the loch?'

'If Captain Rab took his boat over to Aberdeen and stashed it ready to sneak back to the island, then this must have been planned well in advance. He could have topped Old Archie any time, so the witness must have been the intended victim. Somehow, he must have known that the witness was arriving on the island that night. How could he have known? And what does Anthony Woodbead have to do with this? And Yulia Klimova? You thought Woodbead and Yulia were shagging, but maybe you were wrong. Maybe they're partners in crime. Maybe they're in this together with Captain Rab. We have to find out what they're up to and we have to find that witness.'

Jim waggled his spare car key at her. 'What we need is a plan. But first we need wheels. Put your knickers on, Sherlock, we're going out.'

CHAPTER ELEVEN

It took less time to get back to the car, due to much of the walk being downhill. As Jim hunted in his pockets for the spare key, Penny, running on autopilot, pulled the car door handle. The door opened.

'All this time we could have waited in the car, instead of traipsing through the woods getting soaked!' she exclaimed.

'I didn't expect the doors to be open! I thought they locked themselves after a while. Come on, let's stop arguing and get going. Where to, my lady?'

'Homeo, Romeo,' said Penny, giving him a cheeky wink. 'I said I'd be back at lunchtime. I sent Mum and the kids looking for clues along the route Old Archie and the witness must have taken. I can't imagine that anything has survived this weather, but it was a loose end that needed tying up.

'That's the trouble with all of this. We just keep creating more loose ends. Do you want to do a detour up to the loch to see if the captain's boat is there?'

'Can we do it later? Now I have my handbag again, I've just realised that we haven't delivered Elsie's teeth. Thank goodness nobody made off with my bag when the car was sitting with its doors unlocked. Can you imagine the thief's face when he opened it and the first thing he saw was a pair of false teeth floating in wine?'

Penny and Jim laughed, their earlier bickering forgotten, and they agreed to drop the teeth off on the way. Jim steered Phil along the harbour road and up towards the High Street, where he parked outside the library, a Brutalist building rammed in by some 1960s town planner alongside the twee Victoriana, presumably on a rainy day where there was little else to do but drop acid and make bad decisions.

Penny hopped out of the car and, grabbing her handbag, scooted through the rain and into the library. Row upon row of books were stacked on shelves reaching all the way to strip lights in the tiled ceiling. Penny wondered whether, somewhere in there, was a very good book called Frock in Hell, by an excellent author whose name she couldn't quite recall. She made her way towards a desk by the window, where Elsie sat reading a magazine.

'Hello, I'm here to bring these back,' said Penny, holding up the bag of teeth.

Elsie didn't look up. She continued to stare down at her magazine, her chin resting on her hand. 'Just leave it there,' she said dismissively, gesturing with her other hand towards a pile of books on the end of the desk.

Penny shook the bag under Elsie's nose. 'Wine gum?' she asked.

Elsie looked up and reddened slightly. 'I shouldn't have done that,' she said. 'But the woman is so rude, I couldn't help myself. Just as well I have a spare set. Thank you for bringing them back, dear. I didn't know how I was going to explain to the dentist that I'd lost yet another pair.'

'No bother,' said Penny, stifling a giggle. 'Have you phoned Sandra Next Door to arrange to put the gun back yet?'

'I rang her first thing this morning. I was going to apologise, but she said she wasn't talking to me and hung up.'

'Och, she'll come around. Listen, Elsie, I need to ask you…this is a bit delicate…last night, when Mrs Hubbard was upset, you looked like you knew something. We're just trying to understand why we can't find any trace of people and, if you do know something, it would really help if you could tell me.'

Elsie shook her head and stared down at her magazine for a moment. When she looked up again, there were tears in her eyes. 'You don't know what you're asking and I'm sorry, I can't talk about it. You should speak to your parents.' She placed a hand on Penny's and, gazing at her earnestly, repeated, 'Speak to your parents. I promise it has nothing to do with Old Archie's murder, but you're entitled to an explanation.'

Taking pity on the older woman, Penny decided not to press her any further. Instead, she asked, 'Am I right in thinking you said Captain Rab keeps a boat at the loch?'

Elsie looked relieved at the change of subject and, pulling a tissue from her cardigan sleeve, she wiped her eyes and said, 'Yes, the Princess Ellie. He and Old Archie used to take it out fishing.'

'What does it look like?'

'It's one of those cabin boats. Not big, but not tiny either. Blue and white, I think. I only saw it a couple of times when I dropped Old Archie at the loch. His post van was in with young Kenny for repairs, you see, so we only had the library van. It took two weeks to get the part from the mainland, would you believe it?'

'That's ridiculous,' said Penny.

'Exactly what Captain Rab said, maybe with a few less swear words. That's why, when his boat needed repairs, he took it straight to Aberdeen himself. He told Old Archie that unless they have the thing in front of them, they just fob you off. They tell you they're waiting for the part, when really they've given it to another customer instead.'

Penny mentally slotted another piece of the puzzle into place. She thanked Elsie and left the library, battling the wind to shut the heavy glass door behind her. As soon as she had hauled herself into Phil and pulled her seatbelt on, she recounted the story to Jim.

Jim swung the car around and pulled out onto the road, his wheel hitting a pothole, sending a small tsunami over the pavement. He righted the steering and pointed the car in the direction of the village. His face was grim, as he mulled over Penny's news.

'What I don't get,' he eventually burst out, 'is why

Captain Rab, who has been on this island since forever, would suddenly do something like this. He's a horrible old man, but people around here trust him. You don't suddenly turn into a murderer. Which means he's either done it before or something…someone?…terrible pushed him in that direction. I don't know. Maybe Anthony or Yulia pulled the trigger. Whatever. My head's spinning with it all.'

'Let's just take it one step at a time,' Penny advised. 'We'll see what Mum and the kids found then go to Eileen's later to do the internet research like we arranged. Once we have all the information, we can call an extraordinary meeting of Losers Club and make a plan.'

'Aye, and maybe we can discuss that nutrition plan you sent me.'

'Why? What's wrong with it?'

'Two words. Fucking vegetables.'

And with that, they were back to bickering. Jim was firmly of the opinion that chips and ketchup were two of his five a day. No way was he eating "fuckin' wee trees", as he called broccoli, but he'd force down an onion provided it was shaped like a ring and covered in batter. He emphatically disagreed with Penny's suggestion that he shove a courgette in something else shaped like a ring. And, by the way, what the fuck was a spiralizer? Because if it was anything to do with where Penny had just suggested he shoved the courgette, then he wasn't into that kinky stuff.

By the time they reached Valhalla, Jim had worn Penny down and she found herself promising to write a new plan, this time incorporating chicken nuggets.

'Are you coming in for lunch?' she asked.

'Does it involve carrots? Only joking,' he said, holding his hands up as if to fend her off. 'I have to go into work. I'll pick you up later.'

Once more, Jim spun the car around, this time sending a spray of gravel and rainwater over Penny's legs. As she stood in the porch, emptying the gravel from her wellies, she decided that he was probably the most irritating man she had ever met, and she was quite glad that their earlier tête-à-tête had been interrupted.

The front door opened, and Mary emerged to find out what was taking so long. She regarded the tyre marks in the drive and noted the shaking out of the boots.

'What have you been doing to that poor boy to make him take off in such a hurry? Life is always a battle for you, isn't it? You should try to be more low maintenance, like me. I never give your father any stress. We bumble along nicely together. I tell him what we think, and he says "yes, dear." That's how relationships should work – a two-way street. Now, come inside.' Mary ushered Penny into the house and closed the front door, still babbling on. 'I've made us carrot soup for lunch. There was a lovely young girl selling them down at the village shop. Fiona something or other. Said she knows you. Said she grows the carrots herself and they're all organic, whatever that means. Anyway, I bought some tomatoes as well, so it's tomato soup tomorrow.'

Suddenly, Penny didn't feel very hungry. Her rational brain calmly stated that everything was washed and boiled. Meanwhile, her irrational brain screamed, 'It's not carrot soup, it's pee soup! And what about Fiona's cystitis?' She decided to listen to her rational brain but felt more uneasy with every mouthful. After a few spoonfuls, she gave up and, buttering some bread, asked her mother and the twins, 'How did your investigation go this morning?'

'Oh my God, it was big yikes. Hector slipped on the cliff path and nearly died,' said Edith, leaning forward in her enthusiasm to relate the shocking details of Hector's brush with a patch of wet grass and a fifty-foot drop. In fact, her enthusiasm was bordering on indecent, and Hector looked a little hurt. Penny took some guilty pleasure in reminding Edith to eat her soup before it went cold.

'Yes, Hector nearly died and all that jazz. Sorry Hector, I do care, really. But did you actually find anything useful?' she asked.

Hector puffed out his little chest and began, 'Mother—,' but cut himself short when Mary lifted the soup ladle and glared at him. He deflated a little and said, in a more moderate tone, 'You could at least be sympathetic, Mum. What with Freddie, then this, I'm feeling quite stressed.'

'I know, my wee darling. You have a lot on your plate at the moment. I'm glad you didn't fall off a cliff. Now, what did you find?'

'Nothing, really,' said Hector. 'There was no boat on the beach and nothing on the cliff path. We walked the route to Old Archie's, and there wasn't anything to see. There's an alleyway down the street with a clear view of his house. It's quite sheltered, and if I was the killer, that's where I'd wait for Old Archie coming home.'

'We don't think Old Archie was the intended victim. We think it was whoever was with him,' said Penny.

'Nonsense,' exclaimed Len, who up until now had been quietly dipping his moustache in spoonfuls of carrot soup. Penny assumed that some must have gone down the hatch, but he was very orange around the mouth.

'Why do you say that, Dad?'

Len gazed around the kitchen, as though he might find the answer on the front of the fridge, or hiding in the oven. 'Well, it stands to reason, doesn't it,' he eventually said.

Penny was about to take her father to task over his vague answer, but he was saved by Mary, who looked at him in disgust and said, tartly, 'Wipe your mouth, Len.

You look like you've been giving Bugs Bunny a blow job.'

Edith promptly snorted soup down her nose and had to leave the table, clutching a tea towel to her face. Hector, who was either trying not to laugh or had terrible wind, looked pleadingly at his mother. Penny nodded, and he shot away from the table. A moment later, Penny could hear muffled gales of laughter coming from the direction of his bedroom.

'Mum, remember the talk we had about saying inappropriate things in front of the twins?'

'Oh, for goodness' sake, Penny. Stop being such a snowflake. They're sixteen. If they haven't given someone a blow job themselves, they've seen enough of that sort of thing on the internet.'

'I'd tell you that it's up to me to draw the lines, not you, but you're just going to call me a snowflake, aren't you?'

'Pretty much,' confirmed Mary. 'It's my new word. That and Karen. I have the internet too, and I know all about Karens. Sandra Next Door is one.'

'You do realise that actual Karens find that quite offensive?'

'Snowflakes,' muttered Mary, defiantly.

Penny gave up. Mary had never been a traditional parent. Some rules had been normal; don't take drugs, do well in school etc. However, Mary had a passionate curiosity about the world which, combined with her lack of filter and a good dash of mischief, meant that she barrelled unpredictably through life. She was ninety percent endearing and ten percent infuriating. At the moment, the ten percent was to the fore. Penny changed tack.

'I need to ask you about something. As you know, Losers Club has been looking into Old Archie's murder and, while we were doing some research into his background, we came across something strange. We couldn't find any birth records for him, you, Dad and some other people on the island. Why is that?'

'That's very strange. Are you sure you were doing it right? Len, did you tell her about pop-downs and load-ups?'

'Aye,' said Len, 'I gave her all the basics. These internets are complicated, though. Did you try switching the internet off and switching it on again?'

'You can't switch the internet off, Dad. Yes, I did everything right.'

'It's probably because they didn't have computers when we were born,' said Mary, nodding wisely. 'These days they're practically giving birth on the Twitter.'

'Elsie and Mrs Hubbard said I should ask you about it.'

'I don't know why they'd tell you to ask me about giving birth on the Twitter, dear. Your dad took some photos just after you came out. Will those do? You could put them on the internet if you want.'

Penny sighed. She was beginning to lose patience with her parents. 'I mean they told me to ask you about why there are no birth records for you.'

'I have no idea. It's definitely odd. Now, if you've finished your soup, we'll take a run into town to get the twins' school uniforms. Chop, chop, Chunky.'

Mary began to clear the table and Penny looked imploringly at her father, who stood up abruptly and muttered something about going to his shed. A minute later, the back door slammed, and Penny could see him stalking across the lawn, hands in pockets, head down against the wind.

By the time Penny turned away from the window, Mary had left the kitchen and was loudly marshalling Hector and Edith. A little too loudly, Penny thought. Like if she kept shouting at everyone, nobody would be able to get a word in, never mind ask difficult questions. Mary and Len may have fobbed her off this time, but Penny was determined to get some answers.

Reluctant to go back out in the rain again, she nevertheless pulled on her wellington boots, zipped up her damp raincoat and braced herself for a dash to the car, if Mum could hurry up and find the bloody keys for once.

Eventually, Mary appeared, accompanied by two mutinous teenagers whom she had swathed in brightly coloured plastic rain ponchos.

'I look fucking ridiculous,' said Hector, whose red poncho reached almost to his feet.

'Mum, please, please, tell her,' pleaded Edith, grabbing handfuls of her pink poncho and holding them up in disgust. 'If I put the hood up, I'm going to look like a walking penis from behind.'

'Their coats are soaked through from earlier,' Mary explained. 'You didn't take any spares, and this is all I have.' She gave a dramatic shrug and donned her most innocent face. 'It's your fault. It's not like I planned this!'

'You'll just have to wear them,' Penny told the twins, 'and pray that nobody from school sees you.'

The twins sagged and made their way to the car, scuffing their feet in the gravel.

'It's not like you planned this?' Penny asked her mother, noting the words "Hector" and "Edith" writ large across the back of the ponchos.

They returned to Valhalla in the late afternoon with approximately five million bags and two happier teenagers. Penny had swiftly replaced the ponchos with new raincoats and, in a move worthy of the Wankpuffin himself, splashed out on new sportswear for the twins. She considered branded sportswear an enormous waste of money yet understood that it would help Hector and Edith fit in with the other kids in their year. There had been a minor skirmish over school shoes, with Penny firmly resisting trainer styles in favour of the ugly, boring ones from the list on the school website. She'd waved her phone at the twins, shouting, 'Ugly, boring and ridiculously expensive they may be, but that's what it says here. You pick a pair each, and I'll arrange the bloody mortgage to pay for them.'

This had earned her a glare from the shop assistant but, having just done Battle of the Trousers and UN level negotiations on skirt length, Penny was in no mood to care. She'd bought a black marker pen to scrawl their names on everything, because bugger sewing on name tags, then declared herself done. School uniform shops really should come with a free bar, she decided.

The twins lugged their shopping into the house and Penny made a beeline for the kettle. In an ideal world, it would have been her mother's stash of gin, but she had only eaten bread and ice cream all day and didn't think that turning up at Eileen's door pissed as a newt at four in the afternoon would be setting the best example for Ricky and Gervais.

Jim was in the kitchen, once more poring over the crossword with Len.

'I didn't see your car in the drive,' she said.

'I parked it on the road,' he told her. 'I brought my rake and tidied the gravel. I'm sorry about earlier, Penny. My head's battered with all this Captain Rab stuff, and I think the constant rain is getting to me.'

'It's okay,' Penny assured him. 'I'm feeling the same. I just had a meltdown on Hector over school ties. They had clip on ties in London but the ones here are proper ties. Dad, could you show Hector and Edith how to do their ties please?'

'Only if you help us with twelve across. Stranded players are not here. Eight letters,' said Len.

'Castaway. Can I just grab a quick cuppa, Jim, and we'll be on our way?'

'Fine. Make it quick, though or Eileen will be busy with the bairns' tea.'

'I will. By the way, Mum has invited you for lunch tomorrow. In fact, she's insisting on it. She's making her speciality.'

Len, who had been paying no attention, looked up from his crossword and asked, 'Even Reg got his own back? Seven letters.'

'Revenge,' said Penny.

CHAPTER TWELVE

Eileen was at home when Penny and Jim arrived. The kitchen was in its usual state of homely clutter and a large pot of something delicious bubbled gently on the hob. Eileen immediately bustled around, putting the kettle on and explaining that she had already fed the boys and packed them off to their rooms with the electronic baby-sitters.

'They're up there designing forts on Minecraft,' she told her visitors.

'On the subject of forts…' Penny told her about the money clip they'd found that morning and asked whether it was something the twins could have dropped.

'No, they wouldn't have anything like that,' said Eileen, looking concerned. 'I'll ask them, but you're probably right. It sounds like someone else has been there. I'm keeping them in until this murderer has been caught, so they're not allowed up to the woods just now. I'll tell Kenny they've pinched his tarpaulin. He'll go mad and I'll suggest he helps them build another fort in the garden instead.' Eileen tapped the side of her head and gave Penny and Jim a crafty wink. 'There's nae mouches on me.'

She pulled a stool up to the table and squeezed between Penny and Jim. Dragging the laptop towards them, she opened the lid and said, 'I haven't closed any of the windows from last time, so we can get started straight away. Who shall we search for first?'

Jim started to say, 'Anthony Woo—,' but Penny stopped him and said, 'Me.'

'You?' asked Eileen, clearly confused by the strange request.

'Yes, me. And then you. And then we'll try Jim. You see, the thought has just occurred to me that if our parents don't exist, then do we?'

'Good point,' said Eileen. 'I tried asking Mum about it, but she just said I must have been doing it all wrong as usual.'

She reached out to the keyboard and began to type. Within a few minutes, they had their answer. There was a birth record for Penny Hopper, but there was also a death record. Penny Hopper had died as a baby in 1977.

Quickly, Eileen searched for Jim. Again, the infant Jim Space had died shortly after birth in 1976. Eileen hesitated, before finally searching for herself. Eileen Campbell had also died as an infant.

'Who are we?' she gasped.

'I don't know,' said Penny, 'but I've had just about enough of this fobbing off. We need to force some answers from our parents.'

'I haven't even asked my dad yet and, from what I can see, there's no point. I'll probably get the same nonsense as you two,' said Jim. 'It might be better to get them together in one place. Penny, will you marry me?'

'Don't be ridiculous. Why on earth would I want to do that?'

'They'd have to come to a wedding! They'd never suspect it was a ruse to get them together.'

'A pretty drastic way to go about it though. Get shackled for life and wait months before we get answers? Anyway, nobody is going to believe that within a few days of meeting up again, we're suddenly tying the knot, least of all the twins. I've only just reassured Hector that I find you very unattractive and will never shag anyone again as long as I live. No, we need to think of something a bit more credible and a bit less long term.

How about staging a charity bingo night? We can show them some fake leaflets and convince them to come to the church hall. Only, they'll be the only ones attending. The twins won't want to come, so I'd be able to get Mum and Dad on their own. I could book the hall for tomorrow night. None of the other groups will have it booked for a Sunday. Then we sit them all down and make them tell us the truth.'

The others agreed that this might actually work. Eileen pulled up a graphics programme on the laptop and they began to design a leaflet. There was some debate about which charity they should use before Jim pointed out that they might get into trouble if they ran a fake event using the name of a real charity. They settled on inventing their own – The Scottish Children's Welfare Trust. Feeling slightly guilty, Penny made a donation to an actual children's charity, before they got on with the business of designing a logo.

Eventually, poster done, Jim reminded the others that they still hadn't researched their suspects. Eileen flicked back to the search page and said, 'Who's first?'

'Anthony Woodbead,' said Jim. 'We don't have personal details for any of these people, so we'll just have to Google the names and hope for the best.'

Eileen clattered the keyboard. 'The only results are rosaries and necklaces. Hang on, I'll try with quotation marks…two results. Both an old blog.' She clicked on the results, both of which led to an error message. 'I'll try the surname…weird…it says the surname died out. There's nobody in the UK with that surname.'

'Oh for fucks' sake,' said Jim. 'Another person that doesn't exist. Shall we invite him to the Bingo as well?'

Eileen put her hands over her own ears and said sharply, 'Shh! I don't want the boys hearing that sort of language.'

'Eileen, are you forgetting you're married to Kenny? His first word began with an eff!' said Penny. She turned to Jim. 'She's right, though. You need to mind your peas and quinoas.'

'What the fuck is a keen wa?' Jim asked.

'Did you not read your nutrition plan?'

'Aye, well, I got as far as the wee trees, scanned the rest for a mention of chips and decided that some constructive criticism was in order. Constructive criticism duly delivered, and I got told to shove a courgette up my—'

'Jim!' said Penny and Eileen together.

Arms crossed and glaring, Jim looked like an expletive bomb ready to explode, yet somehow, he managed to keep a lid on it. 'Yulia Klimova,' he barked.

'How do you spell that?' asked Eileen.

'A R S E H O L E,' said Jim, determined to finish his previous sentence.

'We've already done a search for you. We're onto Yulia now,' Penny told him sweetly. She gave Eileen what she thought was the correct spelling and they waited for Google to work its magic. Four hundred thousand results.

'Click on "Images",' suggested Penny. 'There might be a photo of her, and we can narrow it down from there.'

Sure enough, within the page of photographs, was a picture of a sallow faced, unsmiling Yulia. Eileen clicked on the image, and it took them to the website of a modelling agency based in Moscow. CEO – Yulia Klimova.

'That puts a different perspective on her phone conversation,' said Penny, relieved that they'd at least found one of the visitors. 'When she said "if Max won't do it then tell Alexander to shoot him," she must have been talking about a modelling shoot. Phew! She's not an international assassin after all. Do we want to rule her out?'

Jim, who had stopped sulking and was now leaning forward, staring at the screen, said, 'Probably. She's definitely having some sort of relationship with Woodbead, and he's as suspicious as they come. However, we have nothing substantial on her, so let's put her to one side for now. What about the Cohens and Pete. Do we even have a last name for Pete?'

'Yes, I checked with Rachel before I left the hotel. It's Smellie,' said Penny.

Jim snickered. Penny ignored him.

'There are about two hundred thousand results,' said Eileen. She clicked on "Images". The photographs appeared to be of much older men and neither Penny nor Jim could spot Peter among them. However, with hundreds of pages to check, they soon ran out of steam.

'Try putting quotation marks around his name and adding Canada,' suggested Penny.

This narrowed down the search results considerably. Now, they were mainly restricted to genealogy websites. Eileen clicked through Smellie family trees, noting down a few possible matches. Canadian birth records weren't available online, so they quickly reached a dead end.

'The most likely one is this guy,' said Penny, pointing at an entry for Peter Smellie, son of Elspeth Smellie née Linklater and John Smellie. 'Try searching for any newspaper reports about Elspeth Smellie. It's a much less common name, so we might get a hit.'

They did indeed find an article which mentioned Elspeth Smellie. It was from a small-town newspaper in Ontario. The article was ten years old and detailed the deaths of Elspeth and John Smellie in a fire at their home in Brody. It was accompanied by a photograph of a smiling couple and a teenage boy. Penny and Jim shuffled nearer to the screen to take a closer look at the photograph.

'What do you think?' Penny asked.

Jim screwed up his eyes and tilted his head to one side. 'I'm fairly sure that's him,' he said. 'Eileen, do another search for his name, but this time add "Brody".'

The only other match was a high school graduation photograph from a few years later. This time, Penny and Jim agreed that the kid in the middle row was definitely Pete.

'I wonder what happened to him after his parents died,' Penny wondered aloud. 'Poor Pete. How awful, losing your parents so young.'

'Tragic,' said Eileen, imagining how her boys would cope without herself and Kenny to herd them into school every morning. They'd probably live in their fort and steal food from the bins round the back of the supermarket, she decided. 'Maybe he became one of those feral kids that you read about. Raised by tigers.'

Penny smiled. 'Aye, I've heard that the tigers of Ontario are a caring bunch. If we're agreed that there's nothing ominous about Pete, let's try the Cohens.'

Having been on the receiving end of Ruth's long-winded tales of her family, it didn't take Penny long to fill in enough details to narrow down the search results for Ruth and Larry Cohen. They appeared to have no concept of privacy, and their social media documented the lives of their daughters, with older pictures showing the couple eating ice creams on a beach with two young girls, right up to the present-day photographs of two handsome young women in gowns and mortar board hats. Ruth's pride in what she called "my babies" shone through in every word.

'We'd pretty much discounted them anyway, and there's no faking this,' said Jim. 'Let's forget about the Cohens. We need to focus on Woodbead and Captain Rab.'

He told Eileen about their earlier adventures in Captain Rab's back garden and the discovery that Rab's boat had been taken to Aberdeen for repairs around the time of the murder.

'What we need now,' he said, 'is a plan. Do you think we can get everyone from Losers Club together in the village pub tonight?'

'Kenny will be home soon, so I can come with you then cadge a lift back with Elsie, assuming she can make it,' said Eileen.

'Dad will have Elsie's number and we can ring the shop for Mrs Hubbard. She'll have Fiona's number. And we can knock on Sandra Next Door's door. We're really stupid. Most of us never exchanged phone numbers,' said Penny.

Eileen shrugged. 'There's no need. I think we've just proved that everybody knows everybody in this place.'

'Haven't you got all the phone numbers from when we joined Losers Club anyway?' asked Jim.

'Data protection,' said Penny. 'Sandra Next Door would be first in line to report me for not keeping her details confidential. She'd love it if I messed up.'

'I wonder why she's such a cow,' said Eileen.

'She's unhappy and she's lonely. She's looking for friends, but her unhappiness makes her push people away. It's easier for her to judge people and find them wanting before they can do the same to her,' said Jim.

Penny and Eileen stared at him, surprised at this rare moment of emotional intelligence. He stared back, as if he considered them a pair of supreme blockheads, then gave an exasperated sigh. 'Stands to reason, doesn't it? What with her Geoff shagging Linda from the shoe shop.'

And he's back, thought Penny.

'We better start ringing around,' she told Eileen, digging her phone out of her handbag. 'I'll phone Dad. You do Mrs Hubbard. Jim, get the wine out of the fridge. Eileen and I are not wasting a Saturday night with no kids. No, you can't have one. You're driving.'

The village pub was busier than it had been the previous evening. Penny, Jim and Eileen were early and managed to grab stools at the bar while they waited for a table to become free. Bertie the barman was pulling pints as fast as he could in an effort to keep up with the rowdy crowd of young people who had taken up permanent residence by the pool table. The noise level rose as their game ended, and a heated argument broke out over the efficacy of the pub cues, with one player decreeing that his cue was shite and another declaring his cue shiter. There followed a loud conversation among the group, where the cues were ranked in order of shiteness and, with both players being assigned cues that everyone agreed were of equal shiteidity, a new game began. Somehow, in all the noise and bustle, Eileen managed to procure baskets of scampi and chips to line their stomachs for the wine ahead. Jim looked at Penny disapprovingly and mouthed the words "nutrition plan" before dousing his chips in half a bottle of ketchup and tucking in.

When some of the early evening bar supper crowd were eventually driven off by the whoops and swears coming from the direction of the pool table, the trio were able to commandeer a table and enough chairs to seat Losers Club. Jim happily growled at anyone unwise enough to ask if they could take one of the chairs. Fortunately, they didn't have to wait long for the other Losers to arrive.

Mrs Hubbard, who lived only a few minutes' walk away, was first on the scene, closely followed by Elsie, who complained that people would talk about her being in the pub two nights in a row. 'They might think we're having a fling,' she confided to Jim, giving him a lascivious wink.

'Well, I wouldn't mind seeing what happens when you take those false teeth out, you saucy wee minx,' he said, squeezing her knee.

Elsie giggled and gave him a playful shove which sent him jolting into Penny, who accidentally deposited half a glass of wine into Mrs Hubbard's handbag. There was a flurry of activity, with Penny apologising profusely and Mrs Hubbard giving Elsie a sound telling off. Eileen, meanwhile, had gathered all the napkins and was doing her best to dry the contents of Mrs Hubbard's bag. A soggy Woman's Weekly, a purse, a packet of tissues; all were laid out on the table. As Eileen continued to pull out the items one by one, Mrs Hubbard suddenly stopped berating Elsie and squealed, 'No!' Eileen looked at the clear plastic tub in her hand and froze. Slowly, she raised it and put it on the table with the other things.

Penny paled and asked quietly, 'Why do you have Freddie in your handbag, Mrs Hubbard?'

CHAPTER THIRTEEN

Everyone at the table went very still, all of them looking at Penny. The tableau held for what felt like a few minutes but was in reality a few seconds, until a harsh voice broke the spell.

'What the hell is that?' asked Sandra Next Door, who was standing behind Penny and Eileen, gazing down at the plastic tub, inside which the hamster lay, unmoving, on a bed of kitchen roll.

'Hello, Sandra Next Door,' said Eileen, turning to look up at her. Then, noticing the man beside Sandra Next Door, she added, 'And hello to you too..uhm..'

'Geoff, pleased to meet you' said the man, offering a beringed hand.

Eileen took the hand and kissed it. 'Pleased to meet you, your Holiness.'

Penny let out a snort of laughter, spraying wine over the table and the contents of Mrs Hubbard's handbag, and the tension was broken as the rest of the group joined in. Wiping tears from her eyes, Penny waved Sandra and Geoff Next Door towards vacant chairs next to Jim. She barely contained a second wave of laughter, as Jim turned to Geoff Next Door and said, 'Pleased to meet shoe.'

If Geoff Next Door noticed, he gave nothing away. Feeling slightly guilty for extending such a poor introduction to the group, Penny marshalled her emotions and said, 'Sorry, Geoff Next Door. We're not laughing at you. We're all very pleased to meet you. Do you know everyone?'

She made the introductions, ending with, 'And, of course, you know Sandra Next Door.'

Sandra Next Door eyed her without humour. 'Why

is there a dead hamster in a tub?'

'Good question. Mrs Hubbard, why is Freddie dead in a tub?'

'I'm sorry, dearie,' said Mrs Hubbard. 'I found him in a box of cornflakes this morning. He was already dead. I popped him in with Old Archie, and I was going to phone you later, but when you said we were meeting in the pub, I thought I'd bring him.'

'He doesn't look frozen,' said Penny.

Mrs Hubbard leaned over to pat her hand and said, 'Three minutes on defrost, dearie.'

'You microwaved my hamster?'

'Oh, he's not cooked. I turned him over halfway through. Will you tell Hector I'm sorry for his loss? And would you mind returning the tub when you've finished with it? I need it for Douglas' sandwiches.'

Penny slipped the tub containing Freddie into her own handbag and flinched as a hand landed on her shoulder. She looked up to see Jim smiling down at her.

'Are you okay?' he asked. 'Here, I brought you another glass of wine. I don't think you drank much of the last one.'

Grateful for the small kindness, she smiled back at him and said, 'I'm fine. Just a bit worried about Hector's reaction when he sees this. He's a sensitive wee soul. Edith bounces back from pretty much anything. Hector takes it all to heart.'

'Ah, they're good kids. A good team. I saw how Edith was with him when we delivered the leaflets.'

Penny laughed weakly. 'When they're not arguing, they're great. They've been a lot more united since we came here, probably because they've only got each other. Once they start school and find their own friendship groups, it'll be loggerheads as usual. We'll give Freddie a good send off in the morning. Do you think I should put him in the fridge? Mum will poop herself if she's first up and goes in there for milk.'

'She won't be first up. You're forgetting that you have Alarm Clock Jim!'

'Does whacking you over the head turn you off?'

'I told you, I'm not into that kinky stuff.'

Penny rolled her eyes. 'Fiona and Gordon haven't turned up. Should we wait or should we get started?'

As if on cue, there was a blast of cool air and the pub door opened. Fiona came rushing in, pulling her hood back and wiping the rain from her face.

'It's blowing a hoolie out there, worse than ever. Gordon's just parking the van. He dropped me off at the door and I still managed to get soaked.' Hanging her coat on the back of a chair, she looked around the pub and waved to an old man who was sitting at the end of the bar. 'Ask Bertie to pour me a double vodka, will you, Kev? And a pint of lemonade for Gordon. Oh, and one for yourself.'

Kev gave her a thumbs up and she sat down next to Eileen. 'Sorry we're late. The van wouldn't start. I rang Mrs Hubbard's, but she'd already left, and Douglas said to bugger off because he was watching Dancing On Ice.'

'Didn't that finish months ago?' asked Penny.

'He said he'd recorded it, and these past two nights were the first time he's had peace to watch it.' Fiona nodded in Mrs Hubbard's direction. 'He thanked me and offered me a hundred quid to take her out every night while I'm A Celebrity's on.'

Penny eyed the bright blue cocktail that was rapidly disappearing inside Mrs Hubbard.

'I'm A Celeb's on for about three weeks and this pub has a big cocktail menu. You'll need to drive a harder bargain.'

They were joined by Gordon, who had collected the drinks from the bar on his way to the table. He pulled up an extra chair and greeted Geoff Next Door like an old friend.

'Do they know each other?' Penny asked.

'Oh, yes,' said Fiona. 'They go to the Sunday men's

group at the Vik hotel.'

Penny's questions about the men's group were forestalled by Jim, who cleared his throat and said, 'Shall we begin?'

The group settled down, and Jim explained what they had discovered so far.

'So, to sum up,' he concluded, counting the points off on his fingers, 'Old Archie and the witness definitely came from Gibraltar, we've pretty much discounted most of the visitors, the witness was the target, Captain Rab had the means and opportunity to sneak back onto the island on the night of the murder, Captain Rab and Anthony Woodbead (or whoever he is) are up to something and myself, Penny and Eileen are dead.'

He glanced at Penny, who took up the baton.

'We're no nearer to finding the witness, so that leaves us two lines of enquiry,' she said, 'Find out where Captain Rab's boat went for "repairs" and, if it really did go for repairs, could it have been taken out overnight without anyone noticing. Secondly, how do we find out what Captain Rab and Anthony Woodbead are up to?'

'Obviously we watch them,' said Sandra Next Door. 'Organise ourselves into shifts and follow them.'

'Good thinking, Sandra Next Door. We should start tonight, but five of us have had a drink so can't drive. Shall we start early tomorrow morning?'

Jim begged some paper and a pen from Bertie the barman and drew up a timetable so that they could keep watch on the hotel and Captain Rab's house.

'If they leave either place, tail them. If you think you might have been spotted, leave and call Eileen. These are dangerous men, so don't take any chances. Eileen, I'm putting you down as a spare, in case anyone can't make it, but your main role will be coordinator. Elsie, do you have anything a bit less conspicuous than the library van?'

Elsie shook her head, no.

'Okay,' said Jim, 'then you and Mrs Hubbard can

go together as a pair in her car. So, that's four pairs of us covering from six in the morning through ten at night. There aren't enough of us for twenty-four-hour coverage. I suggest we rotate every two hours.'

He scribbled some more and, tearing the paper into strips, handed everyone a slip with their allotted times and places. There was a moment's silence, while everyone studied their timetable, followed by a disorderly babble as they begged, bribed and bartered among themselves to swap time slots. Jim sighed and went to the bar for another sheet of paper.

Eventually, timetable sorted and mobile telephone numbers exchanged, the group agreed to meet in the church hall the following night.

'Won't it be closed?' asked Mrs Hubbard.

'No…erm…the Football Club have it booked until eleven,' Jim lied.

Despite her earlier intentions of taking advantage of a Saturday night out, Penny found herself flagging. Her throat was hurting again, and it had been a very long day. The others seemed set on staying awhile, so she decided she wouldn't be letting Eileen down too badly if she asked Jim to take her home. Anyway, they were down for the first shift at six and no doubt Jim would be knocking on the door at five, the inconsiderate git.

Jim was glad to get away early. He was doing a lot of the night work and, between that and sleuthing, he was exhausted. It was making him curmudgeonly, and he could hear himself taking it out on Penny. As they pulled up outside Valhalla, he reminded her to take a Bingo leaflet for her parents and said he'd pick her up at quarter to six.

'Are you sure you wouldn't like to come about four and demand a cooked breakfast?' Penny asked.

Jim adopted his best innocent face. 'Is it on the nutrition plan?'

'I'll get chicken nuggets in there somewhere, but there's no way I can squeeze in a sausage.'

'What did I tell you about the kinky stuff?'

Penny was still smiling as she removed her boots and went into the house. The twins were in their rooms and the grandparents were in the living room watching a German movie. Penny joined them and quickly worked out the game. Mary would close her eyes and translate a line. Len would read the subtitles and tell her if she was correct.

'We must climb the ladder in the nude,' declared Mary.

'We must find the leader in the night,' Len corrected her.

'Hans has gone to the crayon.'

'Hans joined a monastery. Can we stop now? We've been at it for half an hour?'

'Alright, alright. I really think I'm improving,' said Mary, still with her eyes closed.

Len looked at Penny, shook his head and mouthed the words, 'She's not.'

'You can open your eyes now, Mum,' said Penny. 'I picked this leaflet up in town. There's a charity bingo night at the church hall tomorrow. Do you fancy going? The prizes look really good. There's a voucher for that new designer shoe shop in Aberdeen.'

'There's a new designer shoe shop in Aberdeen? Why haven't I heard of this sooner?!' exclaimed Mary, grabbing the leaflet. 'Ooh, you're right. The prizes are good. Look at this, Len. A robot that mows the grass. You've been after one of those for ages. Shall we go?'

Penny felt a twinge of guilt. She'd buy her dad the lawnmower for Christmas to make up for the subterfuge. However, there was no way she was buying her mum more shoes. The woman had about three thousand pairs already. Instead, she offered to take over the German testing for a while. A grateful Len scuttled off to find his newspaper, and Mary once more closed her eyes.

'Put this around him. His loaf is cold.'

Penny looked at the subtitles. "Put this around

him. His body is cold."

'Well done, Mum. You really are improving.'

Penny dragged herself out of bed in what felt like the middle of the night. She had pressed the snooze button for as long as she dared and would have to make do with a quick wash. Her thick, dark hair, once shiny and coiffed, looked like she'd spent the past week wearing a helmet in a wind tunnel. The bits not sticking out at right angles to her head were firmly plastered to her scalp. 'But you still fancy me, don't you, Chesney?' she whispered to her poster.

Jim turned up exactly on time. Penny met him at the door and handed him a flask and a plastic tub while she put on her boots.

'Take these,' she whispered, fearful of waking her slumbering family.

'Why are we taking Freddie with us?' Jim whispered back.

'Snacks, you idiot.'

'I know Mrs Hubbard microwaved him, but I'm still not eating him.'

'Shut up and get in the car.'

They reached Captain Rab's at exactly six o'clock. On the way, they'd driven past the Square where Penny had noted Gordon's van parked outside the hotel. She could see Fiona inside, slumped against the window, her face contorted by the glass as, open-mouthed and pig-nosed, she peacefully slumbered. Penny could only hope that Gordon didn't follow suit. She also hoped that Anthony Woodbead was the only "skinny, baldy, lanky streak of piss" (as Jim had charmingly described him) staying at the hotel, otherwise Gordon and Fiona might miss him.

'Maybe we should have tried to get a photo of Woodbead. Or taken the hotel ourselves,' she said.

'They'll be fine. All they need to do is keep an eye out for a big stick insect.'

They settled themselves near where they'd parked previously, about halfway between Captain Rab's house and Eileen's. Within minutes, Penny could feel herself nodding off. She looked across to Jim and could see he was also flagging.

'I spy with my little eye something beginning with D,' she said.

'Not playing.'

'Come on, you have to. It'll keep us awake.'

'Okay, dashboard.'

'No.'

'Drainpipe.'

'No'

They went through dirt, dog hair and diving school before Penny said, 'Do you want a clue? It's all around us.'

Jim thought for a moment then shrugged. 'I give up.'

'Dark!'

'You can't have dark. It's not a thing you can see!'

'Yes, you can see it. You look outside and say it's dark. Why would you say it's dark if you can't see it?'

'Dark isn't a thing!'

The argument raged on until they were interrupted by a sharp knock on the passenger window. Penny started and fumbled for the button to lower it. Eileen was there with bacon sandwiches.

'I thought you could do with these,' she said, handing the plate over. 'And these.' She passed Penny and Jim two walkie talkies. 'Breaker, breaker, that's a big ten forty, over,' she grinned.

'That's very thoughtful, you gorgeous creature who looks far too fresh for this time in the morning,' said Penny, 'but we are supposed to be incognito, and you standing here in your wellies and Winnie the Pooh pyjamas is a bit of a giveaway. Anyway, if we've got two walkie talkies, who are we walkie talking to, or do you have a third one?'

'Good point,' said Eileen, plucking one of the

walkie talkies out of Penny's hand. 'I'll sneak off. By the way, you *can* have dark. I could hear you two arguing from halfway down the street. What does incognito mean?'

Without waiting for an answer, she turned tail and dashed back towards her house.

'You know, sometimes she's as thick as mince, and other times she has you by the balls. I can never work her out,' mused Jim.

'I heard that, over,' came a voice from the walkie talkie.

For almost two hours, Penny and Jim watched cars come and go, the odd passer-by on foot and a cat in the window of the house next to them, who spent a happy half hour alternating between licking its paws and its backside. Jim and Penny found themselves mesmerised by the feline grooming, with Jim noting at one point, 'It's like three eyes staring at you.'

The boredom was punctuated by Eileen's frequent transmissions.

'This is Winnie the Pooh. Are you receiving, Rubber Duck? Over.'

'Rubber Duck receiving. How can we help you, Winnie?'

There was a long silence, then Eileen's voice came through. 'You have to say over, or I won't know if you're over. Over.'

Penny sighed. 'Over.'

'That's better. Do you and Rubber Glove want a cup of tea? Over.'

'No, we still have some left. Over.'

'Is that left over over or left over? Over.'

'Go away.'

'You didn't say over. Over.'

Just before eight, Jim suddenly sat forward in his seat. He nudged Penny, who had been trying to outstare the cat in the window.

'Look! There's movement. I think that's Captain Rab leaving the house.'

They watched as Captain Rab closed his front door and marched off, straight backed, turning into the lane at the end of the row of houses. Penny scrambled for her seatbelt.

'Quick. If he's going up to the High Street, we can drive round and catch up with him there. Put the foot down, Jim.' She grabbed the walkie talkie and pressed the button. 'This is Runner Duck to Winnie the Pooh. Over. Pick up, Eileen!'

'Receiving. Over.'

'He's left the house and we're following. Can you tell Mrs Hubbard and Elsie to come anyway but that he won't be here? I'll ring Mrs Hubbard to let her know when he's on his way back. Over.'

'Righty-ho. Out.'

Jim floored the car, sending jets of water onto the pavement. He reached the end of the harbour road and turned left, up a wide street parallel to the lane. Stopping at the junction halfway up, they looked left. There was no sign of Captain Rab.

'Go to the top and turn left onto the High Street,' Penny barked. 'We'll be able to look down the lane and see him coming, if he's there. He could turn off towards the woods.'

'Yes, boss,' said Jim and sped across the junction.

He was forced to slow down on the High Street, thanks to a bus whose driver had kindly stopped to let passengers off nearer the shops, rather than at the bus stop further up. As the bus pulled off and strained to reach ten miles per hour, it was all Penny could do not to get out of the car, jump aboard and drive the bloody thing herself. However, by the time they reached the top of the lane, Penny was grateful for the dawdling bus. It gave her time to look down the lane, and to her relief, she spotted Captain Rab marching determinedly up the hill towards them.

'Pull in here,' she told Jim, pointing to an empty space outside the shoe shop.

He parked up, and they watched in the rear-view mirrors until Captain Rab appeared at the top of the lane. The captain hesitated for a moment then turned right, heading away from them. With Penny urging him on, Jim scrambled to pull back out into the traffic, cutting off a BMW and eliciting a warning toot from its owner. The bus had caused a tailback towards the roundabout at the top of the High Street, and it quickly became clear that no amount of invective from Jim was going to change the fact that they were stuck. Penny pulled her hood up and grabbed her handbag.

'What are you doing?' cried Jim.

'Something,' said Penny, grabbing the door handle. 'Because I'm not sitting here while that dick of a bus driver is kind to old ladies. I'm going to follow Captain Rab on foot. When you've managed to turn around, park in the supermarket car park at the bottom and call me.'

She jumped down from the car and slammed the door, feeling a certain satisfaction in the resulting thud. As Phil slowly trundled off, almost nose to bumper with the car in front, Penny ran across the road and frantically scanned the street for any sign of the captain.

Her efforts were soon rewarded, as she spied a short figure with a distinctive march fifty yards ahead. She hurried to catch up with him, then slowed as she got closer, conscious that the rain was her friend in terms of her hood obscuring her face but that he had recently seen her on at least two occasions, so could recognise her. Although, what was the worst that could happen if he spotted her tailing him? It wasn't as if he was going to shoot her in broad daylight on a Sunday morning outside…she looked up at the shop sign above her…crikey, there was no way she was going to die outside Car Kit.

She hurried on, stopping outside the less ominously named Island Treasures tourist tat shop, and watched as

Captain Rab crossed the road and headed towards the supermarket. Thank goodness she'd brought her handbag, she thought, heading after him. If he spotted her in there, she'd just look like she was shopping. It could all be a happy coincidence.

Captain Rab went straight into the store, stopping only to collect a basket by the door. Hot on his heels, Penny grabbed her own basket and made her way through the fruit and veg section, one eye on the captain and the other on a display of half price strawberries. What the hey, she decided, tossing a punnet into the basket. May as well multi-task, otherwise what's the point in being a woman?

The captain didn't mess around. He went straight to the items he needed and joined the queue for the checkout. Lingering behind him in the toiletries aisle, Penny threw a few random items into her basket then joined the next queue along. This was going to be tricky. If he got to the front of his queue first, she'd have to dump her "shopping" and follow him out. If she ended up ahead of him at the tills, then she'd have to delay until he'd paid. And, whatever happened, she must not call attention to herself.

Penny reached the front of her queue first. Keeping an eye on her quarry, she absent-mindedly emptied the contents of her basket onto the conveyor belt, and the check-out assistant began scanning them. A moment later, Penny became aware that the beeping had stopped.

'These are two for the price of one,' said the check-out assistant. 'Do you want me to ask someone to get you another?'

'Mmhmm,' Penny mumbled, her mind elsewhere.

A voice came over the tannoy. 'Steve to checkout three please. One tube of Honeypot lube and a bottle of Lactulose...extra strength.'

Poor soul at checkout three, Penny thought, stuffing a packet of bacon into her bag. They don't know if they're coming or going. She snickered to herself, wishing Jim was here so she could share the joke.

Realising that she'd taken her eyes off the prize for a few seconds, she glanced over to the next checkout to see how Captain Rab was getting on. He wasn't getting on at all. He was staring directly at her. As was everyone else. Struck by a sudden notion, Penny looked up at the little number glowing above her checkout. Oh, bugger.

Red-faced and no longer giving a fig whether Captain Rab was ahead of her or behind, Penny stuffed everything into her bag and paid. As she stepped outside the glass doors, her phone rang. It was Jim.

'I'm in the car park next to the bit where you put the trolleys back. You'll never guess what. I just met one of the lads from football and he said Margaret on checkout three just embarrassed some poor sod with—'

'I'll be there in a minute,' said Penny, hanging up. She wasn't ready to laugh about this. Maybe someday, but not today.

She looked around for any sign of the captain and spotted him talking to another man next to the bottle recycling bank. Frustratingly, the man had his hood up and his back to her. She'd have to get closer. Skirting around some parked cars, Penny bent low and moved behind the bottle bank. I should record this in case it's evidence, she decided, swiping through her phone to find the app. Getting as close as she dared without risking being seen, Penny strained to hear the conversation.

'You better watch your step,' Captain Rab growled. 'If you don't—' CLUNK CLUNK CLUNK 'They'll be coming for you.'

Curses on whichever idiot had chosen this moment to dispose of their wine bottles.

'Leave me alone, you crazy old man. I don't even know you. My—' CLUNK 'cruel—' CLUNK CLUNK CLUNK 'I'm leaving.' CLUNK CLUNK. Jeez, this was a recycler with a problem!

Penny peeked around the edge of the bottle bank. A pair of green wellies blocked her view and she looked up to find a woman staring down at her. The bag of bottles she was holding clinked as she took a step back.

'Hey, aren't you lube and laxatives lady. What are you doing behind there?'

Penny couldn't think of a single reason why a woman with lube and laxatives would be sitting behind a bottle bank in the pouring rain, so she just gave the woman a cryptic smile and said, 'A girl's gotta do what a girl's gotta do.'

She had absolutely no idea what she meant by that, but the woman took another step back then, giving her a pitying look, turned tail and walked quickly to her car.

Penny emerged from her hiding place and looked around. The two men had gone. She could see Captain Rab striding purposefully across the car park, as if to head back up the High Street. Of the other man, there was no sign at all. She stopped the recording, pressed play and listened to the conversation again, just to be sure. Yes, that was definitely Pete's voice.

CHAPTER FOURTEEN

Jim was starting to worry that Penny was taking too long. He was just about to call her again when the car door opened and, breathless and sodden, she hauled herself and a bag of shopping into the passenger seat.

'Follow that man!' Penny cried, then grinned at him. 'I always wanted to say that. No, seriously, follow him, Jim. I think he's heading home. If he turns down the lane towards the harbour, I'll ring Eileen so she can let Mrs Hubbard and Elsie know he's on his way. Then I'll tell you what I found out.'

Having seen the captain off, they went to Jim's house. Penny kept her pants on this time. She laid the shopping bag at her feet and sat down at the table, watching Jim as he bustled around the kitchen making coffee.

He opened a cupboard door and peered inside. 'No biscuits,' he said, 'Did you get anything nice to eat from the shop?'

He leaned over to look in the shopping bag, and Penny hastily kicked it under the table.

'They're not on the nutrition plan!' she exclaimed. Even she could hear that her voice had gone up an octave.

Jim gave her an odd look then, placing the two mugs on the table, sat down next to her.

'Okay, Sherlock, tell me what you found out.'

Penny explained about seeing Captain Rab talking to someone, and how she'd sneaked behind the bottle bank to listen to their conversation.

'Who was he talking to?' asked Jim, agog.

'I'll let you hear it for yourself,' replied Penny, cranking up the suspense.

She retrieved her phone from her handbag and

pressed play. There was some rustling then…

"You better watch your step. If you don't CLUNK CLUNK CLUNK. They'll be coming for you."

"Leave me alone, you crazy old man. I don't even know you. My CLUNK cruel CLUNK CLUNK CLUNK. I'm leaving. CLUNK CLUNK."

Rustle, rustle, clink, clink.

"Hey, aren't you lube and laxatives lady. What are you doing behind there?"

Silence.

"A girl's gotta do what a girl's gotta do."

Clink, clink, footsteps.

"Bugger, how do you switch this thing off?"

Jim made a lunge for the shopping bag and, before Penny could grab it with her feet, he had it up and on the table. With a great guffaw, he decanted the contents and roared, 'Chocolate, strawberries, bacon, tissues, lube and laxatives. What does a girl gotta do with these, Penny Moon?'

Penny's first instinct was to crawl under the table in shame, but Jim's mirth was infectious. She couldn't help herself. Her lips twitched, and she felt a bubble of laughter well up inside her. Within seconds, she had joined Jim and was helplessly wheezing, 'Oh my God, make it stop.'

Eventually, wiping tears from her eyes, she said, 'The irony is that when they announced it over the tannoy, I didn't even realise it was me. One minute I was wishing you were there to share the joke, and the next I was bloody glad you were in the car park and would never find out!' She took a few deep breaths. 'Anyway, calm down and let's talk about Captain Rab.'

Jim mastered himself and played the recording again. Resisting the urge to chuckle at the last part, he said, 'Is that Pete? It sounds like the captain is threatening him.'

'That's what I thought. Do you think we should go to the hotel and check if Pete's okay?'

'We can't. Not without him finding out you were

spying on Captain Rab. We'll tell the others to consider intervening if they see Captain Rab picking on Pete or anyone else. The man is clearly not in his right mind.'

'It might be dangerous,' said Penny, looking worried.

Jim shrugged and raised his eyebrows. 'We'll have to risk it. We can't let him go around terrorising people. The other day, Mrs Taylor told Dad that she'd heard from Mrs Mackie, who heard it from Jimmy Gupta the Baker, that Captain Rab threw a book at Mrs Kindle in the charity shop.'

'That's very strange. Mrs Kindle used to be a dinner lady at the school when we were there. Do you remember her? Nervy wee thing. Wouldn't say boo to a goose. Always gave you extra chocolate custard on a Friday. When it's open tomorrow, we should go down to the charity shop and find out what happened. By the way, is your dad coming to the "bingo night"?' Penny made some air quotes and immediately gave herself a mental kick up the backside for being "that guy".

Jim made some air quotes back at her and grinned. 'Yes. The third prize of a bottle of Lagavulin swung it for him. I feel quite guilty. I'll have to buy him a bottle for Christmas.'

Penny sighed and stared down into her coffee cup, her shoulders sagging. 'I feel the same about my dad and the lawnmower. I'm quite nervous about what they'll all say when they realise there's no bingo. Honestly, I'm feeling very uneasy about the whole thing. It seemed like such a good idea yesterday. Today, not so much.'

Gently taking the cup from her, Jim tucked a finger under her chin and tilted her head up so that her eyes met his.

'We can't let this go, or we'll spend the rest of our lives wondering who we are. And wondering how many more like us there are on this island.'

'I know,' Penny said, tears springing to her eyes.

'But what if they're not even our parents? They're mad as a box of frogs, but I love Mum and Dad. I can't bear not to belong to them.'

A tear trickled down the side of her nose and she hastily wiped it away with her sleeve. Jim leaned forward and put his hands on her shoulders. They were very close now, their heads almost touching.

'Listen to me. Our parents, Eileen's mum, Mrs Hubbard, Elsie. They're all good people. Whatever the explanation, even if it's something terrible, we have to remember that they are good people, and that we've been loved and happy.'

'You're right,' sniffed Penny, smiling weakly at him. 'And we have each other.'

They sat still for a moment, gazing into each other's eyes, the only sound the ticking of the kitchen clock. Penny suddenly became very aware of her own heartbeat and the blood rushing to her face. Jim moved a hand from her shoulder and tenderly brushed another tear away with his thumb. She felt the damp smear cool against her hot cheek. Slowly, he moved his face closer to hers, and Penny held her breath.

"I AM THE ONE AND ONLY. NOBODY I'D RATHER BE."

Penny sprang back and snatched her phone off the table. She looked at the screen. Eileen.

'Hello. Is everything okay?'

'Winnie the Pooh to Rubber Duck. Can I have my walkie-talkie back? Over.'

'Sorry, Eileen. I completely forgot. I'm at Jim's. We'll bring it down now.'

'Are you two shagging?' Penny could hear the sly smile in Eileen's voice.

'Jeez, no. Get the kettle on. We'll see you in five.'

They once more parked Phil behind Eileen's cottage. Before they went inside, Jim put a hand on Penny's arm and said, 'I'm sorry about earlier. I don't know what was going through my head. You looked so bonnie, and I just wanted to…well, you know.'

Penny was about to very carefully reply, when a voice erupted from her pocket.

'Penny and Jim, up a tree, K I S S I N G. See, I said you were shagging. Over.'

Penny yanked the walkie talkie out of her pocket and shouted, 'Mind your own business, Winnie the Pooh!'

'Only if you stop leaning on the transmit button, Rubber Duck. And you forgot to say over. Over.'

Penny could see Eileen at the kitchen window, grinning and waving her walkie-talkie.

'Come, on. Let's see if she's heard anything from the troops,' she said, taking the strawberries from the shopping bag and getting out of the car.

Penny and Jim added their own boots to the neat rows of wellies in the porch and their coats to the overladen hooks on the wall, before padding into Eileen's kitchen. Mugs of tea were waiting for them, and Jim fell gratefully on a plate of chocolate biscuits.

'Here,' said Penny, handing Eileen the punnet of strawberries. 'Can't keep bringing the boys sweeties or you'll be sending me the dentist bill. Where are the boys, by the way?'

'Kenny took them up to the supermarket to get them out of the house for a bit. Ooh, and there's a funny story about that. Mum rang because she heard from Mrs Mackie who heard it from Mrs Taylor who got it from Karen Green that there was a woman in there this morning buying—'

'Sorry, Eileen,' Penny cut in. 'We can't stay long. It's our turn at the hotel at ten. Have you heard anything from the others?'

'Mrs Hubbard rang. She said she saw Captain Rab coming back, then half an hour later she saw someone she thought was Woodbead knocking at his door. Only he didn't answer and Woodbead went away. That's it.'

'We're due to take over from Geoff and Sandra Next Door, so we'll see what they have to say. Gordon and Fiona are taking their turn on Captain Rab. Let me know if anyone reports anything interesting. Do you want to hear what we found out?' asked Penny, taking her phone from her bag and making a mental note to stop the recording before it got to what she was now thinking of as "the lube 'n' lax bit".

Penny and Jim stayed at Eileen's for another fifteen minutes, before making their way up to the Square and parking next to Geoff and Sandra Next Door. Jim wound down his window and Sandra Next Door wound down hers.

'All quiet?' he asked

'Well done for being on time. We saw the tall, thin one leaving about nine. We followed him down to Captain Rab's. He knocked, didn't get an answer, then went up the lane. We lost him after that, so we came back here to wait for him. He hasn't come back,' said Sandra Next Door, before abruptly winding her window back up and signalling to Geoff Next Door to leave. He gave Penny and Jim a cheery wave and, Penny thought, an apologetic smile, then the Volvo pulled away, leaving them a clear view of the hotel entrance.

'I spy with my little eye…,' said Penny.

'No. Just fucking no,' said Jim.

It was an uneventful two hours. There was very little activity around the hotel and, following a brief but unsuccessful endeavour by Penny to get Jim to join in a variety of car games, the pair sank into a companionable silence, each lost in their own thoughts.

Penny was mulling over the almost kiss and how she felt about it. She realised that she probably would have gone through with it but would definitely have regretted it afterwards. It wasn't fair to lead Jim on, and she had to find the right moment to let him know that she couldn't take things further. She still had feelings for Alex, although she wouldn't characterise them as love any more. She was open to the idea of another relationship. After all, the twins would be all grown up and doing their own thing soon, and she didn't want to spend the next forty or so years on her own. But there was the rub. The twins. Mere months ago, they'd had a reasonably happy Mum and Dad, a stable home life and a hamster. All that had been ripped away from them. She didn't think they'd react well to her gadding about with other men, particularly Hector who thought his dad walked on water. She didn't know when, if ever, she would be able to introduce a new man into their lives. If she did, she had to know it was a proper relationship and not just a quick snog over a kitchen table. No, she was definitely relieved that there had been no snogging. Even if a very horny little part of her appeared to disagree. But surely that was just hormones and such like. She'd ignore them and they'd go away. It was just a matter of how to explain it to Jim. And she still had to tell Hector about Freddie, who was currently hidden under a bag of frozen peas. My word, she fretted, everything was such a mess.

Jim, meanwhile, was wondering which dog would make the best pirate. Captain Jack-a-Poo Sparrow, he decided. Pirates of the Caribbeagle.

The silence was broken by Penny's phone, which burst into life just as Mrs Hubbard and Elsie pulled into the Square. It was Eileen.

'Hello,' she said breathlessly, without waiting for Penny to speak, 'we have a situation. Gordon and Fiona have reported that two people have knocked on Captain Rab's door now, and he hasn't answered.

'I hope nobody will be annoyed with me. I phoned the ferry ticket sales number, thinking if he picked up, I'd put the phone down but at least I'd know he was at home. I just got the answering machine. He might not answer his own phone, but he would definitely answer the business number. Either he's sneaked out the back or something's wrong. Should I tell Gordon and Fiona to take a look in his window?'

'Mrs Hubbard and Elsie are here to take over watching the hotel, so hang fire and we'll come down,' Penny instructed her.

She relayed the information to Jim and, without waiting to have a polite word with Mrs Hubbard and Elsie, he accelerated onto the High Street in the direction of the harbour.

This time, there was no bus to hold up the traffic. It was lunchtime. Most people were sensibly tucking into a Sunday roast at home, so traffic was light, and they reached Captain Rab's house in no time at all. Jim parked Phil in front of Gordon and Fiona's van and, pulling their hoods up, he and Penny dashed over for a hurried consultation with the younger couple. They quickly agreed that someone needed to take a peek through the captain's window, and they were just debating who would do it, when Jim became aware that Penny was no longer next to him. He turned and saw her speed-walking through the rain, already halfway to the captain's cottage, her wee arse wiggling for all it was worth as she tried to maintain her pace in a pair of wellies that he reckoned were a size too big for her. Bloody woman, he thought. She's a fucking liability. A damn sexy one. But a fucking liability, nonetheless.

Jim sprinted after her, catching up just as she reached the captain's living room window. She ducked down and he followed suit.

'What do you think you're doing?' he hissed.

'While you were busy forming a coalition government with the Green party back there to decide on who should look in a window, I formed a sub-committee of one and decided to do it myself,' whispered Penny. 'Anyway, it looks like the Green party are joining us.'

She nodded her head towards the street and Jim turned to see Gordon and Fiona hurriedly bringing up the rear.

'Great. This doesn't look weird at all. Four people crouching below an old man's living room window in full view of anyone passing by,' he said.

'One, two, four. It's always going to look weird. Now, shut up while I take a look in.'

Penny's legs were already stiff from crouching down and she used the window ledge to pull herself up. At first, she thought the room was empty, but as her eyes got used to the unfamiliar shapes in the gloomy living room, she thought she could just make out something on the floor at the back.

'Take a look,' she told the others. 'I think there's someone lying on the floor near the back window.'

She shuffled along and the others shuffled behind her, taking it in turns to peek over the window ledge.

'I think you're right,' said Fiona, standing up. 'We need to go and check on him. How do we do that?'

'Follow me,' said Penny.

She sped off, around the corner and up the steep lane, skidding to a halt as she reached the back path. Panting, the others caught up with her.

'Down here and over that wall,' she said. 'Jim, give me a leg up.'

This time, there were no arguments. When they reached the wall, Jim gave Penny a hefty shove and almost didn't think about her arse at all. Gordon did the same for Fiona, and soon all four of them were scooting their way towards the bins in the corner.

They jumped down from the bins, and Penny raced over the lawn to look down into the window at the back of Captain Rab's living room. From this angle, the body was obscured by the table, but she could see a pair of legs and they weren't moving. What was that below his knee? She leaned closer to get a better view. It looked like blood.

'There's blood,' she said, her voice shaking. 'We have to get in there.'

'How are we going to do that?' asked Jim. 'You saw

it last time. He's got the place locked up tighter than a nun's—'

Penny wasn't listening. She ran to the steps and, leaping them, landed neatly by the back door. Her ankles burned, protesting at the sudden jolt, but she paid no heed, so focused was she on finding a way in. Wrapping her hand in her coat sleeve, she pushed the door handle down. The door opened.

'Don't touch anything,' she yelled, making Gordon, who had just been about to put his hand on the railing to follow her down the steps, jump back in shock. He and the others carefully followed her to the back door, where she was hastily removing her boots.

'I know it's an emergency, but if it's a crime scene, we can't track mud and water across it,' she explained, stepping into the kitchen. 'Boots off, hurry up, and don't touch stuff.'

By the time the others had removed their wellingtons and followed her into the living room, Penny was standing by the figure on the floor, ashen faced. She beckoned Jim over.

'It's Captain Rab and there's a lot of blood. Come here and check if he has a pulse.'

'I'm a vet, not a doctor,' said Jim. 'How am I supposed to know?'

'Oh, for God's sake.' Gordon pushed his way to the front and knelt down by Captain Rab.

'I'm the first aider for the men's drama group,' he explained, placing a finger on the captain's neck. 'There's a pulse but it's not very strong. At least he's breathing. Fiona, call the ambulance. I've no idea where the bleeding is coming from, so we'll have to get his clothes off. Penny, I need scissors and towels. Jim, see if you can get his shoes and belt off without moving him.'

Within minutes, they had cut Captain Rab's clothes off and Penny and Jim were kneeling in the pool of blood, pressing towels to deep wounds in his back under Gordon's instruction. The doorbell rang, and Fiona rushed to the front door to let Doc Harris in. He was accompanied by the two island paramedics, who immediately took over from Penny, Gordon and Jim.

After the paramedics had stabilised the captain enough to move him into the ambulance, Doc Harris turned to the group and said, 'They'll take him to the community hospital, although he should really be airlifted to Aberdeen. This blasted weather. We're not equipped for dealing with stab wounds. You saved his life, you know. Well, for now at least. I don't know what we're going to do if he dies. Douglas Hubbard will have a fit if I ask him to move all the ice lollies out of the little freezer.'

'Don't you have any facilities at the hospital?' asked Jim.

'Sadly, no,' said Doc Harris, shaking his head. 'Wendy Chan choked to death on a Curly Wurly last week and we really rely on Aberdeen for these things. This is the first time I can recall there being any violent crime on the island. Anyway, I'll phone the police and let them know. They'll want to speak to you all, of course, but for now I think the best we can do is lock up the house. Has anyone called his brother?'

'I have,' said Fiona.

The others looked at her curiously and she shrugged. 'It's Kev from the pub. Captain Kev. You saw him the other night.'

'Fiona made good use of her time in the pub getting to know Old Archie's pals,' Gordon explained.

'So, does Captain Kev work on the ferry with Captain Rab?' asked Jim.

'Oh, no,' said Fiona. 'They've been estranged for years. Ever since Captain Kev said he wanted to see a bit of the world and started working on cruise ships. It was like he'd betrayed the ferry omerta or something. Captain Rab cut him off and refused to have anything to do with him. He came back a couple of weeks ago to try to patch up the row.'

'You should have mentioned this sooner, Fiona,' Penny said, exasperated.

'I didn't think it was relevant. Anyway, he's far too nice to go around killing folk.'

'Who do you think has a motive to stab Captain Rab?' Penny asked, a dangerous edge to her sweet tone.

Fiona frowned. 'Ah. I hadn't thought of that.'

CHAPTER FIFTEEN

Penny's cunning plan to make Jim eat her mother's homemade tomato soup seemed so petty, considering everything that had happened that day. He dropped her off at Valhalla, then went home to change out of his own bloodied clothes. Exhausted, she trudged into the kitchen, where her mother was setting the table.

'Is Jim not coming for lunch,' Mary asked.

'No, Mum. And neither am I. Fiona and Gordon fertilise their veg with their own pee and poo, and to be quite frank with you, I've had enough of Fiona's shit for one day. I'm going for a shower and a lie down.'

'Is that blood on your trousers? Oh my, that's blood on your trousers. Are you okay?'

'Yes, I'm fine. It's not my blood. We found Captain Rab stabbed in his living room and called the doc. Don't worry. He's still alive.'

'Goodness, I hope he's going to be okay. Is he at the community hospital? I suppose he must be. Do you think they'll let me take him some tomato soup? They never feed you properly in these places. I remember when I broke my leg. Six hours it took them to plaster me up, and not even the offer of a cup of tea.'

'I doubt he'll be in any fit state for soup, Mum. I've just remembered that I need to talk to Hector and Edith. Mrs Hubbard found Freddie yesterday.'

'Ooh, lovely. Where is he, the little rascal?'

'Under a bag of peas in the top shelf of the freezer.'

'Oh. Not so lovely. Still, the twins will at least get some closure. Now, I have some gossip for you. You'll never guess what happened in the supermarket this morning.'

'It was me, Mum. I'm the lube 'n' lax lady,' said Penny, too tired to care anymore.

For once, Mary had nothing to say. She bustled around the kitchen, stirring soup and straightening forks, until eventually she burst out, 'If it's a sexual problem, you can talk to me and your father. We're very open minded you know.'

Penny had a sneaking suspicion that any talk of her own sex life, non-existent or otherwise, would soon turn to a blow-by-blow account of every problem in the bedroom department that Mary and Len had ever had. She would never be ready for that conversation.

'Thanks, Mum, but it was just a misunderstanding. Everything's fine.'

'Because if Jim can't get it up—'

Penny put her hands over her ears and ran out of the kitchen, shouting, 'La, la, la, not listening.'

Hector was determined to take the news of Freddie's death "like a man", or so he said. Penny later heard him sobbing in his room and knocked gently on the door. She found him sitting on his bed, red-eyed and surrounded by tissues.

'I'm so sorry,' said Penny, drawing him into her arms. 'At least he died doing something he loved.'

'He was partial to a cornflake,' Hector hiccoughed between sobs.

There was another knock on the door and Edith came in. She handed Penny her mobile and said, 'Dad's on the phone. I told him about Freddie, and he wants to talk to you.'

As if today hasn't been awful enough, thought Penny.

'Hi, Alex. How are you?'

'Edith says you've killed Freddie and you've been running around with the local vet.'

'It's not quite like that. Freddie escaped by accident when we were taking the suitcases in, and I've been busy with my weight-loss group. Jim just happens to have been giving me lifts because the weather here is foul and Captain Rab isn't very reliable.'

'Who's Captain Rab? Another one of your fancy men?'

'It's my car. And the bloke who was stabbed.'

'What bloke who was stabbed? Are the kids safe?'

'Yes, they're fine. It was the bloke that we think murdered the postman.'

'Postman? What postman? Who is murdering and stabbing postmen and captains?'

'That's what Jim and I have been trying to find out.'

'Aha! So, it's not just lifts, then.'

'It's also none of your business.'

'So, this Jim *is* your fancy man!'

'No, he's not. Did you just phone to be annoying or do you have something useful to say?'

'I'm sending Hector a dog.'

'You can't be serious. Please don't do that!'

'It's already done. I've paid a man in Aberdeen to take it over on the next ferry.'

'He'll be waiting a while then. The ferry isn't running at the moment, and the bloke who has just been stabbed is the ferry owner. You really should have asked me first.'

'Just make sure you're there to meet the next ferry. Right, put me on to Hector so I can make him happy again.'

With a sigh, Penny handed Edith's phone to Hector and left him alone to chat to his dad. She went back to her own room and sat on the bed, unable to get rid of a nagging feeling that she'd forgotten to do something. Then it struck her. She'd forgotten to call off the surveillance on Captain Rab's cottage. And what time was it? Goodness, nearly four. Jim would be here in a minute to pick her up for their next stint outside the hotel. She called Eileen.

'Has anyone told you about what happened to Captain Rab?'

'It's okay,' Eileen assured her. 'Sandra and Geoff Next Door turned up late for their shift at the harbour and saw the ambulance. I've rescheduled everyone to only keep an eye on the hotel. You and Jim are still on the four to six shift, if that's okay.'

'Thanks Eileen. You're a star. Can you tell whoever's there now that we'll be a bit late? Jim hasn't turned up to get me yet.'

'It's Sandra Next Door, so good luck with that. The only person allowed to be late in Sandra-World is the woman herself.'

'Isn't Geoff Next Door with her?'

'No. He's in the hotel. It's his Sunday men's group and he refused to miss it. I think that's why they were late earlier. Heeyooooge argument. I went out to offer them a sandwich and Sandra Next Door's resting bitch face was wide-awake and gunning for Geoff. I reckon them rings he wears are actually knuckledusters to fend her off.'

Penny chuckled. 'What is this Sunday men's group?'

'Gordon told me about it last night. It's an all-male drama group, and I think they like a to have few pints while they're there. They put on a pantomime in Aberdeen every Christmas and Geoff Next Door is always the dame. Gordon is Aladdin this year, if you can believe it. God knows who Princess Jasmine is, but I hope it's not Billy Gray from the chemists because his skin is terrible, and he always looks like he needs a good wash.

'Anyway, Linda from the shoe shop is doing their shoes and costumes. According to Gordon, Sandra Next Door is sick of the whole thing. Linda's been getting shoes delivered to Geoff at home, and he won't stop wearing them in the house. Apparently, it's going to cost a fortune to get the stiletto marks sanded out of the wood floors.'

'That must be what Elsie was talking about when she hinted that Old Archie had been delivering unusual things to next door. So, Geoff Next Door isn't having an affair with Linda from the shoe shop?' Penny asked.

'Goodness, no. Can you imagine him daring to cross Sandra like that? He'd need more than knuckledusters. He'd have to pinch the suit of armour they made for Cinderella last year! Anyway, I'll let Sandra Next Door know you'll be there soon. I'll just meet you at the church hall afterwards.'

Still chuckling, Penny ended the call. Better be ready to go as soon as Jim arrives, she decided. If he's here in the next couple of minutes, we might just make it without incurring the wrath of Sandra.

As she stood in the porch debating whether to put her boots on now or wait until Jim turned up, she saw his headlights in the drive.

'That's Jim here, Mum,' she called. 'Will I see you and Dad at the bingo later?'

'Yes, I'm looking forward to it,' Mary shouted back.

Penny tried to ignore the guilty twinge in the pit of her stomach as she got into the front seat. Jim was right, though. They had to find out why they were dead. They had to gang up on their parents to force an answer. And she couldn't think of another way to get them all in the same room at the same time, unless you counted Jim's way, which would probably scar Hector for life.

'You're very quiet,' said Jim, as they drove through the outskirts of Port Vik.

'I'm just thinking about tonight. My head's fine with it, my heart less so. Let's talk about something else. Who do you reckon stabbed Captain Rab?'

'I've been giving that some thought. Anthony Woodbead was there, then disappeared, so he's in the frame. Could the partners in crime have fallen out? Then there's Captain Kev. He has the motive. The back door was unlocked so, whoever it was, it was someone the captain knew. He must have let them in. It was also someone who didn't want to be seen, otherwise why go to the back door? Finally, it probably had to be someone who was fit enough to get over that wall, because we know he kept the back gate locked. Although, if someone phoned ahead, he might have opened it. But that makes no sense. How would you explain that you were coming to visit but had to come in the back way?'

'Did you see your car key anywhere while we were in the house?' asked Penny.

'Damn! It never occurred to me to look. If the police go in, they'll find it and how am I going to explain that?'

'I have his front door keys. We could nip in and get your car key before we go to the church hall later,' Penny suggested.

'A big part of me wants to say no to that, yet I can't see that I've any choice. It'll be straight in and straight out, though. I don't want anyone to spot us.'

They pulled into the Square, next to Sandra Next Door, and Jim wound down his window.

'Have you been alright here on your own, Sandra Next Door?'

'Of course. Eileen said you were going to be late. Glad you're not. There's nothing to report. Nobody has seen hide nor hair of your Woodbead man since he went to Captain Rab's earlier.' She softened for a moment. 'How is the captain?'

'It sounds like he'll pull through. Mind you, it was a shock finding him like that. Is that you finished all your surveillance stints now?'

'It was supposed to be, but I'm covering the six to eight for Mrs Hubbard and Elsie. There seemed no point in dragging them out at night. Geoff and Gordon are in there,' she said, gesturing towards the hotel. 'They've had a fair few to drink, so Fiona and I are going to do the next shift together then take them home. Eileen has cancelled the last shift. There aren't enough of us to cover it.'

It was like herding cats, Penny thought, watching Sandra Next Door's taillights disappearing into the distance.

She settled back into her seat and was just about to suggest a game of Truth or Dare, when a sudden burst of Chesney set her rummaging through her handbag for her phone. She looked at the screen. An Aberdeen area code, but she didn't recognise the number. It was probably a man about a dog, she decided, debating whether to answer. After a few rings, she reluctantly pressed the green button.

'Hello. This is Sergeant Wilson from Police Scotland. Am I speaking to Penny Moon?'

Penny's heart skipped a beat. Had something dreadful happened? Then she remembered. Something dreadful had happened.

'Yes. How can I help you?'

'I'm trying to establish a few details about what happened today with Mr MacDonald.'

'I'm sorry. I don't know a Mr MacDonald.'

There was a short silence, then Penny heard the clatter of a keyboard before the voice said, 'Sorry. You'll know him as Captain Rab. Can I ask how you made the discovery?'

Penny paused. How was she going to explain how four people happened to be at Captain Rab's house at lunchtime on a Sunday? It wasn't as if he was famously sociable and would have invited them round for a couple of Yorkshire puddings and a roast potato. She decided to go with a bare minimum version of the truth.

'We were meeting friends down at the harbour, and they mentioned that they'd seen someone knock on his door and get no reply. He's quite old, so I took a peek through his window to check he was okay and saw him lying on the floor. We went round the back to see if there was a way in, and the back door was open. One of our friends is a first aider, so we called Doc Harris and stemmed the bleeding until he arrived.'

'It sounds like your actions saved Mr MacDonald's life. Why were you meeting someone at the harbour, if you don't mind me asking? Given the weather, it seems an odd place to meet.'

Bugger, bugger, bugger, thought Penny.

'We'd been visiting my friend, Eileen, and it just seemed a good place to meet Gordon and Fiona afterwards.' As soon as the words left her lips, Penny realised how ludicrous they sounded. Why hadn't she just said something breezy like, "Oh, you know what we islanders are like. Weather means nothing to us."?

'Again, I hope you don't mind me asking, but wouldn't it have been better to meet at this Eileen's house, out of the rain?'

Penny sighed and pressed the speaker button so that Jim could hear the conversation.

'Alright,' she said, 'we were watching Captain Rab's house. I have Jim Space here with me. Just ask your questions and we'll tell you whatever you want to know.'

Jim's eyebrows shot up and he gestured frantically at her.

'Wait a minute,' Penny told Sergeant Wilson. 'I'm just going to put you on hold while I have a blazing row with Jim.' She pressed the hold button. 'What?'

'You can't tell her about Sandra Next Door and Elsie searching Old Archie's house or about us breaking into Captain Rab's garden the first time. I'm fairly sure those are crimes,' Jim said, his voice an octave higher than usual.

'Okay. What about you stealing Sandra Next Door's begonias and us being legally dead. Because I'm fairly sure there are a couple of crimes in there too?'

'Don't tell her about those either. That last one might get our parents in trouble. Don't tell her anything that might get anyone into trouble.'

Penny pressed the hold button again and said, 'Fire away, Sergeant Wilson.'

Under the sergeant's questioning, Penny and Jim gave a censored version of the truth. They told the sergeant about Losers Club's suspicion that Old Archie had helped to smuggle someone onto the island from Gibraltar and that this person was the intended victim. They hadn't been able to trace this person, but it seemed likely he'd witnessed the shooting. They explained how a number of visitors were trapped on the island and that, by chance, they'd seen one of them, Anthony Woodbead, visiting the captain. They'd since established that Woodbead was probably an alias. Furthermore, they had established that the captain had taken his smaller boat to Aberdeen, ensuring he had the ability to sneak back onto the island even though he was supposedly in Aberdeen at the time of the murder. Increasingly concerned about Captain Rab's erratic behaviour, Losers Club had decided to mount some surveillance on him and Anthony Woodbead. Woodbead had called on Captain Rab that morning and nobody had seen him since. The only other person that they knew of who might have a motive to attack the captain was his estranged brother, Captain Kev, who had recently come to the island seeking to make amends.

Penny felt quite pleased with herself and Jim. They had missed out all the interesting parts, of course, but they'd covered the salient points. In fact, she felt quite proud of everything Losers Club had achieved, so it came as a blow when the sergeant said, 'Stop the surveillance now. I don't want you to put yourselves at risk.'

'We're already at risk. There's a murderer on the island!' Penny exclaimed with mounting incredulity.

'Leave the detecting to the police,' ordered the sergeant.

'And leave a murderer free to kill us all in our sleep? What you fail to understand, Sergeant,' said Penny, suddenly aware that Hector may have inherited his pompous streak from her, 'is that Old Archie was one of our own and if we don't get to the bottom of this, who will?'

'We will,' said the sergeant. 'The weather is supposed to clear by tomorrow and the police helicopter should be there by noon.'

'Oh,' said Penny, feeling deflated.

'Okay, we'll stop the surveillance,' Jim said. 'Is there anything else?'

'Yes. Go home and stay there until we get there. Tell the others to do the same. If you've all been poking your noses in, it's quite possible that the murderer is aware.'

'Poking our noses in!' Penny started, but Jim cut her off.

'We'll do that. Thank you for your time, Sergeant Wilson.' He pressed the button to disconnect the call.

'Go home and do nothing? You just rolled over and offered her your belly to tickle!' Penny exploded, the subject of dogs still clearly very much on her mind.

'Calm down,' Jim told her. 'Of course we're not going home. We'll carry on as planned. Now, how about a game to take our minds off things? I bet you £10 I can make you get out of this car without saying anything or touching you.'

'Okay, you're on. How can you? That's impossible. What? You're just going to sit there in silence until I get bored and—'

The foul smell hit her nostrils. She grasped the door handle and flung herself outside, slamming the car door shut in outrage.

Jim pressed the button, and the passenger side window glided down. He looked mightily pleased with himself.

'Silent but deadly. £10 please,' he chuckled. 'And dark is *not* a thing you can I Spy.'

CHAPTER SIXTEEN

Jim eventually managed to persuade Penny to calm down and get back in the car. This was mostly achieved by agreeing that he was indeed a filthy sod, who spent far too much time with animals and not nearly enough in polite human society.

'I think we might have called some attention to ourselves,' he said, as blinds in the flats above the shops were twitched back into place. 'Did you have to shout so loudly?'

'Can you blame me?'

'It's not like you don't do it.'

'Yes, but I hold it in until I'm somewhere I can safely let it out. Like a proper person. Do you think anyone from the hotel noticed?'

'Probably not. Martin was going on about how they'd installed triple glazing in the rooms after guests complained about boy racers keeping them up half the night. I remember zooming around here in my dad's car, hoping the girls at the bus shelter would notice me. They never did. You don't see gangs of girls hanging around bus shelters anymore.'

'That's probably because you frightened them all off. Anyway, these days they're probably all on Tinder or Grinder or whatever it's called.'

'Grindrrrrr,' Jim corrected her. 'Yes, I've heard they do this weird thing these days where you have to go through a period of "talking to" someone before you officially declare yourselves in a relationship.'

'Yep. Gone are the days when you bumped uglies at the school disco and were set for life. Or at least the next few weeks.'

'You may have been ugly, but I was a catch.'

'We are not going down that road again,' Penny firmly told him.

They bickered amiably until Sandra Next Door and Fiona turned up to relieve them at six o'clock.

'So, are you ready for a bit of breaking and entering?' Penny said brightly.

'As opposed to following police orders, going home, being safe in my own bed and not getting arrested?' asked Jim. 'Of course I am!'

He swung the car around, gunned the accelerator and sped off in true boy racer style. He figured he might be able to impress at least one girl tonight.

The harbour was quiet, if you didn't count the waves crashing against the wall and the wind howling down the lanes. At least, there were no people around and only the odd passing car. Sunday evening in Vik, thought Penny. Nowhere to go and even less to do than usual. No wonder her mother had taken up pole dancing.

They parked at Eileen's and walked along the back lane between the gardens, before cutting down the lane at the end of Captain Rab's row of cottages. They'd agreed that a more circuitous route was preferable to some nosy neighbour taking Phil's number plate.

This was quite exciting, thought Penny, as she poked her head around the corner of the lane to check for anyone on the street. Like a movie. She turned to Jim and made a series of hand signals, pointing at her eyes and holding random fingers up.

'What the fuck are you doing,' he whispered.

'It's what they do in films. The soldiers give people instructions with their fingers and then they all go storming round the corner and shoot the bad guys.'

'Stop pratting about. Do you have the front door key ready?'

'Shh. There's a cat at your three o'clock.'

'What does that even mean?' Jim thrust past her and strode towards Captain Rab's front door. Penny hurried to catch up then, hands shaking slightly, she pushed Captain Rab's key in the lock. The door, swollen by a week of rain, was wedged firmly in the jamb, but with one hard push from Jim, it opened.

In the early evening gloom, the furniture was set in deep shadow. Even though they had been there a few hours earlier, the living room felt unfamiliar. The house had a strange, unlived-in feeling. It was too quiet, like its occupant had died and the house was holding its breath, waiting for someone to come along and remove the things that until recently had been touched and treasured by a vibrant soul. All the small things that made a life real, the Port Vik coasters, the spare laces on the table, the turned down corner of a book page. His bag of shopping from that morning was still on the table. All these things which had littered a lifetime lay abandoned. No matter how Penny felt about Captain Rab, she was struck by how little separates life from death. The last heartbeat that turns a home into a house clearance.

She shuddered and gave herself a mental kick. Captain Rab was still alive and probably swearing at the doctors right now, convinced there was nothing wrong with him that a few sticking plasters and a stiff brandy wouldn't fix.

'Let's get your key and get out of here,' she said.

'I was thinking the same thing,' Jim replied. 'Spooky, isn't it?'

'Hang on. Don't start looking yet.' Penny went to the kitchen and, putting her hand inside her sleeve, opened the cupboard under the sink. Bingo!

'Here,' she said, returning to the living room. 'Use these.'

She handed Jim a pair of yellow rubber gloves and slipped on a pair over her own hands.

'It's a new packet, so the police will never know

they're missing,' she told him, stashing the cellophane wrapper in her pocket. She felt a little guilty. Captain Rab would probably be hunting high and low for these at some point. She imagined him spitting nails and ranting about little bastards breaking in and stealing his rubber gloves. Always assuming he wasn't in jail, of course.

Jim began opening drawers and rummaging through the contents. Penny, meanwhile, gazed around the room, trying to think if she were a miserable, sweaty old git, where would she put a key? She half-heartedly upended an ugly orange vase. A paper clip and an old 2d coin fell to the floor. Popping them back in the vase and returning it to its place on top of a china cabinet, she noticed a small glowing light on the desk by the front window. The computer was on. Dare she take a cheeky peek? It wasn't what they were here for, but it seemed too good a snooportunity to miss.

She went to the front window and swished the curtains closed.

'What are you doing?' asked Jim.

'Shh. Keep your voice down. These old places have thick walls, but they're not soundproof. I'm going to have a look on his computer. I don't want anyone outside to see the light from the screen.'

'Well, I can't see a bloody thing now you've closed the curtains,' Jim protested.

'Stop being such a fusspot. It's only for a minute.'

Penny gave the mouse an experimental nudge and the monitor came to life. It was an old computer, and seemingly Captain Rab had never bothered to set a password. She supposed that if you lived alone and had little worth stealing, rubber gloves excepted, there wasn't really a need. This relic would be lucky to fetch a fiver on eBay.

She checked the captain's browser history, unsure as to how she would react if she found out he was into gimp masks and nipple clamps. Half of her would be shocked, she supposed. Whereas the other half suspected he wouldn't mind enthusiastically smacking someone's bare backside, or whatever people in gimp masks and nipple clamps do. With that sort of thing, the captain would definitely be the spanker and not the spankee. Standing there in his yellow rubber gloves, with his wee pigeon chest all puffed up, battering some poor bare-arsed lassie. Bastard.

What the hell was she thinking? A minute ago, she'd been feeling a wee bit sorry for him, and now she had him as master of the Port Vik sex dungeon. Just stick to the facts, Penny, she told herself. He's a horrible old killer, but at least he's not a sex maniac. Probably.

She looked at the browser history and breathed a sigh of relief. It looked like the captain had been researching something called The Red Path. It seemed to be some sort of religious organisation. She clicked on one of the links and it took her to an old news article. Skimming the article, she gathered that The Red Path was a cult in Scotland which had been dismantled in the 1970s. The reporter deplored the injury of several policemen during efforts to capture the leader, who was still at large.

Penny's concentration was disturbed by a rattle at the door. Quickly, she switched the monitor off and turned to Jim, her face a mask of sheer panic.

'Did you lock the front door behind us?' he whispered.

'No,' she squeaked.

'Quick, under here,' he said, gesturing to the dining table by the back window.

Penny scrambled under the table, and Jim lowered the leaf before diving in after her. There was barely room for them both. Now was not a time to be regretting all the divorce chocolate and wine, but Penny couldn't help wishing that her bottom was a couple of inches smaller. She held her breath as she heard the front door give way, followed by footsteps in the hall.

There was a creak as the living room door opened.

She could hear someone rummaging around the room and the whir of the old computer as it came to life. There was a series of clicks, and she knew that someone else was looking at the captain's browser history, just as she had herself a few moments before.

She screwed her eyes shut and silently prayed. Oh, God, please make them go away. I'll be good, I promise. I'll stop taking your name in vain. I'll try to eat some of Mum's tomato soup. I'll stop breaking into places, and I'll never buy lube again. At least, not until I'm the other side of the menopause. I might need a bit of help then, but that's okay, isn't it? Unless you'd like to not give me the menopause? Because that would also be okay. Also, I promise to stop imagining that other people are perverts. I will love my family and even be nice to Jim. Just please, please make them go away.

Penny suspected that one prayer did not make up for thirty years of not going to church. She resolved that when this was all over, she'd be properly thankful for what she had, rather than trying to strike a bargain with God that if He waved an omniscient magic wand, she'd stop thinking about Captain Rab and nipple clamps. It was no wonder that God was ignoring her. He had better things to do of a Sunday. It was His day, after all.

She heard footsteps cross the living room, coming closer. Her heart was racing, and she had to bite down on her lip to suppress a panicked squeal as a pair of wellington boots appeared right next to her. She felt Jim's hand slide across hers, his grip tightening on her fingers as if to say, 'Hold your nerve, Penny Moon.'

Penny Moon held her nerve, even though every one of them was screaming, 'Run, now! Get out of here!'

Jim could feel Penny trembling against him and fought an instinct to put a reassuring arm around her. He held onto her hand, his own heart hammering and watched while the wellies walked around the table to his side. He almost cried out as a voice whispered, 'Well, you have been a busy boy.' For a moment, he'd thought the voice was talking to him.

There was a rustle of paper and the boots disappeared. After a tense moment, Penny and Jim heard the front door being firmly pulled closed. They stayed where they were, listening intently for any sign that the intruder could still be in the house. Nothing. Other than their own shallow breathing, complete silence.

Penny took a big gulp of air and crawled out from beneath the table. Jim followed suit, and they sat on the carpet, shaking in the aftermath of the adrenaline rush.

'Do you remember careers day at school?' Jim asked. 'I don't recall burglar being an option.'

'Probably just as well,' said Penny. 'Neither of us is very good at it. Let's find your key and get out of here.'

They stood up, stretching their cramped limbs, and Jim immediately noticed that something was missing.

'There were some papers on that table. Whoever it was must have taken them,' he said.

'Did you see what they were?' asked Penny

'Not really. I noticed them while I was looking for my key. They seemed to be printouts of newspaper articles and maps. I think there was a certificate of some sort there as well. Sorry, I was too busy checking drawers to take a proper look.'

'I really wish I'd looked at them instead of messing about with the computer. There's not much on there, by the way. It looks like he was reading some old articles about a religious sect in the seventies called The Red Path.'

'Well, they're gone now,' Jim said. Then a thought struck him. 'You do realise that we're responsible for evidence going missing from a crime scene, don't you? We should probably have done as we were told and stayed at home. The police are going to lock us up and throw away the key if they find out.'

'Who's going to tell them? Captain Rab? It's probably something that incriminates him. And the thief is hardly likely to come forward. It's so frustrating that I didn't recognise the voice. Did anything about it sound familiar to you?' asked Penny.

'No.' Jim shrugged ruefully. 'It's hard to hear an accent when someone's whispering. All I could say for sure is that it didn't sound like a local. Doesn't mean that it wasn't a local. It's just that a local would be more likely to say "loon", not "boy". Going by the size of the feet, I'd say it was a man.'

'Or Linda from the shoe shop. Did I tell you about what's really going on with her and Geoff Next Door?'

'Tell me later. I want to get this damn key and leave.'

They didn't find the key. Penny even had a brainwave that they should try the most obvious place, but it wasn't on the hook by the back door.

They returned to the car, discouraged. It was only as she sat down in the passenger seat that Penny realised it had finally stopped raining. The wind was still blowing like billy-o, but the constant patter against the windscreen was no more. She felt her spirits lift slightly.

'Is the chip shop in the Square open?' she asked, noting that the harbour chip shop sign was unlit, and the shutters were down.

'I think so. Are you hungry?'

'Absolutely starving. Mum made soup from Fiona's tomatoes for lunch, and I refused to eat it.'

'Eh, let's rewind a wee bit here,' said Jim, holding up a hand as if to stop her. 'You invited me for lunch. Were you going to tell me it was poop soup?'

'No,' Penny told him brightly, 'but I was a bit annoyed with you at the time. Then Captain Rab was stabbed, and I got some perspective. I decided I'd been a bit petty. But then you farted in the car, and now I'm thinking of new ways to get petty revenge.'

'You don't have that bottle of laxative in your bag, do you?' asked Jim, eyeing her suspiciously.

'No. Although you really shouldn't give me ideas.'

'Fine,' he said. 'Fish and chips. I'll pay if you promise not to take revenge.'

'I can't promise that,' said Penny. 'After all, a girl's gotta do what a girl's gotta do.'

CHAPTER SEVENTEEN

Eileen had arrived at the church hall early and set out chairs in a circle, as they had for Losers Club the previous Wednesday. Penny reflected that a lot of water had passed under the bridge since then. Literally and figuratively speaking. She checked her watch. Quarter to seven. This was starting to feel like last Wednesday, when she had been so anxious that no one would come. Except Jim was here with her this time, looking as anxious as she felt. She noticed him frown as he, too, checked his watch. Eileen was clearly agitated. She had adjusted the chairs so many times that Penny suspected she may have actually achieved the impossible, a perfect circle.

'Come here,' she told them both, opening her arms wide. 'This is far too American, I know, but I think we could do with a group hug.'

The trio clung together for an indecently long time, until Jim said gruffly into Penny's hair. 'For fuck's sake woman. You'll have us air kissing like the English next.'

'We could do loads of kissing, like the French,' said Eileen, grabbing his face and kissing each cheek twice.

'Gerroff!' he yelled, pushing Eileen away and backing into a chair.

'Aw, is wee Jimmy Space running away from the girls,' laughed Penny, walking towards him.

Jim quickly walked backwards, dodging Eileen as she came round the rear. Suddenly, they were teenagers again. With a loud whoop, he ran off, the two women chasing him as he used his football training to escape their clutches, until eventually, all three of them roaring with laughter, Penny and Eileen cornered him by the stage and covered his face in kisses. For a moment, everything was forgotten. Nothing mattered.

Until a voice said, 'Has bingo been cancelled and replaced with an orgy? Len, you didn't tell me it was orgy night. Can I still win some shoes? And, for heaven's sake, don't make your father do anything for that lawnmower that'll put his back out. I'll never hear the end of it for weeks.'

'Hello, parents,' said Penny, warily. 'Bingo night isn't happening. We'll explain everything in a minute. We're just waiting for some others to get here.'

'Oh, I do love surprises,' said Mary, taking her coat off and settling herself down on one of the chairs. She patted the chair next to her. 'Come and sit down. What have you three been up to, eh?'

Penny avoided the question by going over to help her father, who was struggling with the zip on his anorak.

'Here, let me get that for you, Dad.' She examined the zip and noted the fabric caught in the teeth. Wiggling it free, she pulled the zip down and helped him off with his coat.

'Is this one of those moments where the child becomes the parent?' asked Len with a rueful smile. 'You might have to wash my bum one day in the not-too-distant future, you know.'

'Ugh. I love you very much, Dad, but I'm putting you both in a care home.'

'Could you put your mother in a care home first? I could do with the peace and quiet.'

'It's a deal.' Penny gave him a conspiratorial wink and Len smiled back.

Penny watched him as he ambled off to sit next to her mother. Jeez, this is breaking my heart, she thought. She loved these people so much. A whole lifetime of love could be shattered tonight. She couldn't live without answers, yet she was terrified that she might not be able to live *with* the answers either.

She swallowed the lump in her throat and turned

towards the door, where a blast of air announced the arrival of Mr Space and Mrs Campbell. They looked surprised to see only five people there. Eileen and Jim hurried to them, explaining that bingo night wasn't happening and that, if they would just take a seat, all would become clear.

Mrs Campbell was wearing lipstick and a sequinned blouse. Her auburn hair was swept up into a loose bun, the roots forming a silver halo around her forehead. She had clearly made an effort for the occasion. Once more, Penny could feel the guilt hot in the pit of her stomach. If she felt like this, goodness knows how Eileen must be feeling right now.

Even Mr Space was looking quite dapper in his polo shirt and chinos. His short, grey hair was neatly cut and a spot of blood on his chin testified to a recent tangle with a razor. He was shaking an iPhone at Jim and saying, 'If you rang to tell me that bingo night was cancelled, I'm sorry I didn't answer. This blasted thing never rings.'

Jim gently took the phone from him and switched the ringer button on.

When everyone was seated, Penny looked at Jim and Eileen for a cue. It seemed odd that they hadn't discussed this part. They should have worked out a script, or at least agreed who was going to start. She took a deep breath and began to speak, when Jim's voice cut across hers. They both paused.

'Sorry,' he said.

'No, it's okay. You go.'

'No, it's fine. You go.'

'Mon Dieu,' said Eileen. 'Will one of you go because I'm dying here? And I'm not going because we all know I'll mess it up.'

Penny pointed at Jim, and he nodded.

'We are gathered here today,' he began, ignoring Eileen's nervous titter, 'because we need answers. As you know…or as you don't know, sorry Dad, I didn't get a chance to tell you…we've been digging into Old Archie's murder, and during the course of our investigation we checked into the backgrounds of some of the islanders, including yourselves and, ultimately, ourselves.

'Initially, we were looking into Old Archie and couldn't find any definitive trace, so we checked on some people whose full details we knew – that's you guys, by the way. We couldn't find any trace of you either. Then, following Penny's brilliant logic that if there was no trace of your birth then where did we come from, we checked ourselves out. We found our birth records, but we also found our death records. All three of us died as babies.' Jim paused and looked at Penny. Acknowledging the silent cue, she gave him a brief smile and took over.

'I asked you both about it, Mum and Dad, and you both gave me a load of nonsense about the internet. You did much the same thing to Eileen, Mrs Campbell. Mrs Hubbard, who also doesn't exist, wouldn't tell us anything, and Elsie from the library just said that we should ask you. We decided to get you all in the same place so that we could get some answers. We're sorry that we faked the bingo night, but we hope you'll understand why.'

Penny sat back and surveyed her audience. Her mother looked stricken and was holding onto Len's hand like it was a lifeline. Len, however, had bowed his head and seemed to be taking a deep interest in his own knees. Mr Space had paled and was staring at Jim, his eyes glistening. Mrs Campbell, on the other hand, appeared furious.

She stood up, hands on hips, and said, 'I'm not listening to this nonsense. Len, Mary, Ivor, come on, we're going. And you!' She pointed at Eileen, whose face instantly crumpled, tears welling in her eyes, 'You, young madam, are far too easily led. First its aliens. Then you're swearing at some poor waiter in French. Oh, don't think I hadn't heard about that! And now these two idiots have fed you a pack of lies, and you're just lapping it up.'

She looked as though she was about to continue her tirade, when a voice said, 'Sit down, Jeanie. This has gone on long enough. They have a right to know the truth.'

Len lifted his head and calmly gestured to her chair. 'Please. Sit down.'

The wind firmly taken out of her sails, Mrs Campbell sat down and crossed her arms over her ample besequinned bosom.

Mr Space was still staring at Jim. He somehow looked much older and far frailer than he had ten minutes ago. In a tremulous voice, he said, 'I wish you had asked me rather than doing it like this.'

'Would you have told me the truth, Dad?'

Mr Space sighed. 'Probably not. Fair enough. Len, how do you want to do this? Do you want to tell them, or shall I?'

'I'll tell them, Ivor. You can chip in if I've misremembered something.'

Len took a moment to gather his thoughts, then began.

'What you first have to understand is that in the early seventies we were young people living in a world of freedoms that hadn't existed before. Society was changing and it was exciting. I don't just mean the pill and mini-skirts and all that stuff. New groups were springing up to challenge the status quo and universities were hotbeds of radical thinking. It seems unthinkable now, when extremes are seen as frightening, but back then it was common to be members of political groups supporting socialism or Marxism. We were all pumped up on how clever and how much better than our parents we were. Determined to change the world.

'Your mother and I met when we were in our third year at Cornborough University. We both came from small villages in Scotland. Villages which were still relatively untouched by the changes. Where things were still done in the way they had been for centuries. Your grandmother had wanted to go to university when she was younger, but your great grandfather said that education wasn't for girls and made her work on the farm instead. She was determined that your mother wouldn't miss out and, even though the rest of the village thought she was odd, she encouraged your mother to study hard so that she could have a different life. She wanted your mother to have the life she'd never had. She was a strong, independent woman, your grandmother. Your grandfather was a decent man too, although I don't think he ever understood your grandmother pushing Mary to have a life beyond the village.

'On my side, my parents expected me to get a good job in the nearest town, settle down with a bonny local lass and produce bonny bairns. When I started talking about some of the political ideas I'd picked up at university, my father banned me from going back. Of course, I ignored him. In those days, you had student grants and I had enough money to see me through the year without any help from him. We fell out, which is sad because if I had known what was ahead of me, I'd have tried to make my peace with him. He wasn't a bad man. Just set in his ways. My mother didn't have a say in it all. She did as she was told, like the generations of women before her.

'Anyway, that's the background to how things were. Ivor and Jeanie were in much the same boat. I suppose what I'm saying is that we came from very sheltered backgrounds and were ripe for the picking. Cornborough was popular with a lot of Scottish students, so we weren't the only ones. I was studying economics, Ivor was in the last year of his veterinary medicine degree, Jeanie was doing accounting and Minty Hubbard and Elsie were studying English Lit. There were a few others. There was also a man called Thaddeus Height. He was older, a theology student, and he was the leader of one of the socialist groups on campus. He was a very charismatic man, and we were flattered when he asked a few of us back to his flat for drinks after a meeting. We were impressed that he had his own flat. The rest of us were in run down boarding houses or shared rooms with other students.

'Those sessions at his flat turned into a regular thing which in turn evolved into meetings where we began to discuss even more radical ideas. The discussions moved towards religious socialism. Things like living in co-operation with each other and sharing everything. We could see so many parallels between the teachings of the bible and socialist ideologies. You have to remember that, coming from rural villages, we'd had strong religious upbringings. Going to church wasn't a matter of choice. Christianity was with you from cradle to grave. Combine this with the new ideas we were learning...well, you can see how we convinced ourselves that the world needed to go down a different path, and that we would lead them.

'We developed a set of biblical principles, a strict moral code if you like, which we thought society should live by. Thaddeus hand-picked more students to join our meetings and asked us to bring along people whose minds could be opened. That's the phrase he used. "Whose minds could be opened." Just after the final exams, Thaddeus announced that he'd rented a property in Caithness and invited us to join him there. By this time, there were about thirty of us. We called ourselves The Red Path.

'The place was a smallish farm. We set about fixing it up and getting it going. If nothing else, it was good experience for Ivor. Without him, we'd have been sunk at the first lambing. A degree in economics doesn't get you very far when the barley needs harvesting, and in those days, we didn't have the internet. We had to learn it from books. It was hard, but we managed to feed thirty people and make some profit.

'The biblical principles were clear about all profit being for the benefit of the group, and that's exactly what happened at first. We lived happily for a couple of years and the local community regarded us as weird, harmless hippies. Many of us got together and had children. That's where you three come in. We didn't believe in marriage, but there were strong rules about monogamy. Quite a few babies were born and, believe it or not, our little community was a good place to be. We saw a future where you all grew up and spread the word.

'However, it was not to be. Over time, Thaddeus became more distant. He said that we needed to go beyond the farm and lead the ignorant towards the truth through direct action. He didn't say what he meant in so many words, but we all knew he meant violence of some sort. He began to call himself The Bridge, meaning he was a link between God and The Red Path. Some of the group truly believed this. Others like ourselves, who had known him back in the early days, were less in his thrall. Even people who had been happy, committed couples found themselves divided by how, or whether, we should go in the direction that Thaddeus was leading us. Our happy little community began to fray around the edges.

'Eventually, he went on his travels and recruited more Red Path members, meaning there were a lot more mouths to feed, so the farm work became harder. There were also some new, more dominant personalities. Thaddeus started inviting them and his supplicants to his rooms for drinks, just like he'd done with us, and soon there was a group within a group. Except this new group were a tight clique. They didn't share meals with us or help with chores. They'd work on the farm, but outside of that they kept to themselves.

'It was Jeanie here who first noticed something unusual. She was responsible for the accounts, and she spotted that we were purchasing a higher number of supplies than usual. When she queried it with Thaddeus, he pointed out that the Red Path had many new members and said she was worrying over nothing. She told some of us original group members and, suspecting that money was being siphoned off, we began to keep a closer eye on the inner circle.

'It was nothing major. We listened in on conversations, checked bins for any stray papers and encouraged some of the inner circle who still talked to us to share gossip. Jeanie kept two sets of books, so we had an idea of what was really being spent and how much money was disappearing. At night, we'd compare notes, and slowly we built a picture of what they were up to.

'We found out that they were planning to bomb a newspaper office and hijack a plane. They believed that only through extreme violence could the world achieve peace. I don't know. It was warped thinking. It was like they were trying to shock the world into listening to them. We realised we had to leave, but we had no means of doing it. As the inner circle plotted, they became more wary, and we could feel them watching the rest of us. The only vehicles we had were the bus we arrived in and the farm vehicles, and the inner circle had the keys. Thaddeus had kept them in his room from the start, but because we were happy, none of us had questioned it. With so many young children and babies, there was no way we could walk out. Even the oldest bairns were barely toddlers. The nearest place was ten miles away, and none of us felt we would be safe within a hundred miles of Thaddeus.

'It was Mrs Hubbard and Elsie who saved us. They sneaked out one night and walked the ten miles to the village, where they phoned the police. Give him his due, the local bobbie listened and called his superiors. The police were sceptical at first, but Elsie showed them some receipts for chemicals that were nothing to do with the farm. The Anarchist Cookbook had been published not long before and had been in the news, so home-made explosives weren't beyond the realms of possibility. Elsie left the receipts with the police then she and Mrs Hubbard walked ten miles back and did a day's work on the farm like nothing had happened. Looking back, they must have been exhausted. You'd think the police could have given them a lift at least part of the way.

'I don't know what happened on the police side of things. All I know is that the next time Mrs Hubbard went into the village to get some supplies, she was approached by a woman who said she was from the Special Branch. She asked Mrs Hubbard to find out more information about the inner circle's plans and gave her a miniature camera to take some photographs.

'We were all terrified, but we gathered as much as we could. We took it in turns to photograph the inner circle. Elsie crawled through Thaddeus' window one day while he was out. She took photographs of whatever documents she could find. Ivor kept a log of everything we overheard. Believe me, the inner circle were zealots, and I don't think they'd have hesitated to kill us or you, even though you were babies at the time, if they thought we were a threat to their plans. Yet hundreds, maybe thousands, of lives were at risk if we let them go through with it.

'Mrs Hubbard managed to get everything back to Special Branch the next time she went to the village. It seems naïve now, but we signed a letter asking them to help us escape. However, it was also our saving grace, as you'll see in a minute.

'About a week later, in the dead of night, we were awoken by a series of bangs and crashes. Armed police stormed the farm and rounded us all up. There were people running everywhere, babies crying, screaming. Some of the animals got loose and were scampering around the yard. We slept in a converted barn, but we heard shots over at the main house where Thaddeus lived with his inner circle. It was absolute pandemonium. The police rounded up most of The Red Path members and shut us in the barn, yet many managed to escape. Some of them were the mothers and fathers of the babies, and they ran off with the children, leaving their other halves behind to face the music. It was terrible. There were parents who never saw their children again and never knew what happened to them.

'Eventually, they loaded us into coaches and bussed us to the police station in Inverness. We weren't allowed to collect any belongings except whatever was needed for the babies. You three screamed blue murder the whole way there. If I hear a baby crying on the bus now, it takes me straight back. In those days, there were no rights. The police could keep you without charge for as long as they liked. We filled the cells in Inverness for nearly a week. The criminals of the Highlands must have thought all their Christmases had come at once. It was awful, though. Your mother had no coat, and it was freezing. Jeanie here had no shoes. They took all the babies away, including you, and we didn't know if we were ever going to see you again. At heart, we were a bunch of young teuchters, scared witless.

'There was a trial, of course. Thaddeus and many of the inner circle had got away. Even some of the people who weren't inner circle had escaped. Those of us who had signed that letter were separated from the rest and asked to give evidence. With Thaddeus still on the loose, it was a risk, but the letter would probably come out as part of the trial anyway. We agreed to give evidence in exchange for witness protection.

'That's it really. I think the Security Services were involved. They created false identities for us all. They used genuine identities for the babies because there were already birth certificates, so you'd all grow up and be able to get passports, driving licences and things like that. Then they gave the parents legends to support this. Ha! Legends. It sounds like a spy movie. For the few people who didn't have children, they gave them whole new identities, including passports. But they said there were too many of us and not enough time to do it for everyone. That's why a lot of folk have barely been beyond Aberdeen. We were shipped en masse to Vik as part of an alleged newly created government scheme to boost the population of remote islands, and we've been here ever since.

'We couldn't tell you because Thaddeus is still out there. He and a bunch of his followers fled to somewhere in America and started again. As far as we know, The Red Path still going, but they never got the traction that they gained here. Now we have the internet, we can keep an eye on them. However, the reverse is also true. Which is why you can never tell anyone what we've told you tonight.

'The saddest part is that you never got to know your extended families. Jeanie here was one of the lucky ones in a way. Her mother joined The Red Path to be closer to her when Eileen was born. The rest of us had to cut all ties with our families as soon as we went into witness protection. The Security Services kept tabs on The Red Path for years afterwards and found signs that they were still looking for us. We couldn't risk our parents, brothers and sisters being in danger if anyone got the slightest hint of where we were. We couldn't risk it for you three either. Nor any of the other children, and now grandchildren. We wanted the secret to die with us so that you'd be able to live normal lives. Hector and Edith, and your boys, Eileen. They must never know.'

CHAPTER EIGHTEEN

The silence that followed was measured by the steady tick tock of the church hall clock. Ten seconds. Thirty seconds. A minute.

Len sat unmoving, head bowed, as Mary stared anxiously at Penny. Mr Space, his eyes once more filled with tears, opened his mouth to say something to Jim, but no sound emerged, and he sank back, defeated and awaiting his son's verdict. Mrs Campbell, however, appeared to be steeling herself for an argument. She took deep breaths through her nose and glared at Eileen, as if daring her to judge.

Jim leaned forward to clutch his father's hand, and the scrape of his chair against the wooden floor broke the spell. With tears in his own eyes, Jim quietly hugged his sobbing father.

Eileen smiled uncertainly at her mum.

'You were so brave,' she whispered. 'I'm so proud of you.'

Instantly, the fight went out of Mrs Campbell. Her shoulders sagged, and the loose bun wobbled as she reached a hand out to her daughter.

'I'm sorry, my wee darling. Your dad…your dad was one of the ones who ran away. They caught him a few days later and he was jailed. He was in the inner circle, you see. After mum joined, it was like he lost interest in us. Like now mum was here to look after us, he could devote all his time to Thaddeus. He died in Peterhead Prison in 1979 after an argument with another prisoner turned violent. He wasn't a bad man, poppet, just a misguided one.'

Penny had a thousand questions, but she couldn't think any more. She didn't want to think any more. Not while her very core was this twisted mass of shock, relief, pity, love, loss. Her body buzzed, and her face was numb. No, her face was wet. Why was her face wet? She realised that she had been holding her breath and quickly exhaled, then inhaled. The buzzing stopped as she steadied her breathing and allowed the emotions to wash over her.

'I thought…I thought…,' she said, her voice low and ragged as she gasped deep breaths, 'I thought that maybe I didn't belong to you.'

Hot tears flooded her eyes. She let them fall. Let them all fall.

Len's head snapped up and he shot off his chair, grasping Penny's shoulders and gazing directly into her eyes.

'I'm so sorry. So sorry that we frightened you like that. Always know that we love you.'

He gathered Penny into his arms, like he did when she was small, and buried his face in her hair. Mary came too and wrapped her arms around them both. Together, they silently rocked Penny until her sobs subsided.

She pulled away. A string of snot stretched between her upper lip and Len's best Fairisle tank top. Mary produced a tissue from her sleeve and wiped Penny's nose.

'That was disgusting,' she said, looking around for a bin. 'Surely you can have no doubts that I'm your mother now.'

Penny smiled weakly. How *could* she have doubted it? After all, she had her mother's bottom.

Slowly, the emotion in the room subsided. Everyone looked wrung out and exhausted, but Penny had questions. Some of her questions could wait, but others needed answers straight away.

'I know you'll have loads of questions too,' she told Eileen and Jim. 'Do you mind if I ask a couple first?'

She turned to the group of parents. 'The first thing I want to know is, who are we? What are our birth names? And what are your names?'

Ivor Space answered. 'This information never

leaves this room. We never speak of it again. Agreed?'

Everyone nodded their assent.

'Good,' he continued. 'I was born Ian Bisset. Jim, your mother was Lynn MacBride. Your name at birth was Bernard.'

Eileen snorted and even Penny, who was still raw, snickered, 'Bernard.'

Mrs Campbell went next. 'You may well laugh, Iona Boyle. Lord knows what was going through my head at the time. Your father was Grant Boyle, and I was Elizabeth Bell.'

Mary pointed to herself then Len. 'Edith Hutcheson and George Gunn. You were born Beatrice Gunn.'

'Who else on the island is a former cult member?' asked Penny.

'We can't tell you that. It's not fair on them. Some of them have children and grandchildren, even great-grandchildren,' said Len.

'Okay, then here's my final question. We know Captain Rab was researching The Red Path. Was Captain Rab a member?'

'Yes,' said Mrs Campbell. At Mary's warning look, she added, 'We may as well tell them. We've told them about Elsie and Mrs Hubbard, and if he was looking it up, then it's obvious. He was one of those whose partners escaped, Penny. His other half ran, taking their daughter Ellie with her.'

Something clicked in Penny's head and a piece of the puzzle slotted into place. 'His boat!' she exclaimed, turning to Jim. 'Remember? The Princess Ellie.'

'That's right,' said Mary. 'He named it after Elspeth. Poor man. He never got over losing her. He wasn't always a grumpy old git, you know. He used to be the life and soul of the party. A kind, happy man. But all the happiness was sucked out of him after his partner took off with his wee girl. It's sad to see him so bitter when you know what he was like before.'

Something was niggling at Penny, but she couldn't put her finger on it. She decided to let it go for now and sat back, listening to the others as they asked their questions.

'What about Captain Rab's brother Kevin?' Jim wanted to know. 'If he's on the island to visit Captain Rab, then he must have been one of the people put in witness protection. Otherwise, he wouldn't know where to find Rab.'

'Can't fault your logic, son,' said Mr Space. 'Aye, Captain Kev was in The Red Path and was put into witness protection here too. That's why him and Rab fell out. They both used to work the ferry, but Captain Kev wanted to work on cruise ships. Captain Rab said it wasn't safe for him to leave. He was so angry with Captain Kev for putting everyone in danger, as he saw it. They had a huge argument one night, and it ended up in fisticuffs. It was the talk of the island, the two of them fighting on the ferry.

'I know a few of the islanders have gone abroad, either permanently or for holidays, but that's only been in the last ten years or so, and they were the ones with no family ties on the island. As time passed, we all started to feel safer. Captain Kev and Captain Rab's argument was…oh, it would have been the mid to late eighties. Things were still fresh enough for us to feel vulnerable. The babies born during the Red Path days were at most young teenagers, and other children had come along since. We could understand why Captain Rab was so angry, yet at the same time none of us thought there was a need for him to cut off his brother.'

'Do you think Captain Kev could have stabbed Captain Rab?' Jim asked.

His father shook his head. 'Unless he has changed, which I suppose isn't beyond the bounds of possibility given how much his brother has changed, I'd say it's highly unlikely. He was always very laid back. Not a violent man at all.

'The two of them were thick as thieves. They worked on the fishing boats in Buckie from the age of fourteen. Captain Rab went to night school to pass his exams and got a place studying Marine Biology. He was older than us and I've no idea how such a very practical man managed to have his head filled with Thaddeus' nonsense. I think there was a reactionary streak in him.

'When we moved to the farm, Kev joined us. He said he missed his big brother too much. He wasn't a great believer, but he was a good worker and pitched in. Then, not long after we came to the island, the old ferry captain retired and Kev and Rab bought the business. Len here was working at the bank by then and helped them get the loan. Captain Rab said he needed to do something with the sea because it was in his blood. Captain Kev was more the junior partner, but he stuck by his brother for ten years before he decided to make it on his own.

'Given how close they were, the split must have hurt them both a great deal. Captain Kev has come back a few times to try to mend bridges, with no success. I can't see any reason why he would suddenly turn on him after all these years. It's out of character and the anger has long since gone out of the situation. These days, it really boils down to Captain Rab being a stubborn old bugger and Captain Kev propping up the bar in the pub for a couple of weeks every few years.'

Jim nodded, satisfied, and asked Eileen, who had sat patiently awaiting her turn, whether there was anything she wanted to know.

'I have loads of questions,' she said. 'The biggest one is how you managed to keep it secret all these years.'

'It was surprisingly easy,' said Mrs Campbell. 'Remember, you were all babies when we arrived. By the time you were old enough to understand, we had been Len and Mary Hopper, Jeanie Campbell and Ivor Space for years. We had jobs, bank accounts, homes, lives on this rock in the North Sea. Most of the time we didn't think about who we were. We just got on with being who we are. As long as we kept our heads down, there was no reason to believe that anyone could find us. That's why most of us have barely gone further than Aberdeen since we arrived on Vik. Mary, you went to London, didn't you?'

'Yes. We could go anywhere that didn't need a passport,' said Mary. 'Don't forget, there were already people living on the island when we arrived. Some of us married some of them. I expect they would have had to tell them about what had happened. The thought of putting so many people at risk if it got out has kept us all quiet over the years, to the point where we almost forgot that we haven't been here forever.'

'What about Penny being in all the newspapers?' Eileen asked. 'Were you not worried that someone would connect her to you?'

'Yes, it was a slight worry. Although even if they mentioned our names, they were unlikely to be putting our photos on the front page. It's not as if any of us have embraced social media,' said Mary.

'Jeez, Mum. You did that TikTok with Edith!' Penny exclaimed.

'I have no idea what a Tok Tik is,' Mary retorted.

'It's a huge online thing. We need to get her to take it down and make sure the twins don't post any photos of you and Dad on their social media. You may not be on socials, but all the kids are. Nothing is private anymore. You should warn the others.'

'What about our relatives?' asked Eileen.

'You can never contact them,' said Mrs Campbell. 'They'll have read the stories at the time and assumed we went to jail. They were all told that none of us wanted contact, so nobody could tell them where we were. It's the price we paid, and probably the hardest part of all of this is that they, and you, have to pay the price as well. I'll tell you anything you want to know about our family when we get home, Eileen.'

Mrs Campbell stood up. 'I don't know about anyone else, but I could do with a glass of wine and a comfy sofa. Are you ready to go?' she asked, yawning.

Eileen was about to reply, when a sudden burst of Chesney split the air, startling the group. Both Eileen and Penny scrambled for their handbags. Penny got there first, dredging her phone from under the fish and chips wrapper she'd discarded earlier.

'Not me,' she said.

'It's mine,' said Eileen, her brow creasing as she studied her phone screen. She jabbed at the green button. 'Hello? Kenny? Is everything alright?'

Penny couldn't hear the other end of the conversation, but she could tell by the concerned look on her friend's face that everything was not alright. She looked at Jim. He had stood up, poised to help. Saint Bernard to the rescue, thought Penny, with an inward smile. She'd file that one away for later use. There must be some more good Bernard jokes she could annoy him with.

Eileen hung up and Penny focused her attention on her friend.

'Ricky and Gervais are missing,' said Eileen, her face betraying her panic. 'Kenny went to get them for a bath before bed, and they were gone. He's going out to look for them. I have to get home now, in case they come back. Can one of you give Mum a lift home?'

Without waiting for a reply, Eileen grabbed her coat from the hook by the door and fled.

Mrs Campbell started after her, but Mr Space put a hand on her arm.

'I'll give you a lift Jeanie. Do you want to go home, or do you want me to drop you off at Eileen's?'

'Eileen's please,' Mrs Campbell said. 'I'm not having Eileen and Kenny do this on their own. I remember when her and Penny went missing. Do you remember, Mary? Len? They were only about ten. They'd decided to run away and make their fortunes. We found them about fifteen minutes later at the bus stop, but it was the most frightening fifteen minutes of my life. The boys will likely turn up. It's a small island.'

While she was talking, Mrs Campbell had shrugged on her coat and was now clutching her handbag, ready to leave.

Before she could go, Jim asked, 'Do you have Kenny's mobile number, Mrs Campbell? Penny and I will help him with the search.'

'We could help too,' said Mary. 'Len, it'll be almost dark outside. Where's the big torch?'

'It's okay, Mary,' said Mrs Campbell. 'Just get yourselves home. If Kenny needs any help, I'll let you know.'

She passed her phone to Jim, and he copied Kenny's number into his own. Meanwhile, Len and Mary donned their coats.

'That's us off then, Penny-farthing,' said Len, standing on tiptoe to kiss Penny's forehead. 'We'll talk more when you get home. Don't worry about the twins. We'll make sure they have everything ready for school in the morning. Give us a ring when you find those boys.'

The four parents departed, leaving Penny and Jim to tidy away the chairs and lock up the church hall.

'That was a shocker,' said Penny, stacking a chair on top of its vile, brown plastic brethren, which lined the edges of the hall. 'It's weird to think that there are probably aunties, uncles and cousins out there who don't even know we exist.'

Jim gave her a wry smile. 'Understatement of the year. It was a flabbergaster. I can't believe my sensible old dad was in a cult. What a secret to keep!'

Penny was about to stack the next chair but suddenly stopped and set it back on the ground. 'Something's really bugging me. It was when they were talking about Captain Rab's boat. How he named it after his daughter.'

'Good deduction there, by the way, Sherlock,' said Jim.

'Why, thank you, Bernard. What was it they said the daughter was called?'

'Ellie.'

'No. Her full name.'

'Elspeth, I think. Why?'

'I've heard that name somewhere recently. But where?'

Jim thought for a moment. It sounded familiar to him too, but his brain, already overloaded from the evening's revelations, steadfastly refused to join the dots.

'It'll come back to us,' he said, hefting a chair onto the stack. Come on, Beattie. It's good to talk. Let's finish up and phone Kenny.'

'You've been trying to think of BT jokes since we learned our names, haven't you?'

'That's the only one I could come up with. Nevertheless, someone had to say it'

'You're such a saint, Bernard.'

Jim groaned. 'They could at least have called me something normal. I'd rather be Saint Peter. He's got quite a good gig going.'

Penny gasped and held her hands to her face, her eyes widening in horror.

'I know where we heard the name Elspeth. Fu…udging hell! This opens a humungous can of worms.'

CHAPTER NINETEEN

'What? Where? Who? When?' said Jim.

'Never mind that now. We have more important things to worry about. Phone Kenny,' Penny instructed, her desire to irritate him restored to normal levels after the emotional upheaval of the previous hour.

Jim shot her an outraged glare and dialed Kenny's number. Penny could hear the muffled ringing followed by Kenny's best telephone voice informing the caller, 'I'm nae here. Leave a message. And if it's aboot yer car, phone the garage ye feel gype.'

That's our Kenny, thought Penny. Straight to the point. Phone the garage you stupid idiot. She leaned into the phone and spoke.

'Kenny, it's Jim and Penny. If you need help looking for the boys, ring us back.'

Jim hung up and gave her a stern look. 'Right, Sherlock. Spill the beans.'

Penny sighed, mildly exasperated that he hadn't worked it out for himself. 'Remember when we were doing the internet research on the visitors?'

She watched Jim's face as it travelled from frowning man to delighted man, with brief stops at befuddlement and shock on the way.

'That article!' he exclaimed. 'The one about Pete's parents being killed in the fire. His mother was called Elspeth. What was her surname?'

'It was in the ancestry website where we tracked down likely Pete Smellies.'

'Pete Smellies. Sounds like a revolting line of bath products.' Jim chuckled at his own joke then, catching sight of Penny's stony face, said, 'I'll phone Eileen and see if she still has the browser tab open.'

Jim put the call to Eileen on speaker, so that Penny could join in. He apologised profusely for bothering her and asked for news of the boys.

'There's no news,' Eileen told him, a crack in her voice. 'I'm waiting to hear back from Kenny.'

'We phoned to find out where he wanted us to search, but there was no reply,' said Jim.

'He might be somewhere with a weak signal. You know what it's like here. Lots of places where you don't get any reception at all. Try him again in a wee while.'

'We could try the parks and the school,' Jim offered.

'Kenny has probably already looked in the obvious places. I've contacted their friends' parents. There's no point in you randomly running about the place. If we've had no luck in an hour, I'll get people together and we'll do an organised search.'

Penny cut in, hoping that she didn't sound unsympathetic. 'Eileen, remember when our parents were talking about Captain Rab's daughter? They said she was called Elspeth. A minute ago, I realised where I'd heard the name before. It was Pete's mum's name. Do you still have the tab open where we were searching the ancestry sites for him?'

There was a long pause. Penny heard some clicks and Eileen's voice came back on the line. 'Yes, I've got it here. What do you want to know?'

'Her surname.'

'It says née, which as we experts know is French for not. So, it was nae Linklater.'

'Clear as mud. Linklater. Thanks, Eileen. We'll ring Kenny back in ten minutes or so. Let us know if the boys are found. I love you, Winnie the Pooh. Over.'

'Love you too, Rubber Duck. Out.'

Penny tried to push the wave of love and worry for her friend and her boys back down into the pit of her stomach. She couldn't do anything to help them until they'd spoken to Kenny. Or, God forbid, joined an organised search party. Please let the boys be found before it gets to that stage, she silently prayed. I'm not going to promise to be good or try to bargain this time. I'm simply asking you to keep them safe.

Jim's voice broke through her anxious reverie. 'What next, Sherlock?'

She gave herself a quick mental shake and refocused on the task at hand. 'Well, we don't know if Elspeth Linklater was the same person as Captain Rab's daughter. I mean, he's Rab MacDonald now, but he would have had a different name back then. Or his daughter could have taken the mother's name. Obviously, if Elspeth Linklater was Captain Rab's daughter, then that would make Pete Smellie his grandson.'

'Which raises a few questions,' said Jim. 'Like, does Pete know? And, if he does, how did he find out? It's not like Captain Rab would have contacted him, given that he hasn't spoken to his own brother in decades because he thought Captain Kev was putting people in danger. So, assuming Pete came here to meet his grandfather, how would he even know that Captain Rab was here in the first place?'

Penny nodded. 'I agree. None of it makes sense. Although, if Captain Rab *is* Pete's grandad and Pete somehow tracked him down, it makes sense that the captain didn't seem too pleased to see him. Then again, if it was as simple as tracing your long-lost grandad, why did Pete lie and say he didn't know Captain Rab? I suppose if he knows about The Red Path, then he probably knows it's a secret. Still, he could have come up with something more plausible than denying all knowledge. A family rift, or something.'

'I wonder if Captain Kev knows,' said Jim. 'After all, he would be Pete's great uncle. Come to think of it, he could be the one who told Pete. If he was still feeling aggrieved, he could have traced Pete and told him where to find his grandfather.'

'Hmm. From what our parents said, it doesn't sound like the kind of thing he'd do.' Penny shrugged. 'Who knows. Before we disappear down the rabbit hole, let's phone my dad and ask about Captain Rab's real name.'

The call to Len would have been short but sweet, had Mary not answered.

'You owe me a new pole,' she said, her strident tone so loud that Penny didn't need to put her on speaker. Anyone within a ten-mile radius must have been able to hear the rant that followed. There was no need for the Vik lighthouse, Penny mused. Just stand her mother at the top of a cliff bellowing "Get out of the way, you big idiots" and they'd be sorted.

Penny interrupted Mary's hundred decibel monologue. 'I'm sorry Hector broke your pole, Mum. I'll buy you another one. Yes, I'll get the hole in the ceiling fixed. No, he's not being groomed on the internet. He was probably just messing about, making a video for his boyfriend or something. Now, stop talking and listen. What was Captain Rab's name when he was in The Red Path?'

There was a clatter as the phone in Valhalla was placed on the table, and Penny could hear her mother shouting for Len.

She rolled her eyes at Jim. 'Hector broke Mum's pole dancing pole.'

'So I gathered,' said Jim. 'Poor Hector. It must be hard having a long-distance relationship.'

'Yes, it's a shame. They hadn't been together long before we moved, so it'll probably fizzle out. Hopefully, he'll meet someone new at school.'

'They're quite conservative about these things here. Aren't you worried he'll get bullied?'

'Not too worried,' said Penny. 'Hector's very good at making allies, and Edith will tear the nuts off anyone who has a go. Anyway, they're just as likely to get it in the neck from someone for their posh London accents or their famous father. Kids are brutal. Oh, here's Dad.'

She pressed the speaker button, and they could hear Len saying, 'Hello? Penny?'

'I'm here, Dad. I have a quick question. What was Captain Rab's name when he was in The Red Path?'

'I'm sorry, Penny. I can't tell you that. Why do you need to know?'

'Because we think that one of the visitors to the island might be his grandson.'

There was a long silence while Len pondered whether or not to give Penny the name. Eventually, he sighed and said, 'Alright. It was Gifford. Michael Gifford.'

'Mystery solved. Thanks, Dad. We came across the name Elspeth Linklater when we were researching a Canadian guy called Pete, and when you said that Captain Rab's daughter was called Elspeth, we wondered if she could be the same Elspeth as Pete's mum.'

'Ah,' said Len. 'Then this might change things. His partner on the farm…the one that ran off with their daughter…she was called Irene Linklater. Hang on. Your mother is shouting that she forgot to ask about Ricky and Gervais. Have they found them yet?'

'Not as far as I know. Tell her I'll call if there's any news.'

'I will. This is very worrying, Penny. Not the missing boys. Although, of course, that too. No, I mean Irene's grandson turning up on the island. How would he have known to look for Captain Rab here?'

'That's exactly what we're going to try to find out. Make sure you keep the doors locked and warn the others. Is there someone in the police that you're supposed to contact?'

'I'm not sure, after all these years. I'll ask Mrs Hubbard. She might know.'

'Stay safe, Dad. I'll be home as soon as possible.'

'You stay safe too, Penny-farthing. Don't go

poking around.'

Penny thanked her father and hung up, then turned to Jim, who looked as perplexed as she felt.

'This brings us back to all the same questions,' he said. 'I figure we have two options to find out what the fuck's going on. Ask Captain Rab or ask Pete.'

Penny thought about this for a moment, before coming to a decision. 'We can't ask Captain Rab. For a start, the hospital isn't going to let us in at this time of night. Secondly, we don't even know if he's in any condition to answer questions. I say leave him to the police and let's ask Pete.'

'Before we go off down your rabbit hole, I'll just try Kenny again,' Jim said, redialling Kenny's number. Penny heard six muffled rings then the voicemail message cut in. 'I'm nae here. Leave a—'

Jim hung up. 'Have you got the key for the hall door? Let's lock up and go to the hotel. See what Pete has to say for himself.'

The rain had held off, Penny was pleased to note, but the wind was blowing harder than ever, as if indulging itself in a final fit of fury before it would allow the storm to subside. They parked in the Square, the car rocking to the rhythm of a gale that funnelled up the alleyway beside them and came howling into the open space. The tops of the trees around the bus stop, even in late August, were already beginning to breathe their final, glorious, autumnal breath, and the harsh wind stripped the branches, sending wet leaves slapping into the car, where they gilded the windscreen, their vibrant golds and browns barely visible in the dying light of the day.

The town felt almost deserted. They'd seen only one car since they left the church hall. It had driven behind them, its headlights glaring, until they turned off to park in the Square.

'Wanker needs to do something about those headlights,' said Jim. Then, as the car sped by, 'And he's got his fog lights on. What a dick!'

'You've got your fog lights on,' Penny pointed out.

Jim fiddled with the controls. 'Have I been driving all this time with my fog lights on? Why didn't you tell me?'

'Dunno,' shrugged Penny. 'I just thought you were a dick. What are we going to say to Pete when we see him?'

They discussed strategy for a few minutes then, bowing low against the wind, they made their way to the hotel.

The reception desk was empty. Penny leaned over it, wondering if there was a buzzer or bell for late guests. She shifted her weight forward and slid her chest over the high wooden surface, rummaging on the desk underneath to find anything she could use to summon help. Reaching out to lift a printout, she accidentally knocked the computer mouse. The screen immediately lit up and she could see the guest booking system. Ooh, this looks interesting, she thought, slithering further forward and turning towards the screen. Her feet left the floor, and the laws of physics conspired against her pivoting any further on her breasts. If she could just reach to pull the screen a little closer. She stretched out an arm and felt herself slip forward, her hips coming to rest on the high part of the desk and her chin leaning on the edge of the lower surface behind. She kicked her legs, trying to shift her centre of gravity backwards, and her wellies fell off, hitting the carpet with two dull thuds. She knew she should have gotten a smaller size. Pity she couldn't say the same about her knickers, which had ridden up her backside and were currently conducting an impromptu episiotomy. She should have gotten those a size bigger.

'Jim,' she whispered. 'Help.'

'I don't know,' said Jim's voice from behind her. 'The view's quite nice here.'

'Stop ogling my arse and pull me backwards.'

She heard him sigh and turned her head slightly to watch him calmly walk around the desk.

'If you'd just done things the sensible way, then you wouldn't be in this predicament,' he said smugly. 'I'll help if you take back what you said about me being a dick.'

He had come to a halt in front of her and her face was level with his groin.

'I can't do that,' she said.

'Why not?'

'Your flies are undone.'

Jim cursed, his hand immediately going to the offending zip. He gave it a tug.

'It's caught on something.' He moved closer to Penny. 'Can you see what it's caught on?'

'Are you wearing pink boxers?' she asked.

'Yes.'

'Good. Then it's not your willie. You'll have to wiggle it free?'

'My willie?'

'Don't be facetious. Stick your hand down and pull your boxers from behind. Then use your other hand to wiggle the zip.'

Jim did as she said, maintaining tension on the material as he manipulated the zipper.

'I can't get it up. I can't get it up,' he said through gritted teeth.

Rachel entered the lobby and drew to a sudden halt. A woman was bent double across the reception desk, her face in the groin of a writhing man who was ranting about not being able to get it up.

'Erm, what's going on here?' she asked.

Jim immediately froze, then took a small step back. Penny immediately slipped forward, her face mashing into his groin. Jim froze again, conscious that Penny's weight was now entirely supported by his crotch.

'It's not what it looks like,' came a muffled voice from the direction of his penis.

'She was leaning over the desk to look for a bell and she slipped,' he explained. 'I went round the desk to catch her.'

'With your willie?' asked Rachel, a distinctly sceptical note in her voice.

'Well, no. She noticed my zip was down.'

'He couldn't get it up,' said the muffled voice from the penis.

'So I heard,' said Rachel, her eyes sparkling with amusement.

'Look, do you mind?' said Jim, gesturing at Penny.

'Be my guest. Or probably better not be my guest if this is the sort of thing you two get up to,' Rachel said, chuckling to herself.

Jim lifted Penny by the shoulders and pushed her backwards across the desk until her backside cleared the edge. Her own weight did the rest, and seconds later, her feet were once more on the floor. Penny tugged at the bottom of her coat, which had ridden up to reveal rather more belly than she was comfortable with, then slid her feet into her wellies. She looked at Rachel, with her perfect blonde bob and crisply ironed blouse, and wondered if Rachel thought *she* looked windswept and interesting. No, Penny decided, she probably thinks I've been sleeping rough behind the bins at the supermarket.

'Sorry about that,' she said, her face still flushed from dangling downwards. 'We were hoping to speak to Pete Smellie. The Canadian guest?'

'I don't think he's here,' said Rachel, going to a cabinet. 'He went out this morning and I haven't seen him since. He definitely wasn't at dinner.' She opened the cabinet and checked the keys. 'Nope. His key's still here. The Cohens and Miss Klimova are in, if you want to speak with them.'

'And Anthony Woodbead?' asked Jim.

'He went out earlier and hasn't been back. His key's still here as well.'

'That's odd,' said Penny. 'With the weather clearing, the ferry would be going tomorrow. You'd think they'd be packing tonight. I realise Anthony Woodbead was only a day tripper, so he probably only has what he's bought to get him through the week. But Pete was booked to stay as part of his tour, so he must have quite a bit of luggage.'

'No,' said Rachel.

'He doesn't have luggage?' asked Penny.

'No, he hadn't booked a room. In fact, he didn't stay here on the night he arrived. He only pitched up the next day. The Sunday morning.'

'Then where did he stay on the Saturday night?' asked Jim.

'I don't know,' said Rachel. 'But it wasn't here. We had Mr Woodbead and the Cohens. Miss Klimova had already booked ahead for a two week stay. They four of them had a late supper on the Saturday night. I remember because they kept the bar open until 3am, and Martin and I could barely keep our eyes open. Mr Smellie came in on the Sunday morning, soaked to the skin and in desperate need of a hot bath.'

'Can we look in his room? We can't explain, but we need to find out what he's been up to,' said Penny.

There was an awkward pause, before Rachel gave them a rueful smile. 'I'm sorry. I can't let you do that.'

Jim hurried to smooth things over. 'It's okay. We shouldn't have asked. You've been a great help, Rachel. Say hello to Martin for us. Oh, and if Woodbead and Pete come back, please don't tell them we were looking for them.'

They left, thanking Rachel effusively, before scurrying back to the car, the wind at their backs this time speeding them along.

'Right. So, Pete and Woodbead haven't been seen for most of the day. Pete is Captain Rab's grandson, he lied about that and about booking his stay on the island, Woodbead is in cahoots with Captain Rab, Captain Rab was stabbed, Old Archie is dead and the real target of the shooting is still running around somewhere on the island. Is that a fair summation? What the hell is going on?' said

Jim, as soon as they were back in the car.

'I really don't know,' said Penny. 'It sounds like Woodbead was at the hotel so, whatever he's up to with Captain Rab, it certainly doesn't include him killing Old Archie. At least, he didn't pull the trigger. Which leaves us with Pete. Something's just occurred to me. You know what our parents said about keeping their heads down and not appearing in the newspapers or on social media?'

Jim nodded. 'Yes. You were right about that, by the way. They're not savvy enough about social media. We should teach them. Or, even better, get the twins to teach them.'

'Never mind that for now,' said Penny, peremptorily waving the suggestion away. 'I've just realised that someone *was* in the newspapers recently.'

'Who?' asked Jim, running through the list of Red Path members in his head.

'Old Archie.'

CHAPTER TWENTY

'Postie of the Year!' exclaimed Jim. 'You clever thing. If he was in The Red Path, someone could have recognised him, even after all these years. I don't get the connection, though. How would that lead Pete to Captain Rab? It's not as though Pete would know anything about Old Archie or recognise him in a photograph. I suppose his mum could have had old photographs from their Red Path days, but it's a bit of a stretch, especially if he was in Canada. The photograph was only in the Scottish newspapers.'

'You're right. He would have had to have been checking Scottish newspapers and have had the means of recognising Old Archie. It doesn't really get us further forward, but it does raise the possibility that, if Old Archie *was* a cult member, he could have been the intended victim. Which means that our witness was never the target.' Penny shook her head. 'Honestly, it's all a huge muddle now. We need to check if Old Archie belonged to The Red Path.'

Jim was already on it. 'I'm phoning my dad this time,' he said, dialling the number and pressing the speaker icon. 'I don't have the energy for another conversation with your mother. No offence.'

'None taken. You should try living with her.'

There was a rustle on the other end of the line, as Mr Space fumbled with his phone, then a tentative voice said, 'Hello? Am I coming through loud and clear?'

'Yes, you've got it the right way up this time, Dad. Are you okay?'

'Not really. I'm feeling...uh...I don't know what I'm feeling.'

Jim's brow creased and he leaned towards the phone. 'Has something happened?'

'Nothing bad,' Mr Space reassured him. 'Just…confusing. I gave Jeanie Campbell a lift to Eileen's and, before she got out of the car, I said to her, "I know this isn't a good time, but when the boys are back safe and sound, would you like to go out for lunch sometime?" She gave me this queer look, then grabbed me by the ears and snogged the face off me. I'm telling you, Jim, tongues and everything. Then she sits back and says, "Sod lunch. I've always fancied you, Ivor Space. Come round to mine tomorrow and I'll show you what you've been missing all these years." Next thing you know, the car door goes and she's off into Eileen's. This is my first foray into dating since your mum…you know. Do you have any…erm…do you think I need to use…protection?'

'Dad, you're on speaker. Penny is here.'

'Oh, sorry, Penny. You didn't need to hear that. What do you think, though? I know the ladies take responsibility for that sort of thing as well these days.'

Penny stared at the phone, her startled face pale in the ghostly glow of the screen. 'I…I don't think pregnancy is an issue, Mr Space, and she's not likely to have any…erm…infections. I don't expect you need to bother. I have a tube of…ooh…something that will help…erm…smooth the way. I'll get Jim to drop it by in the morning.'

'Okaaaay,' said Jim. 'Now that's sorted, can we tell you why we phoned? Was Old Archie a member of The Red Path?'

There was a brief silence on the other end, then Mr Space said, 'I don't suppose it will make any difference to him now if I tell you. Yes, he was. He and Elsie were partners on and off.'

'That's all I need to know. Thanks, Dad.'

'Before you go, is there any news of Eileen and Kenny's boys?'

'No. I'm away to phone Kenny now. I'll let you know when they find them.'

Jim hung up and immediately dialled Kenny's number. He hung up again a few seconds later. 'Still going to voicemail.'

'Try Eileen. See if she's heard from him. He shouldn't have been out of signal range for this long.'

Jim dialled Eileen's number and she immediately answered, her voice anxious.

'Kenny hasn't been in touch,' she said, before they could tell her that they'd called for the same reason. 'I'm so worried. He should have checked in with me by now in case the boys came home.'

'Do you know where he was planning to look?' asked Jim.

'He didn't exactly give me a list.'

'Write down all the places you can think of. Penny and I will be down in a minute to get the list, and we'll go and look for Kenny. Don't panic. None of them will have gone far,' Jim reassured her.

He hung up and looked at Penny. 'Fuck. We're chasing our tails with bloody Pete, and now Kenny's gone missing. We should have been out there helping to find Ricky and Gervais.'

Penny stared bleakly past the smattering of leaves on the windscreen, yet more guilt twisting her insides. Rationally, they both knew there was nothing they could have done. Running around the island like a pair of headless chickens would have made no difference to where they found themselves now. Yet she, too, was kicking herself. Eileen was stuck at home with her bossy, and apparently quite randy, mother, fretting about her family, and Penny had so far been as much use as a condom on Furry Mancock's mid-morning snack.

As Jim started the car, she leaned back in her seat and gazed out of the passenger side window, towards the alleyway next to the hotel. A flash of white caught her attention and she sat forward.

'What's up?' asked Jim.

'Nothing. I thought I saw something. Probably just the wind blowing chip wrappers around,' she said, looking at the shuttered chip shop. Yet she couldn't rid herself of the uneasy feeling that someone had been watching them from the alleyway.

Eileen's kitchen was spotlessly clean and tidy. The dresser, usually home to an assorted variety of chinaware, important letters, things the boys made at school and worming pills for the cat, now stood neat and tidy, the boys' creations taking pride of place in front of Eileen's granny's cake stand.

'When I'm anxious, I clean,' Eileen explained. 'Don't worry, I've done your list as well. I just want to check it one more time to make sure I haven't missed anything out.'

Penny gave her a hug and confided, 'When I'm anxious, I get the squirts.'

'I'm the opposite,' said Mrs Campbell. 'I get completely bunged up. I can promise you that, after everything that's happened this evening, there will be no movement for at least three days.'

Penny was delighted. 'I have just the thing for you, Mrs Campbell. I'll drop it off with Eileen tomorrow.'

'When I'm stressed, I get cravings for strawberries, chocolate and bacon,' said Jim, with a wink. 'Anyway, Mrs Campbell, what's this I hear about you sexually harassing my dad?'

'Sexually harassing,' scoffed Mrs Campbell. 'The man asked me out for lunch. I just cut out the middleman. At our age, there's no time to waste. And his tongue was as far down my throat as mine was down his. Mark my words, I'll make him a happy man.'

'Hmm. You'll either make him happy or put the fear of God into him,' said Jim.

'Either way,' said Mrs Campbell, nonchalantly primping her auburn bun, 'he'll have had an experience. Your mother, God rest her beautiful soul, has been gone a while now and it's about time he got back in the saddle. I'll make sure he gets the ride of his life.'

'Aye, well, go easy on the whip, Mrs C,' said Jim.

While they'd been talking, Penny had opened the homework laptop and googled "The Red Path cult." Most of the results related to the raid on the farm and the trial in the seventies. However, one article was a "where are they now" follow up from 2018. She clicked on the article and scrolled past the recap of old events, eventually coming to a section which detailed the reporter's efforts to locate the group in the present day.

"Much reduced in number, The Red Path members are known to have fled to Michigan, where they once more rallied around Thaddeus Height. It would appear that the United Kingdom authorities were hard on their tail. Within a few months, the US received an extradition request. Height or one of his followers must have gotten wind of this because, shortly afterwards, the group disappeared. It is, however, hard to disappear entirely, even in an age before computerised records were ubiquitous. Land records show that Height had purchased the deeds to a farm in Ontario, Canada while the cult was still active in Scotland. It is clear that he was planning ahead for the day that they would have to flee their homeland. What is not known is whether the members of the group who gave evidence against him, the so-called outer circle, were aware of his plans and joined him there. Certainly, there has been no trace of them since the trial ended."

The kitchen door opened, and Eileen entered, clutching a sheet of paper. 'Here's the list. It's everywhere I could think of.'

She handed the list to Penny, who quickly scanned it and folded it away in her pocket. Penny tugged Jim's arm, urging him to hurry up, and they hurried back to the car, promising to call Eileen as soon as they had something to report.

The moment they were back in the car, Penny told

Jim about what she had read.

'If the cult ended up in Ontario, Pete's grandmother, Irene, was probably with them. It's safe to assume that her daughter, Elspeth, would have been brought up in The Red Path, even if she and her husband didn't live on the farm. Someone must have taken Pete in when his parents died, and I'm betting it was The Red Path. No doubt Thaddeus Height or one of his minions was keeping tabs on the Scottish newspapers. I think someone recognised Old Archie from the Postman of the Year articles and sent Pete here.'

She pulled Eileen's list from her pocket and gave it to Jim.

'Does anywhere jump out at you?' she asked.

Jim took a moment to read the list. 'We could check the river down by the park. There's a tyre swing down there that someone put up over the summer. The boys wouldn't be stupid enough to go in the river, would they?'

'How did you even pass any vet exams? Think about it, you idiot. Where is the one sheltered spot on this list?'

Penny could practically see the lightbulb go on above Jim's head as he said, 'Ah. The fort.'

'Where is a dry, sheltered place you would go if you'd just killed someone and didn't want to be found?' she asked.

'The woods?'

'And what if you'd had all day to plan your escape and find somewhere in the woods to hole up overnight? Where would you choose?'

'The fort! That explains the money clip. It belonged to Pete. He must have killed Old Archie and spent the night at the boys' fort!'

'Bingo,' said Penny. 'It's also probably one of the first places that Kenny searched for the boys. Remember how excited Ricky and Gervais were about their fort and capturing the murderer? I bet they didn't take kindly to

Eileen banning them from going. Let's hope that Pete didn't go back to the fort today, because if he's there then Kenny and the boys are in grave danger. I suggest we go there right away.'

'Motion seconded and carried,' said Jim, starting the ignition and backing onto the lane.

With a squeal of tyres and a very satisfying boy racer spray of gravel, he accelerated up the narrow lane towards the main road leading to the woods. He drove past the houses, their curtains now drawn against the blustery night, speeding towards the car park at the end. As they passed the lanes to their right, the wind buffeted the car and Jim's hold on the steering wheel tightened. Penny gripped the edge of her seat, sure that they were going to be blown off course, into the cars parked neatly on their left. She imagined the people in the houses, blithely making their sandwiches for work the next day and arguing with their darling offspring that Sunday night is not the time to announce they needed fifty obscure ingredients for a school cookery lesson the next morning, unaware that their metal boxes of pride and joy were within a whisker of being mangled heaps of bitter disappointment.

'Slow down,' she warned Jim. 'We won't get there any faster if you kill us both.'

He ignored her and gripped the steering wheel harder, his own sense of urgency impelling him to shave those vital few seconds off the short journey. His relief at finally being able to do something useful fuelling a determination to…do what? Be a saviour? Thirty seconds wasn't going to make much difference. He glanced over at Penny, pale and tense beside him, and realised she was terrified. Jim didn't want her to be scared. He wanted her to be happy and secure. He eased off on the throttle and saw her relax. This protective feeling towards her took him by surprise, and he resolved to revisit it later, when his brain was less full of cults, murder, stabbing and missing people. And his dad sleeping with Mrs Campbell. He wasn't sure how he felt about that one, nor whether he ever wanted to revisit it.

The car bounced up the short, gravelled incline and pulled to a halt in the car park. Penny jumped out, her ears instantly assailed by the roar of the wind in the trees above. Another vehicle was parked in the corner. As Jim raked through Phil's boot in search of his big torch, Penny took her phone from her pocket and shone it at the other vehicle. A faded sticker in the rear windscreen announced, "Baby Bates On Board."

'It's Kenny's car,' she yelled at Jim above the noise of the trees. 'Have you found the torch?'

'Right here,' he said, holding up a large oblong and directing a beam of light at her.

Temporarily blinded, she raised a hand to shield her eyes, and he instantly lowered the torch, leaving her to blink away the white sun that now filled her vision.

'Sorry,' he said.

'You know when I told you I couldn't take back calling you a dick?'

'I said I was sorry!'

'You drove here like a madman and now we can't go anywhere because I can't see.'

'Well, you're not perfect either, Miss Why-Walk-Round-A-Desk-When-You-Can-Crawl-Over-It! How much time did you waste, dangling there with your arse in the air and your giant camel toe hanging out?'

'My knickers slid up,' Penny snapped, relieved that it was too dark for him to see her burning cheeks.

Jim took a deep breath and silently counted to three.

'I'm sorry,' he said. 'Sorry about the torch, and sorry about the camel toe. That comment was out of order.'

'Was it a really big camel toe?' Penny asked, meekly.

'You'd have made a dromedary proud,' Jim assured her.

'There's no need for that!' she exclaimed.

'Alright! Don't get the hump.'

Penny's vision had finally cleared, and she could see the entrance to the woods in the faint glow from the streetlights in the road below. If she'd thought the woods were spooky earlier, they looked positively terrifying now. Jim directed the torch beam at the path, and they set off, Penny clinging to his free arm.

A few metres in, the wind became a distant swirl high in the treetops, its presence marked below by the crack and thud of branches as they fell to the ground. Penny suspected that she should be glad to be walking in a stiff breeze, rather than pushing through a gale as she had for the past week. Yet she felt as though the eyes of unseen creatures were tracking her every move. As though giants were tearing the trees, throwing great limbs in their rage. Any moment now, one of these great limbs would come crashing down upon them, crushing their skulls and beating them into the mulch underfoot. Or perhaps she was letting her imagination run away with her. More likely, there were a few rabbits in the bushes, and she'd get a sound whack with a branch. She looked up, trying to reassure herself that bits of tree weren't going to rain down on her. She looked left, right, behind her; telling herself that nothing was there. All was black. Except…what was that? A pin prick of light bobbed in the distance.

Penny squealed and wrapped her arms around Jim, tucking her face into his shoulder. He carried on walking, while she clung on, skipping along sideways like a jaunty crab.

'I'm not stopping because you want a pee, your feet hurt or you think you've seen a ghost,' he told her.

'It's not that,' she said, panting with the effort to keep up. 'Look behind you. There's someone there!'

CHAPTER TWENTY-ONE

Jim stopped and turned to look behind him, Penny shuffling round, her face still buried in his shoulder. He switched off the torch and waited a moment, staring left, right and straight ahead to where he presumed the path lay. He listened intently. Nothing. Only unrelenting darkness and the sound of branches falling in the wind.

'I can't see anything,' he said.

'There was a torch,' insisted Penny. 'I could see a bright circle some way back along the path.'

'Well, there's nothing there now. Could it be from when I shone my torch in your eyes? You might still have a bright dot from that.'

Penny was going to protest that she had definitely seen a torch light, but the more she thought about it, the more she began to doubt herself. Eventually, she sighed and admitted that Jim was probably right, and they continued their march, with Jim muttering something about "bloody women with fertile imaginations" and how at least you knew where you were with a sick cow.

Although they walked reasonably quickly, they were slowed by the path disappearing as it twisted and turned. One moment it would be there ahead of them in the torchlight, the next Jim was confidently steering them into a tree. Judging by the level of curse words, he was working himself up into a temper. Penny didn't think she could cope with that right now. It wasn't as if she could even storm off in a huff. Although a swift knee in the nuts wasn't out of the question. Plotting genitalcide was probably a sign of her own rising frustration, she decided. It had taken them about ten minutes to reach the bench earlier. This time, it felt like it had taken days.

Suddenly, Jim's torchlight fell on a familiar object. Thank goodness. The bloody bench at last.

'This is it,' she hissed, detaching herself from Jim and putting a hand on the back of the bench. 'Switch the torch off. We have to carefully feel our way behind the rhododendron bush. If Pete's there, we don't want him to see us coming. Be as quiet as possible and try not to swear, at least not out loud.'

Jim did as he was told, and the world was plunged into darkness. Penny felt him take hold of the back of her coat, and they performed a strange, stumbling little conga around the rhododendron. It was tough going, the little hillocks in the grass catching their feet and branches plucking at their clothing. Penny led the way, letting memory guide her to the spot from where she had previously spied the fort. For a few minutes, it was so dark that she wasn't sure whether her eyes were open or closed. She could hear Jim cursing under his breath behind her and started to wonder if she was leading them in the wrong direction.

Her misgivings were unfounded, and before long, she discerned a faint light through the trees. She reached back to grab Jim's hand. He gave hers an answering squeeze, letting her know that he, too, had seen the light. Together, they tiptoed gingerly forward, testing each step for twigs or anything which might alert the occupants of the fort to their presence.

As they drew closer, Penny could hear the sound of whimpering. She pressed Jim's hand to signal to him to stop, and they rested behind a tree, straining to hear more.

'Please Mister. We just want to go home. Daddy didn't see nothing. Daddy, wake up! Please. Please Mister. We'll take him home to Mummy and we promise we won't tell.'

The high voice was trembling, terror resonating in every word. It was like a knife in Penny's heart. Her eyes were very much open now. She knew this because she was blinking away tears. Tears of panic, horror or white-hot anger, she wasn't sure. The only thing she *was* sure of right now was that whatever it took, those boys were going home to their own beds tonight.

Wiping her face, she whispered to Jim, 'That's Ricky. Let's get a bit closer.'

Once more, they picked their way towards the fort, circling around the edge of the small clearing to get a better view. In front of the small, ramshackle hut, someone had built a fire. The boys were standing behind the fire, and from this short distance, Penny could see that their faces were rigid with fear. Next to them stood Peter Smellie, the long knife in his hand glinting in the firelight. However, it was the third figure which drew an audible gasp from Penny. On the ground in front of the fire, Kenny lay unmoving, a dark patch on the grass beneath his head.

There was an object in the fire. At first, Penny couldn't figure out what it was, until she looked again at Pete, who by this time was walking back and forth in front of the fire, waving the knife at Ricky and Gervais. It was his cast, she realised. He wasn't wearing his cast. He must have been faking the injury all along, presumably because he had a ruddy great knife tucked inside it. The knife itself looked vicious, the long, serrated blade curving upwards towards the tip. Something tickled the back of her brain, and the words "zombie knife" sprang to mind. She had no idea how she knew this. How the hell did Pete keep that thing in his cast without shredding himself, she wondered.

Surroundings assessed, Penny turned her attention to Pete. The boys were tearfully pleading with him to let them go. He seemed agitated, pacing up and down in front of the fire.

'Shut the fuck up and let me think,' he told the boys. 'Your Daddy's dead you stupid little shits, and if you don't keep your goddamn mouths shut, you're next.'

Ricky and Gervais stepped back, cowering in fear against the edge of the fort. Pete seemed to be muttering loudly to himself and Penny shifted forward a little, trying to hear.

He seemed to be having a debate with himself. 'We don't kill innocent children,' he was saying. 'Stupid little fucks should never have come here. They're leaving me no choice. I have to get off this shithole of an island tomorrow. I could tie them up. The Bridge would say tie them up and move them out of the way, but it's safer to just kill them. The Bridge will forgive me. Yes, he will. Or I can say this one wasn't me. It's just a coincidence. They can't tell anyone anything if they're dead. Fuck. This was supposed to be a simple shot in the head and out.'

He stopped pacing and seemed to make up his mind. 'Sorry about this, boys.'

'I'm going in,' Penny whispered to Jim. She felt him catch the hem of her coat as she strode off, but she pulled free and made towards the clearing.

'Fuckity fuck fuck fuck,' said Jim, stomping after her. 'In for a Penny...'

Pete was turning towards the children, knife poised to deliver a blow, when Penny's voice rang across the clearing.

'Not so fast, Peter Smellie. Boys, it's Auntie Penny. Get away from him. Run!'

Gervais didn't need to be told twice. Realising that the cavalry had come, he bolted into the woods. Ricky, however, hesitated, looking at the body of his father. The few seconds of indecision was all it took for Pete to grab him and hold the knife to his throat.

Penny drew to a halt next to Kenny's body. She didn't so much as glance at it. Her focus was entirely on the man with the knife.

'Let Ricky go, Pete. Where does it end? What are you going to do? Kill him then kill me?'

'And then me?' asked Jim. 'Because I'm a much tougher prospect.'

'Then what about the other people who come

looking for the boys? They're getting a search party together right now. Pretty soon these woods will be crawling with people. You can't kill them all,' shouted Penny, the anger coursing through her.

How dare this deluded fool threaten her people. She could feel Jim tense beside her, ready to pounce. Pete was sweating now, despite the cool breeze, his hand temporarily lifting the knife from Ricky's throat to swipe at his own brow.

'And how are you going to get off this shithole of an island?' Penny yelled, hoping that if she could just keep the pressure on, she might distract Pete enough for Ricky to break free. 'There's no ferry. Captain Rab won't be sailing you out of here tomorrow.'

'I know that, you stupid bitch,' snarled Pete. 'Who do you think killed him?' A note of triumph entered his voice as he continued, 'Me. That's who. Old fucker was on me day and night to turn myself in. He knew I was sent by The Red Path to kill Old Archie. Thaddeus saw Archie's photograph in the Evening Express, and it was what he'd been waiting for all these years. Revenge on the traitors who tried to take him down. Well, now I got two of them.'

Despite the anger and growing dread, Penny was secretly delighted. This was just like on telly. The killer won't stop talking and confesses all. She decided to throw in a question.

'So,' she said, trying to sound confident. 'So, you shot Old Archie, then stabbed your grandpa. Big hooray for you. How did you even know he was your grandpa?'

'He came to me. I know, right! He's supposed to be hiding from the big, bad, boogie man, then one look at me and he throws caution to the wind,' Pete crowed. 'Grandpa had been keeping tabs on me and Mom all these years and recognised me as soon as he laid eyes on me on the ferry. Apparently, I'm the spitting image of his brother in his younger days, so the sad bastard said he couldn't bear to turn me in himself. That didn't last long. This morning he told me the storm was clearing and, as soon as it did, the police would be here, and he'd tell them everything. He had to go.'

'Sorry to break it to you, pal,' said Jim. 'Captain Rab's not dead. Which leaves you rather fucked, doesn't it? What were you planning to do? Kill everyone on the island and swim to Aberdeen?'

'Like I'm gonna tell you.' He pulled Ricky closer and began to sidle away from the fire. 'Now, you stay there nice and easy, and me and the kid will slide on out of here. I'll be gone in the morning, and if you're very good boys and girls, I might even let you have him back alive.'

Ricky was visibly trembling. His legs had given way and he clung to Pete's arm around his head for support as he was dragged along, the knife at his exposed throat.

Her bravado instantly dissolving, Penny pleaded, 'He's just a wee boy. Please let him go. Ricky, you'll be okay. I'm going to get you home. I'll find Gervais and we'll take you both home to Mummy.'

Pete gave a high-pitched bark of laughter and said, 'Auntie Penny is lying, boy. You're coming with Uncle Pete.'

He was almost at the edge of the clearing now. Another few steps and he would disappear into the darkness, taking Ricky with him. Penny was desperately trying to think of a way to stall him when a voice from the trees to her left said, 'I don't think so. Stay where you are.'

Penny gasped and quickly glanced around to see a familiar figure emerging into the clearing, the gun in its hand pointed directly at Pete. He instantly froze, his face a mask of shock. Penny could almost see the cog wheels turning in his brain, as he frantically tried to plot a way out of this situation. She couldn't help herself. She clearly watched far too much TV, but she was going to have to say it.

'Never bring a knife to a gun fight. Also, good for you Sandra Next Door. The freezer bag's still hanging off the handle by the way.'

'I know,' said Sandra Next Door through gritted teeth. 'It's not like I do this every day. Just thank your lucky stars that Geoff roped me into doing the props for Annie Get Your Gun, otherwise I wouldn't have a clue how these things work.'

'I don't understand,' said Pete. 'Why the fuck is ageing soccer mom here?'

'You don't get to understand. Put the laddie down and put your hands up because I am not afraid to use this thing,' Sandra Next Door instructed him.

The gun twitched in her hand and Penny felt her heart in her throat as, for a split second, her brain urgently telegraphed that Sandra Next Door was about to shoot.

Pete, on the other hand, appeared to relax slightly. His demeanour became more confident. 'You're not going to shoot me, lady. Look at you. Your hand's trembling so much, you're just as likely to hit the kid. You may know how a gun works, but you sure can't aim.'

'Try me. Just try me,' said Sandra Next Door, her eyes glittering dangerously in the firelight as she brought her other hand up to steady the gun. 'I've had a very long, very shitty day. My husband's pissed as a newt and put one of his high heels through the new lino in the bathroom. You do not want to mess with me right now.'

'You really don't want to mess with her,' said a voice from behind Sandra Next Door.

'What is this? Does anyone else want to join the damn party?' shouted Pete, as Anthony Woodbead stepped into the circle of light.

'My dear chap,' Anthony said calmly, 'you seem to have got yourself in rather a pickle. Tell me, when you were growing up, did you always want to be a child killer? You clearly have no empathy for the boy, but perhaps you should give some thought to how many years it will add to your sentence. And how popular you'll be with the other inmates.'

He held up his phone and pressed the screen.

Ricky's voice rang out, loud and clear, 'Please Mister. We just want to go home. Daddy didn't see nothing. Daddy, wake up! Please. Please Mister. We'll take him home to Mummy and we promise we won't tell.'

'Maybe I'll let this go viral, after I've played it for the judge. Because you, sir, are going nowhere except jail. Now, Sandra Next Door, hand me the gun.'

'If you come anywhere near this gun, I'll shoot you,' said Sandra Next door, a note of grim determination in her voice.

'My dear, I'm here to help, not hinder. I'm also a top-class marksman with a smidgeon more experience than you. Anything you can do, I can do better. Not that you aren't doing well, of course. In fact, you're doing a marvellous job. However, there is a tiny chance that you could hit the child, and neither of us want that. So, if I could just…'

Sandra flicked him a look of disgust. 'You're in it up to your neck just as much as he is. I wouldn't trust you to vacuum my living room carpet. I was watching you while you followed Penny and Jim.'

She risked a brief glance at Jim. 'I didn't go home at eight o'clock. I spotted him,' she tilted her head towards Woodbead, 'following you, so I followed him. He was running up and down those lanes for all he was worth. I'll say something for him, he's very fit.'

'I don't know about that,' said Penny. 'I prefer my men with a full head of hair.'

She noticed Jim surreptitiously run a hand through his own brown thatch.

Sandra Next Door snapped, 'This is no time for your so-called witty remarks, Penny. When the two of you were in the church hall, he broke into your car, Jim. Was anything stolen?'

'I hate to break up the mothers meeting,' Pete interrupted, his voice dripping with exaggerated ennui. 'If there's nothing else, we'll be going now. Good luck with shooting me, lady.'

Sandra Next Door shuffled her feet apart and steadied the gun, taking aim just as Anthony Woodbead leapt forward to grab it from her. There was a brief tussle, followed by a loud crack as the gun went off, the bullet shooting high into the dark trees. Sandra stumbled backwards, leaving Anthony holding the gun. He whirled around and aimed it a Pete. But Pete was inching backwards, holding Ricky in front of him.

'To quote Annie Oakley,' Pete sneered, 'Aim at a high mark and you'll hit it. No, not the first time, nor the second time. Maybe not the—'

The smug speech was cut short by an almighty crash, followed by a hard thud, and Pete and Ricky crumpled to the ground.

The tableau around the fire held for a second, before Penny broke free, screaming, 'Ricky!' as she sprinted towards the still forms in the semi-darkness at the edge of the clearing.

Jim and Woodbead sprinted after her, quickly catching up as she sank to her knees and dragged Ricky out from under his unconscious attacker. He lay still on the grass, his eyes closed. She brushed his hair back from his face, paling at the sight of the streak of blood on his neck. She could feel a wail, a pure animal howl, rising within her, but as her mouth stretched to release it, Ricky coughed, and his eyes flickered open.

'Auntie Penny? Why are you making a funny face?'

'Oh my God. Oh my God. I thought we'd lost you. Where does it hurt?'

'Nowhere, Auntie Penny. He was holding me so tight I couldn't breathe and there was a bang and another bang and he fell on top of me and I got smuffocated.'

'Your neck. Did he cut your neck?'

Ricky raised a hand to feel his neck as Penny searched through her pockets for a tissue. A hand appeared at her shoulder, offering a neatly folded white handkerchief and she looked up to see Sandra Next Door smiling down at her, tears in her eyes. She took the handkerchief and dabbed at Ricky's neck, relieved to see that the wound was small and shallow.

'I've never been so frightened in my life,' said Sandra Next Door. She crouched down and put an arm around Ricky, helping him to sit up. 'You better go and find his brother,' she told Penny. 'I'll look after this one.'

Penny gave her a grateful smile and stood up, scanning the edges of the trees. 'Gervais! Gervais!' Oh, dear Lord, if he'd gone too far into the woods, they'd never find him before morning.

However, her panic was short-lived. She heard a small voice cry, 'Auntie Penny!' and Gervais appeared from his hiding place behind a large tree.

She ran to him, picked him up and carried him closer to the fire so she could check him for wounds. Cuts and grazes, and what would likely be a belter of a black eye.

'I hit the bad man to stop him hitting Daddy with the big branch, and he hit me in the face,' Gervais explained, his voice quivering.

Penny drew him to her and whispered, 'The bad man won't be hurting anyone again. You're safe now, my wee lamb. I'm going to take you over to a nice lady called Sandra. She's looking after Ricky. Then I'm going to call Mummy to come and take you both home. You've been the bravest boy in the world.'

The idea that he was brave seemed to cheer Gervais up. 'Did we catch the murderer? Ricky said if we went to the fort, we could catch him.'

'Yes, you caught the murderer,' said Penny, picking him up and carried him back to the edge of the clearing.

Gervais looked behind her and pointed towards the fire. 'Why is Daddy still sleeping? He missed all the good bits.'

'I'll go and find out,' said Penny, gently setting him down next to Sandra Next Door. 'You stay with Sandra and

Ricky.'

Jim and Woodbead were still crouched over Pete. Penny tugged at Jim's arm and nodded towards Kenny. A wave of dread swept over her, and her heart ached for Eileen, Ricky and Gervais. She had a feeling that today was about to get even worse.

They made their way over to the still body by the fire. Having watched Gordon earlier, they at least had some idea of what to do this time. Penny held her breath as she felt Kenny's neck for a pulse. Time seemed to stand still.

She would never in her life forget the sense of relief when she felt that faint beat beneath her fingers. Close up, the blood on the grass beneath Kenny's head was a thick, glutinous smear and she suspected that the bleeding had stopped some time ago. She and Jim agreed that they shouldn't move him in case they made things worse. Jim called Doc Harris, then went to the edge of the clearing to get his torch from where he'd dropped it in his haste to follow Penny earlier. He was exhausted, but there was still much to do.

'Where are you going?' Penny asked.

'I told the doc I'd meet him and the paramedics in the car park.'

'What about Pete? What if he wakes up?'

'Oh, Pete's not waking up ever again,' Jim said grimly. 'That great crash was a tree limb landing on his head. Given what he tried to do to Kenny here, it's quite ironic that he got his head caved in by a tree.'

CHAPTER TWENTY-TWO

When Penny later reflected on the events of that night, she realised that the long wait for the paramedics was the hardest part. She had been running on adrenaline for hours, reacting instinctively in the face of danger, and in the sudden calm after the storm, she couldn't seem to stop trembling. As soon as Jim left, she beckoned Sandra Next Door and the boys over.

'Daddy has had a bad bump on the head, but I think he's going to be okay. He would probably like it if you looked after him. You can't move him, though. Just hold his hand and talk to him until the doctor gets here,' she told Ricky and Gervais.

She asked Sandra Next Door to sit with Kenny and the boys while she phoned Eileen. Her hands were shaking, and it took several attempts to press the buttons on her phone. At one point she accidentally called Elsie, who was next to Eileen on her contacts list, but hung up before Elsie could answer. Eventually she heard ringing and Eileen's tremulous 'hello?' on the other end of the line.

'Eileen, it's Penny. We've found Ricky and Gervais. They're both fine.'

'Oh, thank God. Where were they? Is Kenny there? Where's Kenny?'

'They'd gone up to the fort, like you thought. Kenny's here, but he's injured,' said Penny. 'Don't panic. He's taken a blow to the head and he's unconscious, but he's alive. Jim's going down to the car park now, to meet Doc Harris. We're off the beaten track, so they need someone to guide them. If you hurry, you might arrive in time to come up with them. But if you miss them, wait in the car park and I'll send Jim back down for you.'

Eileen didn't wait for further information. There was a click, and she was gone. With their car already commandeered by Kenny for the search, Eileen would be on foot, and Penny could imagine her already sprinting up the lane, telling the wind to 'va te faire foutre' and cursing herself for forgetting to change out of her carpet slippers. Eileen shone like a brand-new soul in this world, which to Penny's mind, made this tragedy all the more devastating.

Penny watched as Anthony Woodbead rose from where he had been crouching near Pete's body. He ambled towards the fire, his arms full of branches, and smiled at Penny.

'We need to keep the fire going. For the light, you see. If the fire goes out, it'll be hard for them to find us. I had to use my phone torch to find my way here, and I doubt that'll be much use.'

'How did you know we were here?' asked Penny.

Woodbead shrugged. 'It's like Sandra Next Door said, I was following you. She's very good, you know. I didn't realise that she was following *me*! I'd been watching you since I spotted you both outside the hotel in the late afternoon. I believe you were loudly remonstrating with Jim about his farts at the time. Fortunately, it wasn't too difficult as the two of you seem to spend far too much time either at the harbour or the Square. Admittedly, I lost you for a while when you detoured to the church hall, but the rain had stopped, and it seemed like a nice evening for a brisk walk around town looking for Jim's car.'

'How do you even know what Jim's car looks like?'

Woodbead dug into his pocket and produced something shiny. With a rueful smile, he handed it over. 'Sorry. Jim's car key. After you had your little adventure in Captain Rab's garden, I simply went outside and pressed until something beeped. You shouldn't leave your bag in an unattended vehicle, Penny. Anyone could go through it and find your lube.'

'That wasn't…it was a mistake. Anyway, what were

you doing at Captain Rab's?'

'All in good time, dear lady. More to the point, what were you doing at Captain Rab's? I assume you went back looking for the key.'

Penny nodded miserably. 'We found him in his cottage at lunchtime. He'd been stabbed. He'd clearly let his attacker in the back door, so we thought it must be someone he knew. We were worried that the police would search the house for evidence, and we couldn't risk them finding Jim's key, so we went back for it in the evening. We didn't find it, and someone came in while we were there. I thought it might be you.'

'No. It was Pete. I expect he waited until he thought the coast was clear then tried his luck in case anyone had left a door open after Captain Rab was taken to hospital.'

'So, if we hadn't gone in to get the key, he wouldn't have been able to make off with evidence. It's our fault he stole some papers off the table,' Penny said gloomily.

'Don't blame yourself. He'd probably just have gone round the back and found another way in. Also, he doesn't have the papers. Not any longer.' Woodbead grinned at her and patted his pocket.

'What's in them?' asked Penny.

'Nothing you need to know about. Just some notes that Captain Rab made. Come on, I have something to show you.' He stood up and beckoned to Penny to follow him.

They walked across the clearing to Pete's body. Penny shuddered at the sight. She hadn't noticed in her blind panic to free Ricky, but part of the man's head had sunk in on itself. She felt slightly sick and wondered what Woodbead could possibly have to show her that would make it worth putting her through this.

Woodbead crouched down and shone his phone torch at a thick branch near Pete's head. Something embedded in the end of it glinted in the beam of light.

'Do you see that?' he said. 'It's a bullet. That part of the limb is rotten, and it was probably almost ready to come down in the wind. Sandra Next Door's bullet just finished Mother Nature's job. But it's up to you whether you tell her. She might be upset that she indirectly killed Pete.'

Penny couldn't help giving him a sly grin. 'This is Sandra Next Door we're talking about. She'll be bloody delighted.'

He gave a short laugh. 'Yes. Balls of steel, that one.'

His bout of humour ended abruptly, however, when Penny asked, 'Who are you, Anthony Woodbead? Because we know that's not your real name.'

Woodbead considered for a moment, then said, 'Come to the hotel for lunch tomorrow and I'll explain. I have to make some calls first. I'll see you and Jim there at one. And please, rest assured that I'm not a threat. In fact, I'm quite the opposite.'

They went back to sit with Sandra Next Door, Ricky and Gervais until Jim returned. Sandra had taken off her coat and draped it over Kenny to keep him warm. Penny retrieved the sleeping bag from the fort and wrapped it around the children. Every so often, Woodbead would toss another log in the fire, sending a shower of sparks whirling into the night air. The little group sat quietly, huddled together in the firelight, and a sense of peace washed over Penny. Had it not been for the dead body in the corner, she could almost have believed herself on a camping trip. The silence felt strange, Penny thought. Why was it so strange? Then she realised that the wind had finally died down.

She was close to nodding off when she heard feet crashing through the undergrowth. The sound of voices was soon accompanied by torch beams cutting through the clearing. Voluble swearing heralded the arrival of Jim, who was closely followed by Doc Harris and the two paramedics they'd met earlier.

'You two are filling up my hospital,' he said sternly, glaring at Penny and Jim.

'Ah, come on, doc. It's hardly our fault,' Jim protested.

Doc Harris harrumphed and bent over Kenny. The paramedics had already crouched down and were examining him.

'He's unconscious,' said one. 'Nasty head wound by the look of things. We can't see any other obvious injuries, but it's difficult to tell in this light. We'll need to get him into the ambulance.' He looked around at the trees. 'Goodness knows how we're going to do that.'

'Very carefully,' said Doc Harris matter-of-factly. 'Right, let's have a look at the other one. Jim, bring the big torch.'

Before he could turn away, Penny caught Jim's arm.

'I told Eileen to wait in the car park if she didn't get there in time to come with you. I said you'd go back down for her.'

'It's okay,' Jim assured her. 'I saw her. She came out in her slippers, so we decided it would probably be better if she waited there. She'd only have slowed us down. Mind you, slippers or not, she must have belted up that road to beat Doc Harris to the car park.'

Penny was relieved. She hated the thought of Eileen stuck down in the car park on her own, but at least she knew help was on its way to Kenny and that the boys were safe. Still, she would be out of her mind with worry. Her train of thought was interrupted by Doc Harris, who was kneeling by Pete.

'Aye,' said the doc. 'Dead. We can't leave him here. Firstly, the animals will get him and secondly, we don't know when the police will be here. Hopefully, that's the storm over, but we're in the middle of the North Sea after all. We only have the one stretcher, so we're going to have to make two trips.'

In response, Jim winked at the doc and strode towards the fort. With a great heave, he hauled the tarpaulin off the roof and returned, trailing the enormous plastic sheet behind him.

'Will this do?' he asked.

Doc Harris eyed the filthy tarp and said, 'We'll need to brush the muck off it, but aye, I don't suppose he's in any position to mind. I don't know where we'll put him, though.'

Jim winked once more, took out his phone and dialled a number.

'Mrs Hubbard. It's Jim. Do you think your Douglas would mind moving the ice lollies into your kitchen freezer?'

It was almost midnight when Penny and Jim arrived back at Valhalla, Pete's body securely stowed in the boot of Jim's car. Penny couldn't remember ever having felt so tired. Her whole body ached for sleep. The thought of her nice warm bed with its dip in the middle was all that was keeping her going. She didn't envy Jim, whose journey towards his own bed was being prolonged by a pit stop at Mrs Hubbard's to deliver a corpse.

'Are you sure you don't want me to come?' Penny asked him.

'No, get yourself off to your scratcher. I'll come by in the morning,' he said.

Penny leaned over and kissed him gently on the cheek. 'Are you sure you don't fancy breaking into Sandra Next Door's? She's not back yet and we do seem to have a talent for it?'

'My days of breaking into places are behind me,' he told her firmly. 'At least, that's what I'm going to tell the judge. Do you think the police will arrest us?'

'Quite possibly. They're going to be pretty mad that we've messed up all their crime scenes. Let's not worry about that tonight. The boys are safe, the doc thinks Kenny and Captain Rab are going to be fine and we have some news for Elsie.'

'What worries me is that if Pete told Thaddeus that Captain Rab is here, then it's not a massive leap for him to assume that other former cult members are here too. He might come after our parents.'

Penny sighed. 'Well, he's not coming tonight. Our parents will have to speak to the people who put them into witness protection and figure out what they're going to do. I can't even think about it right now. I'm too tired. We'll sort it all out tomorrow.'

She watched Jim's taillights disappear into the night and turned towards the house. She had expected it to be shrouded in darkness, yet all the lights were on. Curious, she kicked off her wellies in the porch and headed straight for the kitchen, where she could hear raised voices.

Len and Mary were having another showdown, and Hector and Edith had retreated to the table, the hoods of their onesies up and their hands over their ears to block out their grandmother's voice, which was nearing a pitch that only dogs could hear. Oh no, thought Penny, her heart sinking. Not the bloody pole again.

'What's going on?' she asked, wishing they would all just eff off so that she could grab a glass of water and go to bed.

'I will not be fobbed off this time!' screeched Mary. 'Plates missing. Food missing. Your father is spending more time in his shed than he is in the house. And he's still refusing to put my pole in his shed, despite all the evidence that Hector can't be trusted to pole dance properly. I offered to do it myself, but now he says he can't find the key. I have had it up to here with things and people disappearing.'

'Hector, Edith,' roared Penny. 'Go to your rooms and get all the plates, cups and whatever else you're not supposed to have in there. Now!'

Hector and Edith looked relieved to escape. They

scuttled off to their rooms, and a moment later Penny heard the double thunk of two bedroom doors closing.

Penny took a deep breath and turned to her father.

'Dad,' she said in the calmest tone she could muster, 'we all know that the shed is more precious to you than…well, at least Mojo. Therefore, we all know that you certainly haven't lost the key. Which means that there is something in the shed that you don't want Mum to see. Now, we can either stay up half the night listening to Mum rant, or you can come clean and let us all get a good night's sleep. The twins have their first day at school tomorrow, and this is not doing them any good either.'

Len glared at her defiantly. Penny glared back. Mary did the most glaring of all. It was a glaring Mexican stand-off. Then Len let out a puff of breath and sagged in ignominious defeat. He fished down the neck of his good, checked shirt, the one he had carefully ironed so that he would look smart for fake bingo night, but which now looked like he had slept in it, and extracted a chain, on the end of which was a small, silver key. Wordlessly, he handed the key to Mary.

Rather than look triumphant, as Penny expected, her mother instantly softened.

'Oh, Len,' she said, in a tone of gentle disappointment. 'You haven't been helping Elsie again, have you? We talked about this, and you promised not to do it while the twins were here.'

Penny looked from one parent to another, confused as much by her mother's demeanour as she was by her words. 'Promised not to do what while the twins were here?'

Len shook his head and said, 'It's a bit more than that, Mary.'

Mary's tone grew sharp. 'Not the hard stuff, Len? You swore you'd never do the hard stuff.'

'No, no,' said Len, becoming irritated with her accusations. 'It's probably better that you see for yourself.

Penny, you come too. We may as well get it all out in the open.'

Penny and her mother quickly donned their wellies and followed Len across the sodden lawn to the shed. He hesitated at the door.

'Now, Mary,' he warned, 'you're not to go off on one.'

'What do you mean "go off on one"?' Mary said, her voice rising. 'I am the calmest person you are ever likely to meet!'

'Shh. Please,' Len pleaded. 'The last thing I need is Sandra Next Door poking her nose in.'

'Have you got sex slaves, Len? Is that what it is? Because I'll report you myself if it's sex slaves,' Mary said.

'No, I got rid of the sex slaves before the twins arrived,' said Len. Then he looked at Mary's face. 'I'm joking,' he protested. 'It's not sex slaves. Open the door and see for yourself.'

Mary put the key in the lock and turned it. There was a click, and she slowly turned the handle. Penny wasn't sure what she had expected, but it certainly wasn't this.

At first, she couldn't see. Blinded, she shielded her eyes, slowly lowering her hand as they adjusted to the light. Then the sweet, sickly smell hit her nostrils and she was transported straight back to university and a pair of shoes filled to the brim with vomit.

'Holy shit, Dad,' she said, as she surveyed the neat rows of plants, with their slender jagged leaves.

'Oh, Len,' said Mary. 'Not again.'

Penny was stunned. 'Is this your project with Elsie? Growing weed?'

'We only sell it to the pensioners,' Len explained. 'Mrs Richardson has awful trouble with her arthritis, then there's Mr Gill. He has MS. It's a cruel, cruel disease. I grow the stuff and Elsie delivers. It's not like we're drug dealers, Penny-farthing. We sell it at cost. It's a community service'.

'So, when Elsie does the rounds in her library van and…,' said Penny.

'They get a bag of weed with their bestseller,' Len finished for her.

'And you knew about this?' said Penny, whirling round to face her mother.

'I told him to stop while the twins were here. I didn't want them to have any…bad influences,' said Mary. She held out her hands in supplication. 'I'm so sorry. I should have warned you. I honestly thought he'd stopped months ago and had filled the shed with junk. As soon as you split with Alex, I said, "Len, Penny will probably come home, so you have to shut down the farm." Didn't I say that, Len?'

'You did, Mary. Don't blame your mother. It's my fault,' said Len.

But Penny wasn't listening. She was looking at the door behind them, where two heads were peering around the jamb, their features obscured by the hoods of their onesies.

'Hector. Edith. You may as well come in,' she said, expanding her arms to take in the contents of the shed. 'It turns out that Grandad is the island drug king pin.'

'Well, I wouldn't say that,' said Len, 'Although I am quite pleased with how this crop is coming along.'

'It's okay, Mum,' Edith drawled. 'We already know.'

'You do? How did you find out?' asked Len, beaming with delight at his clever grandchildren.

'It's not a good thing, Len,' Mary sharply reminded him. 'They should never have known about this.'

Len immediately looked contrite, but asked again, 'How *did* you find out?'

'We were looking for Freddie, and you'd left the key on the kitchen table,' said Hector. 'But that's not all he's got in here, Mum. Look at the back of the shed.'

Penny looked and, beyond the glow of the lamps,

she could just make out the dark triangular shape of a tent. Threading her way through the neat rows of plants, she strode up to the tent and politely knocked…brushed?…at the door.

There was a brief hiss as the zip was pulled down and a man's head poked out of the opening.

'Yes, how can I help you?' he enquired, politely.

Penny hesitated, unsure as to how she should respond to this, but was saved by her father, who said, 'It's alright, Mustafa. This is my daughter, Penny, and my grandchildren, whom I believe you've already met. And this,' he said proudly, putting an arm around Mary, 'is my wife.'

'Ah, yes. The daft old bat. Please to meet you, Mary. Now, if you will please give me a moment, I will put some pants on.'

The zip hissed back up and Penny looked at her father, astounded.

Mary gave Len a stern look. 'Well, at least we know where the new camping stove went.'

CHAPTER TWENTY-THREE

It was the day that simply wouldn't end. Penny sat on the arm of the sofa, struggling to stay awake, her bleary eyes fixed on the hole in the living room ceiling that had until recently housed Mary's pole. Beside her, squashed together on the three-seater, were her father, the twins and the short, dark-haired man that her father had called Mustafa, who thankfully was now wearing her father's pinstriped suit trousers below a T-shirt which declared him as being a "Bodacious Babe". Mary, holding court from the armchair, had nominated herself chief judge and interrogator. Currently, Len was in the dock.

'Let me get this straight,' she was saying. 'You got up one morning and just happened to find a man in the shed, so you decided to keep him.'

'Not quite, my love.'

'Don't you "my love" me! I will be your love again when we get to the bottom of this, and not before. Now, where were we? Oh yes. Found man in shed. Decided to keep him. Why did you decide to keep him?'

Len spread his arms in a gesture of innocence, nearly knocking Mustafa's cup of tea out of his hand in the process, and said, 'My lo…Mary, I didn't "decide to keep him". He asked if he could stay. Mustafa, tell her.'

Mustafa gave Mary what he hoped was a winning smile. It soon vanished under her withering stare, yet he was not deterred. He had faced much worse than the daft old bat.

'The shed was open, and I needed a place to hide. When Len came in the next morning, I said, "Foos yer doos and can I please stay?" I told him there is a bad man who shot my friend. I ran away, and nobody can know I am here.

Len was very kind, and he gave me scones and sausages. I was kind to him and looked after his plants. Then when the weather is fine, he will take me to Aberdeen.'

Mary opened her mouth to say something, but Penny got there first.

'Mustafa, are you the person who saw someone shoot Old Archie?'

Mustafa nodded glumly. 'He kept me safe all the way to his house then, bang, he was lying on the floor and blood was everywhere. I thought the man was there to kill me, and I am feeling very bad that he killed Old Archie. I was behind the door and the man didn't see me. Then he came in to look at what he had done, and I pushed him and ran away. He ran after me, but I was very fast. I ran and ran until I came to these houses. I was going to hide from him in a garden. It was raining very hard, the shed was unlocked, so I lived in the shed.'

Once more, Mary opened her mouth to speak but was interrupted by Penny.

'Why are you here at all? I mean, on the island.'

'It is a long story,' said Mustafa.

Great, thought Penny, like we haven't had enough of those already tonight. She gave Mustafa an encouraging smile, and he continued.

'I am from Morocco. I was working for a charity in Libya which documents human rights abuses. Every day my role was to interview people who suffered torture and rape. Many of them were from other countries, where the situation was much worse, and they were trying to go to Europe. I started to hear stories of a man called Bashir who was involved in smuggling weapons through Libya to other nations. They would end up in the hands of people who committed bad crimes...child soldiers, genocide. He was also involved in smuggling people out through Libya. Powerful and dangerous people. Many of them are connected to terrorist groups.

'I started to get more information about this man

and found out that he is in the British government, where he has a different name. I didn't know who to tell. I didn't know who I could trust. If Bashir found out that I knew about him, he would kill me. Eventually, I told my friend at the charity, Fatima. She is also British, and her brother is high in your police.

'They sent a man to talk to me and I showed him what I had found. He told me to go home to Morocco and they would send instructions. One night, the man came to my home and told me to pack my things, we were leaving. He put me on a boat to Gibraltar. Another man met me there. It was Old Archie. He told me all about foos yer doos, quines and loons on the boat on the way here. I am very sad that I shall never meet yon glaikit coo Elsie to tell her that he loved her.'

For a third time, Mary opened her mouth and Penny cut her short.

'Who was the politician?'

'I cannot say,' said Mustafa. 'I had instructions to meet someone here who will make sure I am safe. I am…how do you say it?...a star witness. I don't know if he is on the island now or if he came at all. Len told me there has been no boat to Aberdeen because of your lovely British weather, so I decided to disappear. Len is going to help me.'

Mary opened her mouth to speak, and Penny was about to jump in with another question but stopped when she caught sight of her mother's fierce expression.

'That's all well and good,' declared Mary, 'but what I want to know is this. Where are my plates?'

Len eyed the twins guiltily. 'I'm sorry you got the blame for all the missing crockery. I kept taking food out to Mustafa and forgetting to bring the plates back.'

'It's okay, Grandad,' said Hector. 'While we're in confession mode, Edith and I didn't break the pole by accident. It was a bit wobbly anyway, and we were sick of it blocking the view of the telly, so we tried to unscrew it.'

Edith handed her grandfather his penknife. The tip

was missing from the blade.

'We're sorry. You did a very good job of putting it up,' she said. 'We thought it would be easy to take down. By the way, is Mustafa wearing my T-shirt?'

Len was mid-way through explaining that he'd run out of clean T-shirts to lend Mustafa, and Mary was mid-way through a tirade about her pole, when Penny stood up and loudly clapped her hands.

'If we're back to ranting about the bloody pole again, it must be time for bed. Come on, you two. You have school in the morning. Mustafa, I suggest you sleep on the sofa tonight. We'll sort everything else out in the morning. By the way, do you know the name of the person you were supposed to meet here?'

'Yes,' said Mustafa. 'It's a man called Anthony Woodbead.'

The next morning, summer arrived. Not that Penny noticed. She stumbled around the kitchen, putting cornflakes in Mojo's dish and serving Hector a bowl of Kitty Kat Kibble. The twins, having become accustomed to sleeping late and seemingly spending half the night scouring the fridge for snacks, were sullen and uncommunicative. They reluctantly posed for "first day at school" photographs, their scowling little faces belying the #soblessed added by Penny when she posted the pictures on Instagram for the benefit of their father. Len and Mary's bedroom door remained firmly closed and Mustafa didn't stir from the sofa.

The moment the twins turned the corner at the end of the drive, Penny locked the front door and made a beeline for her bedroom.

'Sorry, Chesney,' she said, blowing a kiss at the poster, 'Usually by this time you've been treated to the sight of me in my big knickers. Not this morning.'

She got into bed and burrowed down beneath the covers, turning her back to the light that seeped through the edges of the curtains. It was warm, and the familiar dip in the mattress cupped her bum perfectly. She felt herself drifting off and idly wondered if Jim was up yet. Did he say he had work today? Had she told him about meeting Anthony Woodbead at lunchtime? Penny couldn't remember. She supposed he would come with her. She'd like that. When she kissed his cheek last night, he smelled of the fire and the woods. It was quite nice really. A bit prickly, but nice. With that pleasant thought, and a few others which may have contained nudie bits, Penny fell asleep.

Her slumber was short-lived. Barely an hour later, Penny awoke to the sound of the doorbell ringing. The doorbell didn't so much emit a ding dong as an annoying buzzy screech. Multiple presses were guaranteed to raise the dead, so Penny was quite glad that Pete was tucked safely away in Mrs Hubbard's ice lolly freezer. She'd rather have seen him brought to justice than dead, but the thought of zombie Pete appearing at the front door was simply too much. If he was going to come back as a zombie, Penny decided, then far better that he visit Sandra Next Door. She'd beat him to death again for getting bodily fluids on her new rug. There was another buzzy screech, and Penny reluctantly dragged herself out of bed, intending to tell whoever it was to bugger off.

As soon as she opened the door, Penny realised that telling the visitor to bugger off would have been a waste of breath. He was immune to buggering off. Freshly shaved and dressed in light blue chinos and a short-sleeved shirt, Jim looked disgustingly well rested.

He smiled down at her, winked and wandered inside, heading for the kitchen. Penny looked down at today's pyjama offering. "Furry, Lazy and a Little Crazy."

'It's the cat in the picture!' she shouted after him. Damn, there was no point in explaining. He was just being his usual pain in the backside self.

By the time she reached the kitchen, Jim was

already settled at the table, with Len's newspaper spread before him.

'I thought you'd be at work today,' Penny said.

'No. Mrs Taylor's dog has fleas. Dad said there's no point in me doing this one. I'd only have to start from scratch.'

Penny rewarded him with a grin.

'Did I tell you that Anthony Woodbead asked me to meet him for lunch today?' she said casually.

Jim frowned. 'No. Why has he asked you out for lunch?'

'Dunno. We just hit it off, I guess.'

'Not with that baldie stick-insect you didn't. I heard you saying you liked a man with hair,' said Jim, pointing to his own head.

'I was just saying that to annoy Sandra Next Door,' said Penny. 'Anyway, I'm joking. You can come too, if you like. He's going to tell me what he's been up to on the island, although I think I already know. *I* also have a little surprise for *him*.'

'You're going to be all mysterious again and make me guess what you're thinking, aren't you? That game is my second least favourite, after I Spy.'

'No, not this time. Stay there. I'll just be a minute.'

Penny went to the living room and knocked gently, before opening the door and popping her head around it. Mustafa was sitting up in bed watching This Morning.

'Do you want some breakfast?' Penny asked.

'I was going to get up, but I heard a stranger,' said Mustafa.

'It's alright. My friend Jim is visiting. Come through to the kitchen and we'll tell you all about how we found Old Archie's murderer. Then I'll find you some clean clothes because we're going on a trip. Don't worry. It's a good trip, and you'll be very safe.'

Jim's eyes widened when Penny entered the kitchen with a man in a bodacious babe T-shirt. For a moment, he thought she was going to tell him that she and Alex had kissed and made up. Then he remembered that, unless Alex Moon had magic fairy dust up his arse, there was no way he could have reached the island.

'Jim, this is Mustafa,' said Penny. 'He's been living in Dad's shed. He's also the man who witnessed Old Archie's murder.'

It was certainly not what Jim had expected with his tea that morning. He'd been thinking more along the lines of a nice boiled egg with some soldiers. Not this bombshell!

'I'm quite glad you didn't make me play the guessing game,' he said. 'Come, sit down, Mustafa and tell me all about it.'

Mustafa repeated the tale of how he had come to Vik, once more refusing to name the politician and pleading with them to help him to safety. In return, Penny and Jim gave him a potted version of how they'd solved Old Archie's murder, merely saying that Old Archie had been a member of a cult in his youth and that the leader had sought revenge for past disagreements.

'So, at least you know that the murderer wasn't after you. As nobody has been in or out of Vik for over a week, you're probably safe for now. However, there's one part we skipped. The name of the man who was with us when Pete was killed. It was Anthony Woodbead.'

Mustafa's eyes lit up and his face broke out in a wide smile. 'Then I am saved!'

'We're meeting him for lunch,' said Penny, glancing down. 'You might want to put some pants on.'

Port Vik was positively festive in the sunlight. After a week of unrelenting rain, there was an air of joyous release about the town, as the residents emerged from their homes to shop, sip lattes and stop for a gossip in the street. Small huddles of people greeting one another turned the pavement in the High Street into an obstacle course and the bus stop in the Square had a long queue of pensioners who had arrived with the early bus and were now on their way home to the villages and farms.

The car park in the Square, which had until recently been almost the sole preserve of the Losers Club surveillance team, was full, and Jim had to circle around a few times until a woman with two unruly black Labradors returned to her car. He pulled over and jealously guarded the area, while the woman roared at her over-excited charges to get in the darn car or else they would never be allowed treats again. It was a canine merry-go-round. One would jump in and the other would jump out. She eventually gave up and threw a handful of treats in the boot, at which point the one that was out realised that, if he didn't get in quick sharp, his playmate would snaffle all the treats. Problem solved, she slammed the boot shut and gave Jim an apologetic smile. Penny decided it was just as well the windows were up and that she couldn't hear the curse words that Jim was muttering under his breath. Mustafa heard them, though, and was delighted to learn some new Scottish words.

By the time they reached the hotel lobby, it was ten past one. Penny had begun to worry that Woodbead wouldn't be there and that, whether or not they'd been on time, he would have found a way to discreetly sneak off the island and avoid explaining his part in this debacle. Which made her wonder, how had Pete planned to leave the island this morning?

It was, therefore, with a sense of relief, that she spied Woodbead chatting with Rachel by the reception desk. He turned to them and for a moment seemed taken aback to see that Penny had brought an extra companion. He quickly regained his composure and held his hand out to the man, smoothly saying, 'Anthony Woodbead. Pleased to meet you.'

Nevertheless, his composure faltered slightly once more when the man replied, 'Mustafa Alaoui. I am too pleased to meet you.'

Woodbead looked quizzically at Penny, who said, 'I'll explain everything over lunch.'

'Ah,' said Woodbead. 'About that. There are some people who want to talk to us first. A Sergeant Wilson and some of her colleagues.' He turned to Rachel. 'Do you think you could find somewhere for Mr Alaoui to sit while we talk to the police. Preferably somewhere he won't be seen. He's had rather a tough few months and I'd prefer not to make them any more difficult than we need to.'

Rachel smiled at Mustafa and said, 'That's no problem. Why don't you come back to the kitchen with me, and we'll get you a nice cup of tea until the coast is clear.'

As she ushered Mustafa away, Woodbead explained, 'I've told them we were having a drink in the hotel when your friend Eileen contacted you because her sons and husband had gone missing, and purely by chance we found Pete when we went looking for them. He had knocked Kenny unconscious. He confessed to having killed Old Archie on the orders of the leader of a cult, who held a grudge against old Archie from many years ago. He told us that he stabbed his grandfather following an argument. He threatened to kill Ricky and a branch hit him on the head and killed him. That's all we tell them.

'They don't need to know about Sandra and the gun. They don't need to know about you breaking into Captain Rab's place. They don't need to know about The Red Path. And they certainly don't need to know about Mustafa. Stick to the story and if they ask any difficult questions or want to interview anyone else, I'll give them a certain number to call. That should put an end to the matter.

I've had some explaining to do, by the way. Apparently, you told Sergeant Wilson that you'd seen me at Captain Rab's and I was the chief suspect!'

Woodbead led them to the hotel lounge, where a tall woman in black Police Scotland uniform introduced herself as Sergeant Wilson. She briefly gave the names of her colleagues, some of whom were in plain clothes, but Penny paid scant attention. She was entirely focused on trying to remember the version that Woodbead had instructed them to tell. She recalled how quickly Sergeant Wilson had broken down their story last time and wasn't sure how she was going to fare against the clever police officer. She definitely must not say "and by the way, we messed with all your crime scenes, stole a gun and tried to shoot someone."

Under Woodbead's watchful eye, Penny and Jim repeated the abridged version of how they solved a murder, rescued a dying man and saved two children and their father from a maniac. All in a day's work.

Sergeant Wilson and a very tough looking man, who wore a smart suit but looked like he'd be more at home in a pair of shiny shorts in a boxing ring, asked probing questions. What time had this happened? Where were they when that happened? How did they know about this, that and the next thing?

Penny could feel herself starting to become confused, and Jim looked like a rabbit caught in the headlights. Their answers grew shorter as they tried to avoid adding embellishments which would invite more questions or, even worse, catch them out in a lie. Eventually Woodbead broke in.

'We're going round in circles here, Sergeant. Your autopsy will clearly show that Mr Smellie died from a blow to the head. There's a big branch up in those woods with his blood on it and a tree which bears the marks of a branch having come off. It's clear that neither I nor these people caused his death. Now, I am sure that all the other witnesses will give a similar account yet, rather than traipse around verifying what you already know, can I suggest you call this number first?'

He handed over a business card. The Sergeant was about to protest, but the smart boxer, clearly recognising the telephone number, laid a hand on her arm, leaned in and whispered something to her.

She cleared her throat and snapped, 'Fine. Give me a minute,' before walking with her colleague to the other end of the room.

Penny strained to hear the muffled phone call, but the sergeant kept her back to them. Finally, roughly shoving her phone in her pocket, she strode back across the room and said in a tight voice, 'We won't need to talk to you again today. Thank you for your *help*.'

That last was said with slight sarcasm, but Penny and Jim didn't object. They were simply relieved to have got off so lightly. Both had been ready to buckle under the interrogation and be led off in handcuffs.

After the police had left to retrieve the bodies from Mrs Hubbard's freezer, Woodbead went to the reception desk and pressed a bell. The bell that would have saved a lot of embarrassment had it been on the desk the night before. Rachel appeared and he thanked her for looking after Mustafa, before requesting in his most charming voice whether it would be possible…and he was so sorry, he really didn't want to put her to any more trouble…but could Rachel conceivably see her way to serving lunch in the lounge so that he could have a private word with Mustafa, Penny and Jim?

Rachel was putty in his hands. She gave him some menus and promised to bring Mustafa through just as soon as he finished showing the chef his mother's recipe for fish chermoula.

Penny, Jim and Woodbead settled at a table by the window, where they sat in comfortable silence watching the people in the Square outside. An elderly lady with a tartan trolley was laughing with a girl who looked sufficiently like her that Penny assumed she must be the woman's granddaughter. Elsie pootled past in her library van. Hopefully she would not be making any special deliveries today. A group of schoolchildren walked along the pavement, their teachers herding them into a rag-tag crocodile, which soon lost form the moment the adults looked away.

Feeling calm again and curious to hear Woodbead's side of the story, Penny asked, 'So, Mr whoever you are, what brings you to our fair island?'

Woodbead sat back in his chair, stretched his long legs out and pondered for a few seconds, as if deciding exactly how much to tell her. He seemed to reach a conclusion and sat forward again, pouring himself a glass of water to wet his whistle while he related details that he assured Penny and Jim were known to very few people.

'You're clever chaps…chapess,' he said, inclining his head graciously towards Penny. 'You've no doubt worked out by now that I'm from the Security Services, and that I'm here for Mustafa. Years ago, some of my colleagues stashed rather a lot of former cult members on the island—'

'We know all about The Red Path and the witness protection,' said Jim.

'Good,' said Woodbead. 'That will save us a bit of time. I suspect that what you don't know is that the former cult members weren't the only people we stashed here. We've been using the island for decades. Captain Rab and Old Archie were recruited to help us shortly after they arrived here. We needed people who knew their way around a boat, you see. They had to be unencumbered by wives and children and able to travel at short notice. Rab and Archie fit the bill perfectly and have been smuggling people onto the island for us for over fifty years. Captain Kev too, in the beginning, but he went his own way.

Penny and Jim were listening intently, astounded that the island with which they were so familiar was home to so many secrets.

Woodbead, who appeared to be relishing their astonishment, continued, 'I know. Shocker, eh? I don't know how much Mustafa has told you, but he has some valuable information and we needed to get him to a place in the UK where he wouldn't be found. Old Archie met him out in Gibraltar, and the plan was to keep him here until we needed him. My job was simply to come here and do a debrief. Make sure there wasn't any new information we didn't already have.

'You'd think that would be simple, but nobody factored in the Scottish weather. Good lord, you lot can certainly do a good storm. While you were poking your noses into Old Archie's murder, I made contact with Captain Rab and realised that the whole thing was entirely connected to The Red Path. Admittedly, at first I assumed that someone had found out about Mustafa and tried to kill him. Slight panic on at HQ about that one. However, as soon as Captain Rab told me Pete was his grandson, it was clear that Old Archie must have been the target.'

'Surely Pete must have told The Red Path about his grandfather being here. Even just knowing about Old Archie living on the island, they might figure out that other former cult members are here,' said Penny.

'Remember I said I had to make some phone calls? That's what they were about. Captain Rab had been gathering information on the cult for years, trying to find out what had happened to his grandson. He handed over that information, or most of it, to me. Pete took some documents yesterday and I retrieved those from his pocket last night. The Red Path have been on the move for years, constantly avoiding law enforcement. However, with the information that Pete let slip to Captain Rab during their conversations and the research done by the good man himself, we were able to locate the cult.

'A party of heavily armed agents should be arriving at their compound right about now. If they've already sent someone else to the island, we should be able to find out whether any of their number are missing and stop them before they arrive. I don't think anyone here is in danger, but we won't be using the island for witness protection again. Just to be on the safe side, you know.'

'One more question,' said Jim. 'How was Pete going to get off the island?'

Penny was pleased he'd asked. That one had been irritating her.

'Captain Rab's boat, of course,' said Woodbead, surprised that they hadn't figured it out for themselves.

'But Captain Rab's boat is in Aberdeen for repairs,' said Jim.

'Did you check on that? It's been here all along. Really, if you're going to investigate murders, then you really do need to be a bit more thorough. Mind you, Sandra Next Door can come and work for us any time. The woman is a natural. By the way, I meant to give you this. A little memento, as we won't meet again.'

Woodbead dug in his pocket and pulled out a small, shiny object.

'Well, there was no sense in leaving it in the branch. We'd only have to explain to the police how it got there, and nobody wants that. Keep it, give it to Sandra Next Door, whatever.' He waved his hand airily and passed the bullet to Penny.

The door creaked open, and Rachel came in, accompanied by Mustafa. She took their lunch order and quickly left them to continue their conversation. Mustafa seemed relaxed and happy to finally connect with his handler.

'It is so good to see you, dickhead,' he said, beaming at Woodhead.

Jim had the good grace to look shamefaced.

EPILOGUE

The beach was reasonably crowded that Saturday, the sand festooned with the beach towels of semi-naked locals, who were taking full advantage of the Indian summer that followed the storm. Among their number was an odd little party, consisting of elderly people, the middle-aged and a couple of young boys, all of whom had no obvious connection but were proud to call themselves Losers Club.

Mrs Hubbard, her trousers rolled up to her knees, was digging her toes in the sand and telling the rest of the group how, now that the corpses were out of her freezers, she'd made a batch of strawberry ice cream and had taken some up to the hospital for Captain Rab. She gave Elsie a poke in the ribs with her elbow.

'This one here came with me. I thought her and Captain Rab would never shut up. The two of them talked for two hours solid. I felt like a right gooseberry.'

Elsie blushed and undid a button on her cardigan, which she had refused to remove on the basis of, as she'd whispered to Fiona, 'Bingo wings. Nobody needs to see that with their sandwiches.'

Fiona had tried to encourage Elsie, pointing out that the rest of them were in Losers Club because they needed to get rid of a few pounds, and she was the only one among them who didn't need to feel self-conscious.

'Speak for yourself,' said Jim.

He, Gordon and Geoff were lying on their respective beach towels, their hairy bellies like three wee clootie dumplings above their shorts.

Sandra Next Door tutted, moving Geoff's stilettos to one side so that she could stretch out on the sand and watch Ricky and Gervais as they played at the water's edge.

Their father was still in the hospital, but the boys appeared to have bounced back from the experience, boasting to anyone who would listen that they'd catched the murderer and hitted him on the head. Within days, the tale had expanded to the boys single-handedly solving the entire mystery, using their cunning detective skills to figure out where the murderer was hiding and carefully planning his capture down to the last detail.

Eileen seemed happy and relaxed now that Kenny was on the mend. She was a bit thick, but my goodness she kept a tidy kitchen, thought Sandra Next Door approvingly. She'd visited Eileen and the boys a couple of times since Kenny had been in hospital. In fact, she'd even gone for drink at the village pub with Fiona. Sandra Next Door had friends.

'Is Penny coming?' she asked Eileen.

'She said that she was taking the twins to meet the ferry,' said Eileen. 'I'm glad that Captain Rab is pals with his brother again, otherwise we would be without anyone to run the ferry. Mrs Hubbard says Captain Kev visited him in the hospital and, what with him almost dying and Kev being the only relative he has left, he realised what a miserable old, pardon my French, git he'd been.'

They chatted for a while, until Eileen declared that they'd waited long enough and began to unpack the picnic basket. Everyone had contributed something, and Fiona promised that all her vegetables were thoroughly washed. The group's trepidation about the tomatoes was soon set aside as Eileen opened a cool-box next to her and revealed what she called her "piece of resistance".

'Lashings of ginger beer,' she giggled, handing the bottles out.

The subsequent toast was interrupted by the arrival of Penny and the twins. Hector was holding a small bundle of black and white fur in his arms, its little nose buried in his armpit, where it had discovered all the best stinky smells.

At Eileen's squeal, the baby Border Collie yipped

and scratched to get down so that he too could join in the fun. The sausage rolls on the picnic blanket may have influenced his decision. He couldn't say. He was only a few months old and far too young to be responsible for accidentally eating the big hairless things' lunch.

'Oh, he's gorgeous,' said Eileen. 'Have you decided on a name for him yet?'

'No,' said Edith. 'We couldn't agree. As per usual.'

Penny looked at her friend's delighted face and somehow knew exactly what Eileen was going to say.

'Timmy!'

GET EXCLUSIVE MATERIAL

Hi. I hope you enjoyed Losers Club. My background is blogging on social media where I write funny stuff about my day and talk to my readers all the time. I miss that connection with the readers of my books, so I've set up an exclusive subscriber zone on my website. If you'd like to sign up for my newsletter and access exclusive content, such as free chapters and stories, please visit my website at www.theweehairyboys.co.uk.

You can find me blogging as Growing Old Disgracefully (or Yvonne Vincent – Author, if you're only interested in book stuff) on Facebook and @theweehairyboys on Instagram.
Thanks for reading.

Yvonne

P.S. The wee hairy boys are my dogs.

AND FINALLY…

My thanks to Fiona, Fiona, Dawn, Louise, Vicky, Jen, Kevin, Anette, Pete, Eilidh, Debbie and Paul for your advice, support and expertise.

All profits from pre-orders of this book have been donated to the Cetacean Research and Rescue Unit, a small marine conservation organisation in Gardenstown, near Banff in Scotland.

Ingram Content Group UK Ltd.
Milton Keynes UK
UKHW012140130323
418508UK00006B/703